MW01615394

THE CASE OF THE EXPLODING SHOP

A totally gripping, breathlessly twisty crime mystery

MICHAEL LEESE

Detectives Roper and Hooley Mysteries Book 4

Originally published as
Just Kill Them

JOFFE BOOKS

Revised edition 2021
Joffe Books, London
www.joffebooks.com

First published by in Great Britain in 2019
as *Just Kill Them*

Cover art by Nick Castle

ISBN: 978-1-80405-010-1

CHAPTER 1

Greenwich Peninsula, London

Sheila Reynolds couldn't remember when she had last enjoyed herself so much. Despite the early morning — it was just after 6 a.m. — she had been talking and laughing for more than an hour.

She was glad she had taken a little care with her appearance. She'd chosen an outfit that complemented her slightly plump figure, while carefully applied make-up hid a few lines which was never a bad thing.

As the light improved, it was apparent that her fellow believers, both men and women, had been equally careful and wanting to look their best. After all, this was one of the few times they would get to see their hero in the flesh.

At last, the doors of the O2 Arena opened, and the new-found friends shared smiles, gentle pats on the back, and even a few high-fives. Soon, they poured in, excitedly exchanging tales of record share prices and special dividend payouts.

They were here to worship John Ryder, the tech mogul they credited with making them considerably wealthier than they might have been. It may not have been the typical stadium crowd — there were far too many business suits for that — but it lacked for nothing in enthusiasm.

The decibel count hit triple figures as, up on the stage, the musicians marched into view. The invitation had stated "Expect the Unexpected" — but, even so, these were household names who had never before appeared on the same stage.

The band launched into the Fleetwood Mac track, "Go Your Own Way", bringing howls of approval. At the final note, the lights dimmed before returning full beam to reveal an unfeasibly handsome man. The screaming hit fever pitch as he glided along. His ponytail, fashioned from thick blonde hair, moved in rhythm with his every move. The man's presence was undeniable. He was in superb shape, a little over six feet five and weighing 270 pounds.

Sheila was surprised to find that she was standing up, waving her arms and shouting so loudly she was going hoarse. She felt a hot flush of embarrassment at the thought of explaining her voice loss to her teenage children.

All around her, thousands of middle-aged people shared the same expression of surprise at just how carried away they had become. But, as if on an agreed signal, they all gave a collective shrug and went back to enjoying the show. They'd come from all parts of the world to see him.

Behind Ryder, the band had started on "Gimme Shelter" by the Rolling Stones. He was even joining in on his air guitar, a winningly bashful grin on his face.

TV cameras zoomed in, capturing the scene in super-high definition. Public appearances by this man, described by *Forbes* magazine as a "Technology Titan", were such a rare event that broadcasters were live-streaming the footage to a global audience of millions.

Ryder took his time before gesturing for the audience to sit down. Then, the music faded away, and the singer handed over the microphone with the care of an athlete passing on the Olympic flame.

Silence settled over the crowd. Ryder looked out at his adoring fans. He concentrated hard, tightened his grip on the mic as he raised it to his lips . . .

Then the screaming started.

CHAPTER 2

Nearly seventy miles away, close to the Kent coast, Detective Jonathan Roper and Chief Inspector Brian Hooley were onboard a Eurostar train about to head under the English Channel.

They had extensive experience of cross-border crime. Just a year ago they had thwarted a plot to set off a nuclear bomb in London. Now, they were on the way to Paris — where they had been booked to deliver the keynote address at an international conference about the seemingly unstoppable rise of transnational crime and how Scotland Yard was dealing with it.

The DCI was a burly man, standing a little under six foot tall, and his greying hair betrayed the years of experience that made him one of the Met's more accomplished "thief-takers". He'd recently divorced from his wife of more than twenty-five years and as a result, was partly estranged from his two children.

Right now, his blue eyes were sparkling as he listened to the announcement that they were about to head under the Straits of Dover.

Beside him, Roper was in his element. "Did you know the tunnel section is 50.45 kilometres or 31.35 miles long?"

DCI Hooley let the information wash over him; his companion had been throwing facts at him since they left London.

As Roper chatted away, DCI Hooley thought it was noticeable that, when he was nervous, Roper talked incessantly. He wondered if it was another expression of the type of autism by which he was affected. The younger man was a brilliant detective, and his condition had given him the ability to spot things others missed. It was a massive advantage for an investigator but came with its own set of problems.

Talking of problems, Hooley was reminded that his younger colleague had only yesterday had to deal with a complaint. As Roper drew breath to launch into another barrage of stats, he interrupted him. "I gather your meeting went well?"

Roper stared at the floor. "I take it you mean the meeting with the HR people."

The DCI kept a straight face. Roper would open up or not. There was nothing he could do to change things. After a pause — long enough to unsettle the normally phlegmatic senior officer — Roper started speaking.

"It went much better than last time. The new head of HR said it was clear that I was trying to be as helpful as possible. In fact, he said he couldn't quite understand why there had been so much fuss before."

DCI Hooley kept his thoughts firmly under wraps. He'd been at the previous meeting and seen, as well as heard, the shouting. It was mainly why there was now a new head of the HR department. The previous incumbent had gone off sick for six months, before announcing he was leaving to travel the world to "find himself".

The DCI had also thought it was a bit of an overreaction. All that had happened was that the complainant had lost his temper after Roper refused to go into detail about his "Rainbow Spectrum". Despite the man's outburst, Roper had remained silent, refusing all entreaties to speak. This had triggered yet another outburst which the HR boss attempted to deflect by asking the DCI if he, in his role as Roper's boss, could help to explain.

Hooley had been relaxed about the request and started by saying it wasn't arrogance that had made Roper mute on the subject. It was his unfortunate experiences at school, which had persuaded the younger man that he should only share the information on a "need to know" basis.

"I've got a need to know!" shouted the complainant, a long-serving detective constable who wasn't known for his patience. This had prompted an intervention by the HR chief, which in turn, led to threats of violence.

In the subsequent disciplinary hearing, the detective constable had claimed he was the victim of being "verballed" by the head of HR.

"I never said 'I'll rip your head off.' What I said was that I 'thought it was a bit off'. I meant it was a bit off that he was defending Detective Roper. It didn't feel fair to me."

In the ensuing inquiry, neither Roper nor Hooley were able to help. At the time the DCI had been laughing so hard he accidentally caught his shin on the edge of a desk, which was extremely painful and rendered his recollection vague. Meanwhile, Roper explained that, once the shouting started, he had stopped listening.

The DCI couldn't help smiling at the memory. He was also secretly glad that he had never had to explain what the Rainbow Spectrum actually was. In truth, he wasn't entirely sure he understood it, despite Roper's many attempts to explain. What he did know was that, on multiple occasions, Roper had used it to help crack some of the most challenging cases the Yard had had to deal with. His support appeared to enhance Roper's ability to spot the details that most other people missed.

Hooley was aware that he and Roper were regarded as an unlikely partnership. The "Odd Couple" was one of their politer nicknames, and it was the older man's stoic personality that was the key to it — since it allowed him to shrug off the type of comments that many would find insulting.

The problem was Roper's lack of social skills. It meant he could make unflinchingly direct personal observations.

Most of the time, Hooley was broadly impervious. He had learned that attempting to bite back with a sharp response made little if any difference.

As the train rushed into the tunnel, the DCI studied Roper in the reflection cast by the window. He was dressed, as always, in his work "uniform" — a skinny black suit, paired with a white shirt, black tie and shoes polished to a brilliant shine.

The DCI knew this was pretty much the limit of his companion's work wardrobe, not that he was a gift to fashion. The real problem for Roper was his hair; thick, black and curly. It seemed to have a life of its own.

Emerging into the daylight on the French side of the tunnel, Hooley smiled as he took in the scenery and settled back for the journey to the capital. A moment later, both of their mobile phones began to ping frantically as they were deluged with incoming traffic.

Hooley grabbed his handset and read the first message. "Bloody hell."

He rarely swore, but this was extraordinary.

CHAPTER 3

As he went to speak into the microphone, a fireball engulfed John Ryder.

Sheila Reynolds was close enough to feel the heat and be dazzled by the light. She froze in place, then felt a tremendous blow to her face as people scrambled to get away.

The only thing that kept her on her feet was the sheer volume of people, all pushing and shoving. A man she had moments before exchanged polite smiles with slammed into her left shoulder as he made for a gap in the crowd, spinning her round into a woman who lashed out and clawed at her face, driven out of her mind by the screaming and shouting. To say it was pandemonium was an understatement.

Sheila Reynolds stumbled and fell to the floor. More people fell on top of her and soon she was trapped, unable to move anything except her head. That too was suddenly covered by another body, and she frantically jerked to try and breathe.

She died in abject terror, suffocated to death.

Those lucky enough to stay on their feet were screaming and jostling each other in the rush for the exits.

Inspector Barry Asmus, on crowd duty outside, ran into the building as the first of the audience ran out.

"I've got people running out of the auditorium," he said, talking into a radio set that linked him with the Arena security teams. "They're shouting about a bomb. What can you see on your video feeds?"

He listened to security explain all they knew so far — that something had happened on stage and that people were making for the emergency exits — as he jogged out through the vast concourse area and past the various food outlets, concessions stalls and restaurants. The place was huge, and this part was like a large out of town shopping centre.

Running through the doors to the outside space, he immediately saw several police officers running towards him. As he got on his personal radio to talk to area command, he waved them over. He quickly went through what he knew, emphasising that it looked like many fatalities. Still, there was no evidence of any terrorist activity, as there had been in previous attacks on concert venues.

Asmus was told that senior officers were on their way, but for now, he remained in charge.

As he was talking, two men, chalk-white with shock, ran up. They were gesturing wildly at the doors they had just emerged from, talking so fast it was almost gibberish, but they quickly slowed down, apparently calmed by his presence.

"It was a bomb or something. It got John Ryder, and then everything went mad."

As the men staggered off, Asmus was grappling with the classic dilemma — how to save lives without destroying the crime scene. He knew that the Counter Terrorism Command, the Area Major Incident Team, AMIT and other security services would be on their way — so he wouldn't be alone for long — but for now, it was his call.

His concentration was broken as a frightened woman ran past, leaving the scent of her perfume behind: Chanel No5, his wife's favourite. It triggered an almost painful feeling as he recalled her telling him not to be late home for their twenty-sixth wedding anniversary dinner that night. It was ironic that he'd only volunteered for the O2 duty to cut the chance of being caught up in a significant incident — but all his hopes of getting home had disappeared with the explosion. He sighed. She was a copper's wife who understood when duty called.

Irritated at himself for getting caught up in his thoughts, he took a moment to think things through. Hundreds, if not thousands, of people, had made their way out by now. People were crying, and many were glued to their phones, either talking or checking to see what had been posted online.

For some reason, a woman started filming him, and he suppressed his irritation as he thought about what to do. Until someone could prove otherwise, he was going to assume a bomb had gone off. Which left the big question: were more primed to explode?

A group of uniformed officers were standing close by, waiting for instructions. He made his mind up. He needed to get more help inside the auditorium.

"We need to get everyone out," he said to the officers. "Be cautious. This is a frightened crowd, so go in slowly and carefully." Asmus looked intently at the men. To him, they seemed impossibly young and were no doubt, scared. "I'll join you as quickly as I can. Do your best and keep calm. You will save lives. Now go. I'll be right behind you . . ."

Even as he spoke, more officers turned up, including a Sergeant. He needed people everywhere and made another snap decision.

"Sergeant, it's vital we get as much information as we can. Can you organise a few officers to start collecting mobile phone footage and any key witnesses?" The man didn't waste time on words; he nodded and took off to get on with his task.

Asmus often complained about TV police shows, but they did get one thing right: you needed to move fast and grab as much intelligence as you could. At this stage, there was no way of knowing what the most critical information would be.

Checking the time, he was amazed to see more than twenty minutes had elapsed. He'd already done what organising he could. Now he needed to get eyes on what he was dealing with.

As he jogged back towards the exits, he noticed that the security gates had indeed been opened, as promised. Uniformed guards were waving people through. They were all deferring to a tall black man.

"You're doing a good job, keeping things moving," he said to him. "You may have saved a lot of lives. There are some badly frightened people here."

The man laughed grimly. He looked at home in the mayhem. "Did two tours in Afghanistan so this sort of thing is a lot easier than walking around and trying not to tread on an IED." He glanced over the restaurant stands. "Hope you're not feeling hungry though. All the catering staff legged it at the first sign of trouble. Can't say I blame them, really. Minimum wage not exactly the incentive to stick around."

While the man had been talking, more police officers and paramedics were streaming in. Asmus didn't waste any time on talk, just waved them towards the arena.

"We have people down on the ground and others still trying to get out. Just get in there and do what you can."

Asmus liked to think he was pretty fit, but by the time he reached his destination at the front of the auditorium, he was out of breath. He didn't stop as he spotted steps that would get him onstage. It would give him a more unobstructed view of what was going on.

To his surprise, he noticed two paramedics already there. He ran over and saw that they were treating a blackened body on the ground.

They watched him approach; their expressions were grim. Asmus spoke first. "Is this who I think it is? And how did you guys get here so fast?"

One of the paramedics replied. "In answer to your first question, yup, it's John Ryder. I don't know how he's alive. The answer to your second question is we are based inside for all major events because nowadays you never know." He paused. "I saw what happened because I was standing in the wings. He was about to say something; then there was a blinding flash of light and a huge bang. My ears are still ringing."

Asmus immediately got on his radio to command.

"Inspector Asmus here. I have credible witnesses describing what sounds like a bomb. I think we have to assume there may be more and we have people still in the main hall. They have conditions ranging from shock to likely broken bones. They're going to need help getting out, although the exits are pretty clear. Good job there's a lot of them, it allowed a lot of people to move through. But we need the bomb squad, and we're going to need more ambulances."

CHAPTER 4

Brian Hooley banged his fist on the table. "This is ridiculous. We're off on a jolly to France while all hell is breaking loose back home. Can you start thinking about the quickest way back to London, and how long before we arrive in Paris?" His impatient, rapid-fire delivery, contrasted with Roper's calm and collected response, made it seem as though entering the tunnel had induced some sort of role reversal.

Roper took his time checking details on his phone. "We're about thirty minutes out of Paris. Going back on the train is almost certainly the quickest way. We could fly — but that would mean getting out to Charles De Gaulle and then having to get in from Heathrow."

"I agree — get us on the next train."

"There's a problem with that. The booking website says there's no more space on the train, or the next one or the one after . . ."

Fortunately, Hooley was now getting a grip. Usually, he was the one telling Roper not to get over-emotional. He realised he was feeling guilty because their trip to Paris suddenly felt like a waste of time.

"The boss should be able to pull some strings. Or at least I hope she can. I'll get in touch with her and see if we can get on the next available Eurostar as extras, or whatever they want to call us. I don't care if we have to stand all the way."

"Perhaps we could travel in the driver's compartment?"

Despite the serious circumstances, Roper's bright-eyed response made him smile. The world could be going to hell, but Roper's inner geek was never far away.

Hooley picked up his phone and began compiling a message for Julie Mayweather, the newly appointed Commissioner of the Metropolitan Police, or the "boss of all bosses" as Hooley called her on the rare occasions they were together and no one else was around.

He pressed send and sank back into his comfortable seat. The sudden realisation that matters were, for the time being, out of his hands had a strangely calming effect.

"Anything on the news yet?"

"They're just starting to run the first reports. People down at Greenwich have already been tweeting photos and comments from the scene. Scotland Yard hasn't put out a statement yet." Roper paused and looked intently at his phone. "The Press Bureau has just confirmed there's a major incident. The BBC says there are dead and injured. A couple of the papers are reporting an explosion. Terrorism cannot be ruled out."

Hooley tapped the screen on his phone.

"I've had nothing since Julie's office alerted us, which makes me fear the worst. It usually means the first responders have walked into something much bigger than they expected."

Roper turned back to his screen and sat back, his eyes wide.

"The BBC has just put out a 'News Flash'. O2 incident confirmed as a bomb. More devices may be hidden in the building."

He read the alert out loud, causing Hooley to groan.

"What's going on down there? Is anyone saying who might be responsible? Please don't tell me we have ISIS gunmen down there shooting up the victims?"

Roper shook his head. "There are no details like that, either official or otherwise. But the BBC has put out another flash to say that people are being evacuated from the area."

The DCI was convinced he could feel his blood pressure going up the further the train carried him away from the major incident. He glared at his handset, hoping that sheer force of will could compel it to reveal what was going on and get him and Roper back to London.

The loud beep announcing he had a message made him jump. He stabbed at his screen and called up the text.

"Many dead and wounded. No further details at this time. French authorities are holding a Eurostar at Gare du Nord. There are spaces. A group of French schoolchildren were due to go out to London for a few days, but that's been cancelled in the wake of the incident."

He didn't recognise the name on the message but it was from one of Julie's team at Scotland Yard. He acknowledged receipt and got a reply almost instantly.

"Almost certainly a device has been detonated. The commissioner is now heading for the scene. She wants you to call her when you arrive back in London. You and Roper are now officially on the case."

CHAPTER 5

The young woman was dressed in the green fatigues that marked out medical responders. She was small, dark-haired and nodded as Asmus talked to her. She had been working on the wounded closest to the stage when he had found her.

"My biggest concern is getting people out of here." He looked around, his gaze taking in the activity all around the vast space. It looked chaotic, but he got the sense there was an order in what was happening, and the earlier panic had settled into a sort of grim acceptance. "Can you organise a check of how many people are going to need carrying out of here? The living and the dead, please. You'll find me here when you're ready. Your best estimate will do; it will help me make sure all the key responder teams have the information they need. For the time being it's down to those of us who are here right now, but that will change soon, once the more senior commanders are on-site and rolling out the response."

She didn't waste words. "Okay," she said, running off towards one of the bigger groups of people. Asmus wanted to get everyone, including fatalities, out, but he knew had to be realistic and give the living priority.

He needed to take a moment to make sure he wasn't missing something. He slowed his breathing and calmly looked around the area. He recalled a briefing he had two days ago by one of the teams responsible for safety in the event of a fire, or similar.

As well as pointing out the dozens of exits from the auditorium itself the man had been especially proud of two things.

"We have vents that open in the event of smoke or fumes, which is a unique feature of the dome. All around the perimeter are Perspex shutters. In the event of an emergency evacuation, they slide upwards. They're our final emergency exits if you like to think of them that way. They were last tested, supervised by me, last week without a hitch.

"The building's undergone a huge makeover. Since its rebranding from the Millennium Dome, its whole interior has been redesigned. It makes us one of the most impressive domes in the world."

At the time Asmus had been impressed, and as he took in the relative calm, he hoped this was a sign that the extra exits were making a difference. There was a trickle of people moving out at a steady pace. Not everyone had been able to rush for the exit.

He heard loud barking and looked up expectantly. Two police handlers appeared with sniffer dogs, with two more behind. They knew what they were doing and headed off fast to quarter the area between them.

His radio squawked, and a deep voice came on. "Chief Superintendent Tom Horsely here. I'm designated on-scene commander by AMIT, but I'm still a few minutes out. Your Sergeant has told me what you're doing, and I wanted to say well done. You should have the first of the bomb teams there already — and soon there'll be more than enough officers to do everything you need.

"But there's a problem. There's a Health and Safety assessment underway, even as I speak. You don't need me to remind you that, if they're concerned about the possibility of a second bomb, they'll fall back on protocols which means you have to pull out of the vicinity, together with any other responders who are with you." He paused and there was a distinct note of tension in his voice. "What's your view about the possibility we might have a second bomb?"

"The honest answer is I don't know. If I thought it was very likely, I would have pulled back already. What I can say is that the first device was very small and maybe it was only aimed at one person — John Ryder."

There was a brief pause again before the senior officer responded. "Understood. My advice is to keep doing what you're doing and do it as fast as you can."

With that, he was gone. Asmus shrugged. He knew the officer could have ordered everyone out already. The man had just warned him he was on borrowed time.

He looked up to find the doctor running towards him. She stopped in front of him and caught her breath. "I've counted twenty-five bodies in the vicinity of the stage. We have a total of thirty-five injured who will need assistance. Of those, nine people are in serious to critical condition."

It was cold comfort, but these figures were a bit better than Asmus had hoped for. "Okay. This is the situation. We need to get everyone out now, as fast as we can. Gold Command may well issue a withdrawal notice at any moment."

Her face was screwed up in irritation. While he shared her view, he knew he had to be realistic — there was no way he could ask others to risk their lives.

"There are real concerns that there might be another bomb. If they give the command to leave, that's it. We have to go. Which is why we have to work as fast as we can."

He thought she would argue, but instead, she smiled as she looked over his shoulder. "Will that lot help?"

The inspector looked over to see a large group of paramedics trotting in. Even better, they were carrying stretchers.

He turned to the doctor. "All yours."

She ran towards the new arrivals and started issuing urgent instructions. Within minutes, the first of the wounded was being carried out.

To his relief, the inspector realised that even the dead were being taken away. He would have hated it if a second device exploded and bodies were either damaged or had to be dug out of the rubble. There was enough pain for the families already without suffering that.

Asmus glanced up at the stage and saw that Ryder had gone. He wondered if the man was going to make it and why he had been singled out. He had always thought the entrepreneur was a modern-day hero to millions.

He resisted the urge to go and check on the medical teams. They were doing their job, and the numbers on the ground were thinning out and real progress was being made. He knew he was pushing hard, but there was no other way.

Five minutes later, his radio squawked. "Tom Horsely here. I've managed to get you all the time I can, but that's it. We're pulling back until we can confirm the area is safe. You need to get everyone out."

He was gone without waiting for a reply. Asmus saw that the last few bodies were being picked up and ran over to help chivvy things along.

"Okay, people. We have to move out now."

The last few paramedics ran on ahead, including the doctor — until, at last, Asmus was the final one inside and it was time for him to get out as well. He stepped smartly towards the exit. A fleeting smile crossed his face. If he got blown up, his wife would kill him.

He never reached the doors. The pressure wave picked him up and carried him back into the now-deserted arena. It happened so fast that he never knew anything about it.

CHAPTER 6

As her jet banked for the run into London City Airport, Valentina Ferrari made some last-minute checks on her make-up. She doubted there would be photographers around, but you never knew.

She was the current head of the European Union's Competition Commission and next year she planned to run for the Italian presidency. Donatella Versace had approached her and offered to be her personal dresser, so she knew she looked good.

Her outfit today was an understated pantsuit. She'd been measured for it during a trip to Washington a few months back. Donatella herself had supervised, joking that the outfit was a bargain. "You look a million dollars, and it only cost $10,000."

She reflected that the fashion boss had been more than proven right. It was the type of thing she could often wear, always look elegant, and send a message that here was a woman who meant business even if the price was beyond ordinary Italians.

She had flown into London as part of a wide-ranging inquiry into the technology business. Among the issues were claims that technology companies were abusing their market dominance to extract high prices from consumers — as well as abusing data protection laws.

As the plane taxied to a stop, she thought about her upcoming meeting with lawmakers at the House of Commons. Even though Brexit was stalling UK politics, she wanted to brief British MPs and seek their support.

After a few moments, her security detail informed her it was safe to leave via the front steps. She walked a short distance across the tarmac and into the back of a gleaming black Range Rover, with blacked-out rear windows. The Italians might make the most glorious sports cars — regrettably, her surname was her only link to the Ferrari motor company — but you had to give the Brits credit for making their own luxury cars. Her vehicle was one of a matching pair with the second Range Rover carrying security people supplied by the British. They had provided her driver and his front seat companion as well. The cars swept out of the airport, preceded by a pair of motorcycle outriders, and an unmarked Jaguar saloon. As they headed into London, Ferrari glanced up at the towers of Canary Wharf. She never failed to be moved by the thoughts of the billions that flowed through the London financial markets.

The rest of Europe looked on enviously. The markets in France, Germany and Italy were hardly trivial, but they all bowed down before the might of the City of London and its multiple layers of expertise.

Ferrari dismissed these thoughts. She wanted to go over, yet again, the critical points of the report that had brought her here today. The car was so comfortable and silent that she was barely aware of the journey, and it was surprisingly smooth until they joined the Victoria Embankment at Blackfriars.

Ferrari sat in the front Range Rover, behind the motorcycles and the unmarked car, and with the second Range Rover behind her. The plan was to continue along the Embankment until Westminster, where regular traffic would be halted to allow the small convoy to sweep past Big Ben and straight into the Palace of Westminster via New Palace Yard.

Suddenly the two police riders turned right and disappeared with lights and sirens blasting.

Buried in her documents on the state of the UK economy, Ferrari was unaware of the exchange that had just taken place, nor did she notice as her driver looked in his rear-view mirror and tensed slightly. Her assistant was similarly absorbed in his reading material.

The driver murmured into his throat mic, which triggered a response from the other vehicles as people swung round in their seats to look behind them. About a hundred yards away, a pair of motorbikes were edging their way through the line of slow-moving vehicles. Both drivers were in heavy black leathers, their faces hidden behind black visors.

The bikes moved closer before they disappeared behind a red double-decker bus and stayed out of sight for the next few minutes. At last, the traffic started to speed up — and the driver of the first Range Rover released his vice-like grip on the steering wheel.

"Has anyone got eyes on those bikes?" he asked.

"Negative," came the response from the team in the rear Range Rover. "They're still behind the bus, as far as we can tell."

Somehow sensing her driver's concern, Ferrari looked up and glanced out of the window. Moments later, she was thrown back in her seat by a surge of power as the driver hit the accelerator.

It was too late. The first motorbike was alongside them, and the pillion passenger wielded the type of battering ram used by police to smash open doors. It made short work of the rear window, sending shattered glass into the car and covering the terrified IMF boss.

"Get down, get down! Hit the floor!" The driver was screaming at her, but stark terror froze her in place. His urgent instructions were far too late.

A long thin shard of glass had penetrated her left eye — but, even as her body started to react, the second bike was alongside them, and this time the pillion passenger was armed with a shotgun, carefully sawn off to maximise impact.

He calmly poked the weapon through the back window where Ferrari was still sitting, unmoving. The gunman fired at point-blank range, blowing Ferrari's face right off and covering her screaming assistant in blood, bone and sinew.

The spray was so powerful that it went straight into the face of the driver. Somehow, he managed to produce his gun. He fired, wildly, unable to see anything for the blood that had coursed into his eyes — but the bullet only found the security guard sitting next to him. The man slumped, bleeding profusely from a shoulder wound.

By the time the driver had wiped the blood from his face, it was all over. His ears were ringing from the shotgun blast, and he was severely disorientated. He could see the team from the other Range Rover were out of their vehicle, guns drawn and shouting in impotent rage.

One man looked about to fire at the fleeing bikes — but stopped himself as he realised he would be in danger of hitting innocent bystanders. There was nothing they could do.

The incident had lasted less than ten seconds — but, judging by the number of people taking pictures with their mobiles, the first images were already online.

* * *

Meanwhile, one of the most controversial stores in the UK was situated close to Sloane Square. It was called Diamonds and Pearls. A temple to modern consumerism, it promoted itself with the slogan, "Always exclusive, always expensive."

Large, shaven-headed men with earpieces guarded the doorway and customers had to be appraised by one of a bevy of super-skinny models wearing towering six-inch heels before they were admitted. Credit cards were carefully inspected and, if you could produce one that had no spending limit, you were welcomed with open arms. Occasionally, just such an owner was turned away simply because the women had the power to do it.

There were two queues, and the one that stretched from right to left was the one to be in. This was the preserve of the Instagram "Rich Kids" who had cash and connections. This queue moved at a decent click as people were allowed in to be relieved of their money.

The other queue went from left to right and moved very slowly. People who arrived before dawn considered themselves blessed if they got in before lunchtime. These people were called "No Mo's" — as in "no money."

But for Paula Brown, it was heaven. Today, her seventeenth birthday, she had risen at 3 a.m. and woken her dad who, with a lot of grumbling, drove her to Sloane Square, arriving just after 4 a.m.

Despite it being early summer, there was an early morning chill. Her father asked if she wanted to stay in the warmth of the car a little longer. But she wasn't having any of it, ushering him away before he could embarrass her.

She got out, leaving behind the sandwiches her mother had made. Her dad would be making short work of those. She'd asked for cheese and pickle — his favourite. She took her place and settled in to wait. While she hadn't wanted to be burdened with a coat, she had been sensible enough to choose several layers — so she resisted the urge to shiver and told herself that all would be fine.

By 9 a.m., the sun had chased away the early morning chill, and Paula was feeling thirsty, but it would have to wait; no one would be seen dead drinking out of a plastic water bottle, not outside Diamonds and Pearls.

As she stood there, her attention was grabbed by a grubby, white van that had screeched to a halt right outside. To her amazement, the driver, wearing a ski-mask, jumped out and ran up Sloane Street, towards Hyde Park. The masked man leapt onto the back of a waiting moped which tore away even as he was settling into place. The pair were almost out of sight as the van exploded.

The pressure of the blast blew the teenager to pieces. Where just moments before there had been more than thirty people on the pavement, was now an empty street. The store was a smoking ruin.

CHAPTER 7

"The Royal Family has refused to leave London. A Buckingham Palace source said it would send out the wrong signal at a moment of crisis."

Roper looked up after reading out the latest news flash. Hooley was shaking his head in disbelief. They were still half an hour from St Pancras station and had been reading news reports and eyewitness accounts of the events.

Frustration at being so far from the action was etched into the DCI's face. "Good for them," he said, adopting a fierce expression. "We can't have people thinking the Royal Family are in a panic. There must be real concern at the highest levels for them to have even considered such a thing."

"Can you remember anything like this happening before?" asked Roper. He was tugging hard at his earlobe, a habit he only adopted at moments of highest stress.

"You're doing that thing," Hooley replied, tapping at his own ear. It brought the younger man up short. The DCI was relieved; he'd once seen him make his ear bleed.

Before Roper could say anything, Hooley responded to the original question, holding his hands up in what might have been seen as a gesture of surrender. "I can't remember such a feeling of being under siege as I have right now. For me, this instant news can still take some getting used to. I worry that it will make me lose my sense of detachment, which is crucial in this type of crime.

"I'm itching to get in there. But that's silly — what can I, or you for that matter, have done? We're not first responders nor have any medical skills. Much better for us to wait and see what develops." A fleeting smile moved across his face. "This couldn't happen now, but in the old days, I can remember the press team at Scotland Yard leaving announcements that something had happened until really late in the day, so that the morning papers could have it. As police officers, it meant you had a chance to get on top of things before you had to talk about them. Now there's no chance — you see police officers having to respond in real-time, and it shows what happens when things go wrong."

His mouth suddenly dry, he grabbed a water bottle and chugged half the contents down. It was usually Roper who did that. More role reversal.

The DCI went on. "I heard you say the terror threat level has been raised to 'Critical', but to be honest, I think we all know that it's not going to do a lot of good right now. It makes you appreciate what a tough bunch they must have been during the Blitz. That was a lot worse. Hopefully, this is the closest we'll ever come to something similar."

His gloomy thoughts were interrupted as his phone beeped. Grabbing it, he saw it was a message from Mayweather.

"PM has convened COBRA," he read. "'All the key players in attendance. Need you both there. Both of you will have full access to all information.'" He checked the time. "We've got an hour. That should be plenty of time. What do you think?"

Roper shrugged and nodded.

Hooley could be sceptical about the motives behind COBRA meetings, feeling they were sometimes only convened so that politicians could try and give the impression they were in charge of events, rather than reacting to them. This time, however, he knew they needed as much critical information as they could get their hands on.

"Make sure you've got that Rainbow Spectrum of yours at full blast. We're going to need to bring a lot of firepower to bear."

It was his Rainbow Spectrum which allowed Roper to make connections that other people couldn't see. Hooley privately admitted that the whys and wherefores were beyond him, but he knew it worked. And that was all he needed.

The DCI glanced at his watch and muttered to himself. Only a few minutes had elapsed since he had last checked — it felt longer. The countryside had long given way to the suburbs, and it was clear they were approaching their destination as the houses became more and more packed together. He just had to hope problems outside St Pancras wouldn't delay them.

Ten minutes later, he groaned out loud as the train slowed and the driver's voice came over the intercom apologising for the hold-up "because of signal problems". He was wondering how long they would be when the train set off again. Five minutes later, they glided into the station.

"We need to run," he told Roper and watched in bemusement as his colleague grabbed his bags, leapt off the train and disappeared into the distance. He sighed and followed more slowly.

Roper reappeared. "I thought you wanted to move quickly. I've been telling you, you need to get more exercise, and this is a good opportunity. A quick run now will help counter the stress."

The DCI looked at him. "Yes, thanks for the advice. But if I start to run about with all these bags, I'm going to have a heart attack."

"You said we needed to run!" said Roper indignantly.

"I know, but I meant it like 'get your skates on'. I don't actually want to put skates on — I just meant we had to move as quickly as possible. And this is me moving as quickly as possible."

Roper shook his head in apparent disgust but remained at his boss's side.

An unmarked black Jaguar was waiting for them at the taxi rank, the uniformed driver standing outside of the car to deter complaints from other drivers. They just had time to buckle up before they were racing east to Whitehall.

Roper turned to Hooley.

"Do you think this is terrorism?"

Hooley suspected this was leading up to something. "It's tough to see it as anything else. Why? What's on your mind?"

Roper leaned back. "It's a funny thing, but my Rainbow Spectrum says it isn't a terror group."

"How can that be?" said Hooley. "We haven't had anywhere near enough detailed information yet to draw any conclusions. We must keep an open mind. The only thing I am sure about is that they are related. When we find out what links them, maybe that will help say if it is terrorism."

Roper was gazing out of the window. "You always say that we need evidence, but sometimes my spectrum works out answers from the most basic of information. I'm not sure I can explain how it has done it this time, at least not how quickly it has happened, but the signs are obvious. And it never changes once it has done something like this."

Hooley took a moment. "It wouldn't be the first time that Rainbow Spectrum of yours has worked things out before anyone else. I'm happy to keep an open mind, but I will need some persuading."

Roper looked over to his friend. "Don't worry. The moment I get more, I will be letting you know."

CHAPTER 8

Armed police teams, supported by Army troopers, were on the streets as Roper and Hooley arrived for the COBRA meeting in Whitehall. The soldiers' grim expressions, and the fact they were carrying assault rifles, underlined just how dangerous things were.

As soon as Roper spotted the soldiers, his hair started to stand on end, and even Hooley felt a cold shiver run down his spine. Although armed officers had become a regular sight in the capital, to see such a display of concentrated firepower on the streets of London was still unusual.

Hooley hated to see assault weapons so openly displayed — but he knew that there was little choice in the matter. Those in charge were being forced to consider the awful prospect that more attacks were imminent.

Security was tight but efficient. Soon they were hustled inside the building and into the COBRA meeting itself. The room was relatively narrow with much of the space taken up by a large wooden table. It had the feel of a bunker, which was appropriate given how under siege those present were feeling. Inside, it was standing room only — with just the most senior people getting a seat; Julie Mayweather was sitting towards the top of the long table.

Some sixth sense made Mayweather look up as they walked in and she acknowledged them with a tight smile, waving them over. They took up flanking positions on either side of her, like a pair of mismatched bodyguards.

"I hear some sort of claim has been made, but I was already in here when the information came through. I don't think it's made the news yet."

Hooley held his hands out in a "not as far as I know" gesture while Roper checked his phone.

He looked away in irritation as he remembered there was no chance of getting a signal inside this room. It was a sign of his anxiety that he had forgotten such a thing; normally, he had a memory of an elephant.

Hooley leaned forward. "That's a pretty intimidating mix of armed people out there. Is that going to be repeated all across London?"

Mayweather gave a sharp nod of the head. "It's one of those moments when we need to send out a clear signal that we're doing everything we can to keep people safe."

"Any name yet on the copper who was killed at the O2?"

The way she kept her eyes down and her shoulders tightened made an icy chill run through him. Even Roper could sense something was wrong.

"It was Barry Asmus." Her voice was barely above a whisper.

Hooley didn't know what to say, not here, not in this wood-panelled room that was packed with the great and the good. Mayweather was just one of two women present. The rest were all white and middle-aged men, the majority in well-cut suits. "The funny-handshake brigade," Asmus had called such characters — although he had always been ambivalent about the people at the top levels of the security and services. After all, he was a white, middle-aged bloke himself.

Hooley looked up as a sudden silence descended. The Prime Minister had arrived, flanked by the Home Secretary, the Cabinet Secretary, in his role as the most senior civil servant, and the head of the Secret Intelligence Service, or SIS.

With everyone shuffling out of the way there was just enough space created for him to reach the head of the table at the far end. Hooley knew multiple rooms made up the COBRA complex. Surely, they had something bigger than this?

James Harold, the PM, was a tall man in his early forties. His dark hair framed a long, thin face, which lent him the look of a mildly disappointed headmaster. He had risen to power on a pledge to reunite a country heavily divided after a referendum on whether the UK should stay in Europe. It had caused a great deal of bitterness, and Harold was seen as the man who could heal the wounds.

He was also seen, unusually for a politician, as a man who never used two words where one would do. He reached the end of the long table and gazed around, briefly looking at each person as if expecting to find answers to this catastrophe.

Pulling off his glasses, he wiped them carefully with a cloth he produced from an inside jacket pocket, then gently replaced them. He was the centre of attention. He might be a man of few words, but he understood how to communicate. Still standing, he leaned forward and placed his hands on the brilliantly polished surface of the table.

His bright blue eyes locked onto Mayweather.

"We start with you, Commissioner. Then I want to hear from MI5 and MI6. Just tell us what you know."

Before Mayweather could say anything, one of her aides entered and started forcing his way through the crowd. He found it tougher going than the PM but finally handed her a sheet of paper. She read it carefully, taking her time — even though she was conscious of the scrutiny on her.

Finally, she looked up and made eye contact with the PM. "We have a claim of responsibility. A group calling itself the Cohort has posted on social media sites including Facebook, Twitter and Snapchat."

In this room where power held sway, the names of the digital giants seemed to echo loudly. An already intense atmosphere became electric with everyone wanting to hear more. The various intelligence chiefs were especially unhappy that the police had got this sort of information before they did.

Mayweather went on, "They claim that they are, and I quote, 'dedicated to putting right the wrongs of the world. John Ryder was targeted because his company exploited other human beings. Valentina Ferrari was only interested in helping herself. Diamonds and Pearls was an abomination when people all over the globe are dying from hunger.'" She stopped. "That's all for now. There are no demands; no boasts about how they defeated us and unless someone here says otherwise, no one has ever heard of this group until today."

There was the faintest sigh as everyone simultaneously breathed out.

The PM spoke into the silence. "Is there any chance this is a hoax?"

Mayweather gathered herself, squaring her shoulders as she took a breath. "We don't think so. The claim was sent to my most secure email account. Very, very few people have access to it. Plus, they attached video footage of each incident. I'm told here that it's very high quality, far better than you would get from most mobile phones."

Everyone in the room started shouting questions, except for Roper, who went very still. Only the way his eyes sparkled showed how fast his mind was working as he contemplated this information.

Hooley looked at Mayweather. "Is it just me, or does that claim sound a bit odd? I can't quite put my finger on it, but something jars."

To the surprise of both, Jonathan leaned in close. "Actually, Brian, I should congratulate you. You appear to have got to the point unusually quickly. This group has issued a note to try and justify themselves and almost made it sound like a shopping list. It doesn't sound genuine. I can't recall anything like that before."

Hooley, who was stinging from what he saw as patronising praise, said, "Well excuse me, Mr Sherlock Holmes, but do you think there has ever been a series of attacks like this before?"

Roper stood up again. "Well, of course. That is exactly the point and that's how we shall find out who is behind this."

CHAPTER 9

When he named his company, John Ryder hadn't indulged in false modesty. It was always going to be called the Ryder Corporation, and from the beginning, he declared it would become one of the biggest brands in the world.

Like most of his predictions, it turned out to be true — and it wasn't long after he set up in Silicon Valley, California, that his business was dominating technology sales. His mobile phones, laptops, tablets, desktops and wearable technology became a byword for cutting edge capability, coupled with a fabulous design that made the most cynical consumer go weak at the knees.

He had also been quick to spot the potential of the Personal Assistant market and came out with a winning product that had the added gimmick that users could choose the names and gender for the device, something that was quickly copied. He was a serially successful man: it was claimed that he only had to think of an idea before it became a must-have item — bringing him riches that turned the company into the biggest corporation on earth, with a stock market valuation over a trillion dollars.

But today that success was in danger of crashing down. The news that Ryder was fighting for his life — and not expected to survive — had seen the corporation's share price take a pounding. It was predicted that, when New York opened, the company would lose a third of its value at a stroke.

With the time difference between London and the USA, there were still a couple of hours to go before the Wall Street bell was rung to kick off trading on the East Coast. There should have been time to do something.

Ryder's deputy, Peter Moran — a man who had never known anything but success — made things worse when he broke down during a live video conference which had intended to reassure markets all over the world. For a time, it seemed that chaos would be the order of the day since there wasn't the experience available to come up with a strategy — but the spell was finally broken when the woman in charge of the London operation, strategically the most important outside the US, took centre stage.

Josephine Taggert had been looking on in dismay. She knew that this was a pivotal moment, and it was important they quickly started acting in unison. John Ryder couldn't do it for them, so they needed to do it themselves.

"If I may have your attention." She spoke very slowly and very loudly into her screen microphone. Everyone on the video call stopped and waited to hear what she had to say.

Her mildly protruding eyes somehow underline the urgency of what they were facing. It helped that she was known to have risen to her position through hard work and ability, not the backstabbing that was sometimes the case. She was the reason why Ryder had chosen London, rather than Seattle, for what was to be a significant announcement.

Taggert held her hands behind her back, something she found calming, and today she needed all the help she could get. She hoped the tiny tremors she could feel running through her body wouldn't show up on the screen carrying the live transmission.

She took a deep breath and tried to take her time. "Don't rush, you need to get this right," she told herself. It was good advice, straight out of the manual, but very hard to do when your body was pumped with adrenalin.

She started to speak but realised her mouth had gone bone dry. She needed a drink of water, or she would be unable to talk clearly. Her assistant, Mary Lou Healy, a petite redhead, had spotted the warning signs and soon handed her boss a glass. She took a couple of sips and relaxed.

"John is our friend, our leader and our inspiration — and he is in the biggest fight of his life. We still don't know exactly what happened, but we have our people at the hospital, and I'm afraid that the news is not good. He is suffering from multiple injuries, including forty per cent burns to his body." She stopped and looked down at the floor before gathering herself to carry on. "I need to give you the real picture. The doctors say his chances of survival are less than five per cent, and even if he does somehow survive, he is going to be very sick, requiring extensive surgery. It might be many, many months before he is released from hospital.

"At the moment, he is in an induced coma and free from pain. He is getting first-rate care, and we are talking to the finest burns doctors around the world. All any of us can do now is keep him in our thoughts and pray for him."

Several of those listening had been crossing themselves as the scale of the injuries was revealed, and others were muttering under their breaths. They might work with the technology of the future, but old habits die hard.

Taggert took another sip of water. "I think it is clear that, for the immediate future, it is our responsibility to take this company forward — and on this, I do have some positive news. It is fair to say that, even though John is fighting for his life, he is still here in spirit. I can tell you now that he flew into London yesterday because he wanted to announce a new product that he believes will take us to the next level."

With that spectacular statement, she pulled her left hand out from behind her back, holding what looked like their current mobile phone.

"John has been working on this in great secrecy, and he only told me about it when he arrived in London yesterday. I didn't even know he was coming, let alone planning to make a big announcement."

She carefully rotated the phone so that everyone could get a close-up view of the product.

"Look closely. John believes this is the future."

CHAPTER 10

The COBRA meeting was breaking up, each department chief anxious to get back into the thick of things. As Hooley turned to go, Mayweather placed a hand on his arm.

"I'm going to see Sandra Asmus this afternoon. She and Barry were so close; I hate to think what she's going through."

Hooley felt a wave of intense emotion and fought back the tears that threatened to flow. He regained his composure so quickly that only someone who knew him well, like Mayweather, would have noticed.

Keeping his gaze low, he said, "I'll call her tonight."

She studied him intently and asked, "I wonder if the kids are still at home? Barry was so proud of his children."

Hooley sighed and patted her hand in a distracted way before turning and walking out. That was the thing about grief; sometimes you could talk for hours, other times you could think of nothing to say.

He found Roper waiting near the exit. "I'll meet you back at the office. Give me a few minutes on my own to walk back and think about my old mate; then we need to crack on. He'd have been really cross if we started moping at the start of a big investigation."

Since Mayweather had got the top job at the Met, all three had left the Special Investigations Unit and handed it over to a new team. Roper and Hooley were now the key members of a tiny unit that reported directly to the Commissioner. Their new home was one floor up from their old haunt in Victoria, so it was still an easy walk back from Whitehall. Roper nodded at his instructions and strode off. He didn't appear to be making any effort, but his long legs soon carried him from view.

For Hooley, it was a time to cast his memory back to when he and Mayweather had first established the Special Investigations Unit. Back then, Hooley's number one priority had been to find a hard-nosed Sergeant to take charge of day-to-day operations. It was a high-profile job, and there was no shortage of hopefuls putting themselves forward. But, while they were all pretty good, Hooley, recently promoted to detective inspector, was determined to hang on to see if he could find the perfect fit.

Which is when Barry Asmus appeared; a freshly minted Detective Sergeant with the maturity of a twenty-year veteran. He had already mastered the knack of looking like the sort of copper you wouldn't want to mess about with.

"If you want to be part of the Old Bill, you need to act like part of the Old Bill," he'd told an approving Hooley at his interview. "Otherwise, why should anyone take any notice of you?"

In no time the pair had bonded, developing a near-telepathic ability to anticipate what each other needed. They had socialised together, and their wives had also got along well.

Hooley smiled as he recalled a joint birthday party for their children. Asmus's eldest daughter had been sent to bed for throwing a tantrum, soon to be followed by Hooley's daughter — who lost the plot over a game of pass-the-parcel.

They'd spent a decade working closely together until Asmus had decided he would prefer to be back on the "front line" and had taken his inspector exams and moved down to Greenwich, not far from his home just outside Bromley.

At about the same time, Hooley's marriage started to come under pressure with his wife increasingly resenting his long hours. She was left alone to cope with a couple of rebellious teens. He'd never found it easy to talk to his kids, and now it was impossible. By the time divorce became inevitable, he was estranged from his children, who were angry at the hurt he had caused their mother.

Despite his personal chaos, Hooley and Asmus had remained in touch — and only just a week ago they'd met up for a pint and a curry. Asmus had been in good form and was full of plans for the future. He'd been approached by a company that provided security advice to top football clubs. Asmus wasn't much of a soccer fan, but the pay was good, and the work was interesting. With the biggest clubs awash with cash, they were a prime target. The fact that he had been so close to retirement made his death more poignant.

Quicker than he would have liked, Hooley arrived in Victoria. There would be plenty more grieving to come, and he needed to find out who was behind these terrible events; that would be the best way to pay tribute to his friend. It was a painful irony that one of the first people he would have called in to help today was Barry Asmus.

Lost in his memories, he suddenly realised that autopilot had brought him to the cafe that he and Roper liked to use. It reminded him that he was hungry, so he called his younger colleague and was presented with a shopping list of sandwiches and muffins.

Food and drinks handed over — Roper had the lion's share — the DCI fired up his computer and checked his emails. He was pleased to find he had been sent the links to access all aspects of the investigation.

From MI5's super-secret database to the AMIT controlled data flow, everything they would need was there. As well as highlighting any previous events that might link to the attack, he often thought the system was like one of those breaking news blogs that appear for the most significant stories — some of it fascinating and some of it dull.

There were many advantages to being on excellent terms with the chief constable of the Metropolitan Police. Not having to engage in an arm wrestle for information was one of them.

Satisfied he had what he needed, he turned to look at Roper — who appeared to have developed the ability to inhale muffins in one go, judging by the ease with which he had just consumed one.

Even through his grief at losing a good friend, there was one question that was nagging away at him. Now he was with the only person who would know the answer.

"How many people will we need?"

"All of them that want to help. It might get a bit complicated."

Hooley raised a quizzical eyebrow, but there was no response. He realised he was going to have to ask.

"Complicated. Why's that?"

"Most people would rather work remotely; that way they don't have to talk to anyone they don't want to. That leaves just two people who want to come in — and they don't like each other, so can't be here at the same time."

Hooley was about to get stuck into his reading again when he realised that Roper was looking at him intently.

"What? Am I missing something?"

"Actually, it's a question of what's missing, that you're missing. Along with everyone else."

The DCI could feel the signs of a tension headache coming on. "I tell you what. Rather than wasting time with me making a load of guesses, why don't you explain what those words mean?"

To his surprise, Roper got up and closed the door. When he looked at his boss, his expression was unusually sombre.

"It doesn't look like any of the known terror groups are behind this. The intelligence services are reporting that all of them, from the IRA through to IS, were taken by surprise; IS itself has been trying to find out who was behind this."

Hooley guessed that this was real-time intelligence and had not yet been disseminated widely. Roper maintained his own, tightly knit circle of contacts. The DCI had no idea who they were or how they communicated.

"You picked this up since we got back to London? Would you have been able to get this in Paris?"

A shrug provided the answer, it meant probably, but it happened faster when they were at the home base, and Hooley felt a sense of justification in ordering the rush return to London. It placed Roper on his patch and gave him the ability to reach out to the people who provided him with these golden nuggets of information.

"Are you passing this information on?"

A sharp shake of the head. "Everyone else will know soon enough — and I don't want to explain how I know about this."

A rueful expression crossed Hooley's face. He understood why Roper had shut the door and why they had their room regularly swept for bugging devices. He didn't think anyone would try and eavesdrop — but better safe than sorry.

It was a paradox of being an investigator. Sometimes the things you knew could get you into big trouble, but if you didn't know them, you couldn't make any progress.

"So, what do you make of this information?"

CHAPTER 11

Julie Mayweather stood up, stretched her arms to ease some of the knots in her back, and looked out at the River Thames. She'd always quietly envied Roper's view from his South Bank flat near Tower Bridge, and now she boasted something similar. It came courtesy of Scotland Yard's move from Green Park to this new setting looking out over the Victoria Embankment and close to the Houses of Parliament at Westminster. It was only a short distance, but the move took the Yard closer to the political heart of the country.

Her working life had changed more dramatically than she had anticipated. She still found it extraordinary to be taking regular calls from the heads of the intelligence services, senior civil servants and sometimes even the prime minister himself.

All the more reason to remind herself that she now called the shots — as well as moving in highly politicised circles, the crucial job was to prevent crime. She might not be arresting people anymore, but she could make life easier for those who did. She was delighted that she had been able to persuade her superiors that she should keep her links to Hooley and Roper as they pursued their highly specialised, and unique, approach to fighting crime.

This wasn't a case of "thinking out of the box"; that sounded too close to "management speak" for her liking. What she valued was having a small number of people who brought a genuinely different way of thinking about the threats they faced.

Knowing that Hooley and Roper were on the case was a comfort. Even though she was already throwing considerable resources at the problem, she always worried that, with most of the task force needing to follow proper process, it would be easy to overlook some apparently insignificant detail.

As soon as she had met Roper, it was apparent that he was different. How he would fit in was less obvious. What had surprised her was the way Hooley too had picked up the baton, seeming to relish his new role as part mentor, part-enabler. She smiled. Who said you couldn't teach an old dog new tricks?

Cheered by this thought, she picked up her reading material, a briefing update on the latest stage of the investigation. The teams of investigators were doing a formidable job of sorting out the details but were a long way from finding who was behind it.

She put the document down and gazed out of the window, just as a heavily laden barge came into view, heading west. At the prow was a scruffy-looking dog, its tongue sticking out as it took in the scents, the canine version of a big grin on its face.

"Lucky dog," she thought, then perked up as she thought she heard Roper and jumped up to check.

Stepping through her door, she saw that he and Hooley had run into the immovable force that was the group of officers who policed the outer office.

It was the pair's first visit since she had taken over three months ago and so they were a new and unwelcome intrusion, at least as far as her guardians were concerned. As she took in the scene, she couldn't help a brief snort of laughter that brought all eyes turning in her direction.

"It's okay, they're with me," she said, waving them into her inner sanctum and motioning for them to take the two chairs in front of her desk.

The DCI noted, with approval, that the chairs were brand new. He had spent so much time sitting on one of the old chairs it had almost moulded to his backside.

Noting his gaze, Mayweather said, "I don't like spending money on office trimmings, if at all possible, but I decided the least I could do for anyone forced to sit and listen to me was to make sure they had somewhere comfortable to sit."

It was a characteristic piece of self-deprecation and brought a fleeting smile to Hooley's face. It was one of the reasons she was one of the more popular holders of this job than had been the case for a couple of years. The rank and file would back a "thief-taker" over someone perceived as a political operator every time.

There was a pause as the three adjusted to their new situation. For years Mayweather had been their direct boss. Now she was the overall chief of all police, and they had moved on to head up their own unit.

After a few moments of unspoken contemplation, they decided that nothing had really changed, apart from some technical stuff about lines of accountability.

Mayweather leaned forward. Despite the undoubted pressure she was under, she hadn't lost her air of competent authority. It was that professional poise that had, many years ago, first convinced the DCI that she was someone he would be happy to follow, no matter where she led.

Pointing over to the now-closed door she raised one eyebrow and said, "I expect we have ten minutes, at most, before someone knocks on that with 'urgent information', so I'll be quick. I have made it plain that I expect you to get full co-operation from everyone on this inquiry. Inevitably there will be some turf wars — so I rely on you, Brian, to decide which battles need to be fought and which can be left alone. If you want some arses kicked, by all means, let me know, but I also know you're quite capable of holding your own." She paused, drawing out the moment. "This is the first big test of the new unit. Are you both happy that you have the resources and space you need to make this work?"

Hooley grinned. He knew she would prefer to hear about action rather than platitudes.

"We're working on some promising lines. Thanks to Jonathan, we got a couple of hours' head start on the news that none of our allies was able to identify the group behind this. I know this sounds basic stuff, but time can be such a critical factor."

He checked with Roper. "Are you happy for me to fill in some details of this?"

A quick thumbs-up gave him the go-ahead.

"We're still thinking this through, but we've been working on a picture of which people had the strongest links to John Ryder. In other words, if this isn't one of the big terrorist organisations, our focus is turning to his own family and senior executives, to his PA and gardener. We're even looking at people who are close to him in a business sense, maybe the sort he meets at these tech conferences that seem to take place every few weeks."

Mayweather looked delighted but still determined to challenge them. "You're not doing this in a 'nothing can be ruled in, and nothing can be ruled out' manner, are you?" She meant the type of lazy detective work that saw people covering their backs rather than doing real police work.

"On the contrary. We've already brought in extra people to help establish our own list of key players. We've also started the first deep background checks. There's a lot of work, but we're on it, and our people know what they're looking for."

Mayweather turned to Roper. "So, this works well for you?"

"It does. I did worry at first because I like knowing everything, but Brian and I talked it through, and now I find it easier this way. It makes me feel better able to make suggestions and follow feelings." He paused. "One more thing. As you know, I've been hoping to get a few more people involved. One of those is Isabella Morris . . ."

"Remind me which one is Isabella?" said Hooley.

"She's a forensic linguist."

"And you've told me about her before?"

"Not in so many words."

"So, what will she be doing?"

"She's brilliant at language and digging out hidden meanings. It struck me that, since the police have already received a message about these attacks, then she might be invaluable. Her job will be to work out what the real meanings are, or if the words are being made up to send us on a wild goose chase. She'll be one of those who might be working out of the office. She spends a lot of time in Cambridge but enjoys getting away to Scotland when she can. She enjoys the peace and quiet up there."

This wasn't the first time Mayweather had heard of forensic linguistics and would have welcomed the chance to learn more, but there was no time — and she could tell by the gleam in his eye that Roper was close to diving into a complex discussion.

She headed him off. "Sounds fascinating, Jonathan, and I look forward to seeing what a difference she makes. The other thing we need to decide now is the official name of the unit. At the moment I am just giving people your actual names and explaining you report directly to me."

"Actually, we agreed on that on the way over here," said Hooley. "We didn't want anything too specific, so we are going with, the 'Data and Analysis Support Unit'. It sounds sort of technical and probably a bit boring."

"I certainly agree about it sounding boring. So, what about the unofficial name? Are you still going with that?"

Roper was smiling. "We'd like to be known as the Odd Bods."

Hooley looked at Mayweather, stood up, and shaped a bow. "I have reached my pinnacle. I am now the Chief Odd Bod."

CHAPTER 12

Josephine Taggert was familiar with the phrase "You could have heard a pin drop", and now she was finding out, the hard way, what that meant. Her big announcement had been greeted with total silence. If she didn't front up now, the argument would be lost.

Even though she had heard others say that video conferencing took the emotion away, she could almost feel the intense feelings being directed at her as executives from around the world looked at her on screen. She could feel goosebumps exploding up her arms and fought back a sudden urge to shudder. Now was not the time to fail. She took a deep breath, focused on breathing and regained control.

Taking a firm grip on the phone, she held it aloft. "I know this looks like one of our regular phones, but John believed this would have the power to transform the market and give us an unassailable lead. When I show you what it can do, I think you'll agree."

Several people nodded, but not enough. Taggert pressed on and, holding the phone in her left hand, it seemed to unfold as she pulled it into a new shape. This had long been one of the most sought-after abilities: a flexi-screen that could fold into a phone or other device. Had Ryder actually succeeded where others had failed? She pulled hard on the screen to show how robust it was.

Holding up a finger, she called up a video clip, hit play then showed her audience how it looked. Now there was tentative applause, and several people called out.

Despite her deep anxiety for her boss, Taggert couldn't help smiling. "This is what John was going to show the world this morning before he was the victim of that vicious attack."

It was unbearably poignant. Someone had set off a bomb at the moment of his greatest triumph. She felt herself tearing up but pushed on, conscious that others were dabbing at their eyes.

"As I have already said, John kept this all very secret. All he told me was that he had already arranged for each of you to receive some of these new sets — and he has pre-recorded a special message which will talk you through, in detail, their capabilities." She held up both hands, palms out. "Before any-one asks, I haven't seen the message yet either. I just know that we are due to get one and, obviously, I don't know what the subject matter is all about. I don't even know for sure when it will arrive, but I think it's soon." She took a breath then added, "Jenny, I think it might be best if I shut up for a minute and hand over to you. I've given you all the news I have."

The Jenny in question was Jenny Mitchell, at Ryder Corp in Silicon Valley. Her image appeared on everyone's screen. She had distinctive long blonde hair and, despite being in her late twenties, was acknowledged as the best thinker in the company. She was now in charge of the global operation.

"Jo, thank you for this — and I agree, you have done exactly what John would have wanted. I am amazed, quite frankly, that he managed to keep this to himself and, if it works, well, the sky's the limit. Just when you start to think that John Ryder has already left his mark on the world, he comes along with another, even bigger, idea. We must do everything in our power to ensure this gets all the success it deserves." She looked thoughtful. "My instinct is that we're going to need you over here to make sure that happens, but we both need to think that through. Let's talk again in a couple of hours and decide what's best. Given that this has happened in London, there's an argument that says we keep our best people there, at least for now. But, one way or another, we need to make a firm decision. With John out of the picture, this is no time for being indecisive."

She stopped talking, and the two women looked at each other, both conscious that what should have been a pivotal moment bringing the company ever greater success might actually be the beginning of the end.

The video conference broke up, with Mitchell saying they should all get back in touch once they had received their packages and messages.

Her assistant was looking at her expectantly. "You know what, Mary Lou? What I'd really like right now is an ice-cold glass of wine. But that's not going to happen any time soon. You and I have work to do. We've got to talk to everyone here and get them up to speed."

The pair were about to leave when Mitchell popped up on the video screens. It was slightly odd to see so many versions of her.

"I think we should delay a public announcement for a few days, to let things die down," Mitchell began. "Unless John has already got a marketing drive going?"

Taggert shook her head. "Some basic information was released under embargo. I think we can buy a few days by confirming there's a new product, but in the circumstances, we would rather not do a marketing drive right now. Before all this kicked off, we had a media call booked to follow what should have been the big unveil at the O2. That's been put back until an hour from now. I can use it to update everyone on his condition and mention the new screens. That will get the basic information out there. We can decide the next steps while we wait to find out what's happening to John. It will also help give the impression we are being proactive and not just waiting on events."

A sad smile appeared on Mitchell's face. "Okay. Give me a call the moment you have any news and definitely speak to me in two hours from now."

The two women exchange another look of silent agreement, with Mitchell mouthing "good luck" as she turned away from the screen, leaving the pair in London to make their way out.

As they reached the doors, Taggert stopped and shook her head in frustration.

"Is everything okay?" asked Healy, looking anxious. Ryder was a bit like a father figure to his staff, and they were all in deep shock.

Taggert puffed her cheeks out. "In one way it's a bit silly — but I forgot to pass on John's joke. He wants to call this new phone the 'Y' phone, as in 'Why are all other phones so useless?'"

CHAPTER 13

The office had been built in the mid-1990s and was showing its age. This part was usually only used by Roper and
Hooley — although another four people could have been
easily accommodated. A short stride away was a larger space
with up to twenty desks.

The bigger office had been unused for weeks, but it was
slowly filling with people as detectives were pulled in to work
under the pair's guidance. In reality, it was mainly the DCI's
guidance, since Roper had a unique motivational style that
often left people looking like they had steam coming out of
their ears.

Hooley found it more comfortable if he dealt with the
detectives in this room and made sure to keep the younger
man at arm's length. This was an arrangement which suited
all sides; Roper could find dealing with "normals" as exhaust-
ing as they found him.

A new batch of detectives had arrived, and Hooley was
on his way to welcome them to what he had started to call
the "Research Room", if only to separate it from all the other
teams. He was almost out of the office when Roper's voice
stopped him. "I still don't understand why you keep having

to meet everyone. I have sent perfectly clear instructions on email. Only idiots could fail to understand."

Hooley turned back. "I know this sort of thing goes in one ear and out the other, but you really should try and understand that people don't like being spoken to like that."

He broke off and sighed. He'd chosen the wrong form of words, and Roper was now distractedly tugging at his ears.

Thirty minutes later, he returned feeling jaunty. He walked back in to see that Roper was having an agitated telephone conversation.

"No, no. I think you should stay in Washington. We're talking about the biggest company in the US."

Hooley knew what was going on here: Roper was talking to his girlfriend, Sam Tyler. They normally spoke over a video link, not a simple phone call, so this was unusual — and, from what Hooley could hear at this end, it wasn't going well. Even from where he was sitting, the DCI could make out the odd word of what was a shouted response.

Roper's knuckles were going white from the gripping the phone so hard, and he was listening so intently that he lost his bearings and became entangled in his chair, only stopping himself from hitting the floor by grabbing his desk with his free hand.

Finally, he managed to get a word in. "You will be playing a central role. You already know everyone over there, and they can all help you. We desperately need to find out if anyone has ever heard of this lot, the Cohort."

There was another long pause as he listened. This time the volume had been dialled down, a hopeful sign.

"Of course, I'm not just saying that. You know I never say things just to try and persuade people. I don't believe in doing things like that." Pause. "I'm not making things up. I don't know how to make things up." Another pause. "No, that's okay. This is hard for us all. But right now, we can't say what is going on, so we need to cover the key places."

When the conversation ended, Roper sat down and stared into space.

Roper referred to Sam as his girlfriend, but most of their time was spent far apart since she worked in Washington in a sought-after role as a data cruncher for various US government organisations, currently with Homeland Security. What little time they had to themselves was spent over video calls, and they could sometimes go months without talking. Hooley had no idea how they coped, but Roper insisted they both liked it that way.

The telephone exchange seemed to have left Roper a little stunned, so Hooley decided to leave him be for a few minutes. While he had been out of the room, more and more information had been generated by hundreds of investigators on the case. Half a dozen items on his screen in Victoria were marked: "Secret. Top Priority."

He read the highlights while he waited for Roper to calm down. Despite their markings, there was nothing especially startling in the documents, which was a concern since it meant little progress was being made.

Roper interrupted his thoughts. "I can't see anything new there. What about you?"

Hooley shook his head. "Nah, nothing at all. But we are making progress of a sort, even if it's partly to do with eliminating things. Your suggestion that it wasn't Ryder's family proved right. Our guys were able to track the immediate relatives, and they all have alibis. There weren't that many of them, so it didn't take long. We'll keep looking."

Roper didn't respond. Instead, he became preternaturally still. Hooley recognised the pose — he had accessed his Rainbow Spectrum. This typically took a few minutes, although Roper had told him he had no sense of time while he was doing it.

He blinked his way back into the moment and started talking.

"Eliminating the family members is helping. When I look in my Spectrum, there is still a lot that doesn't make sense and doesn't fit properly. For a start, that name, the Cohort, is a problem. My Spectrum always assigns a colour to a piece of information. It doesn't matter what the colours are, just that the closer the colour match, the more relevant the different pieces of information." He paused. "Well, most of the colours are light — but the Cohort shows up as black. That is a big problem."

Hooley nodded. "I don't have your Rainbow Spectrum, but my gut has been telling me something wrong. It just doesn't seem to fit."

"That's very interesting," said Roper. "The other thing I cannot make fit, no matter how many different ways I think about it, is the murder of Valentina Ferrari."

"Really?"

Roper shrugged. "I've got a couple of ideas, but it is complicated."

"Fair enough, but the moment you feel confident, let me know.

"Between you and the detectives out there doing the legwork, we need to keep pushing this inquiry forward."

The DCI decided to re-read the latest reports. Working with Roper, it was easy to fall into the trap of thinking he too had a computer-like ability to absorb information. He was reading a preliminary assessment of the deaths at the O2 when he thought he heard Roper saying something about the gym.

"Sorry, Jonathan, I was miles away. Did you just say something?"

Roper looked him straight in the eye. "I said, I've booked you in for some over-50s spin classes. We're going this afternoon."

Hooley froze. What Roper had said was plain enough, but given they were just starting out on the biggest case they had yet dealt with; he was struggling to make sense of it. Finally, his mind accepted what he had been told, and he frowned.

"I think, in the circumstances, we can leave that. A major terrorist inquiry must take priority."

For most people, the glacial way the DCI spat out his response would have frozen them in place. But Roper wasn't most people. Totally unflustered, he said, "Well, you're quite wrong about that. This investigation is going to put you under a lot of stress, and you need to protect yourself, or you will have a heart attack or a stroke. You're a classic victim — you work hard, don't eat well or take enough exercise, and no doubt you are still drinking too much."

Hooley rarely shouted, but this tipped him over the edge.

"Not now, Jonathan! We can talk about this after the case, and I will do all the bloody cycling you like, but for now, can we please get on with some detective work!? *That* is the priority."

Hooley glared angrily at Roper, defying the younger man to say anymore, but he wasn't to be deterred.

"You've gone red in the face, look a bit sweaty — and the fact you've lost your temper shows that the stress is already getting to you. You are going this afternoon, and that's final. I have calculated it very tightly, and you will only need to be away from your desk for thirty-five minutes. That includes the walk there and back, getting changed and doing fifteen minutes exercise. It might not sound much but little and often is very effective. Especially for someone like you who has let themselves go and needs to do something about it. I'm doing it to keep you company. I won't hear no."

Hooley was experiencing a bizarre mix of emotions. He was charmed that Roper was going to such trouble on his part and outraged at the brutal way he was being told what to do. Realising that shouting would get him nowhere, he spotted an escape route.

"I haven't got any gear here," he announced with a triumphant smirk. It wasn't often he got one over on Roper.

Roper matched the smirk with a broad grin as he reached down and produced a kit bag, which he held out in front of him.

"I anticipated you might say that. All the stuff we bought you six months ago is here. All of it unused and with the labels attached, I notice. That is changing today."

For the second time, the DCI was flabbergasted. He stuttered as he mounted a protest.

"Did you break into my flat to get that? If so, how did you get past that alarm system? The bloke from M15 said it was state of the art and totally foolproof! He claimed it would even keep the Russians at bay." Hooley stopped mid-rant and shook his head. "Why am I even asking?"

CHAPTER 14

Peace had broken out. Hooley was resigned to his fate, and in just a few hours he was going to be led to the gym.

Before they left, he wanted to throw his contribution into the mix since it was all too easy to leave the heavy lifting to Roper. He thought he might have just the thing in the shape of an outline briefing on Valentina Ferrari which he had asked his research room to prepare. It had come directly to him so hadn't yet been widely released.

Printing out a couple of copies — he didn't share his younger colleague's comfort with reading on screen — he waved them at Roper to get his attention. Handing one over, he said, "This is an initial appraisal. I've put in a request for a couple of Italian speakers to join our growing team. Hopefully, they'll be able to talk to the Italian Security Services to get more depth and context."

"This is very interesting," said Roper. He had dropped the printout on his desk, having read and absorbed the contents.

The DCI pointed at one of the bullet points. "This stuff about allegations of taking backhanders is interesting."

As usual, Roper surprised him. "I think that came about when she was looking into allegations of over-pricing by the

Italian pharmaceutical companies. It was said that she was paid off to stop her investigation."

"Really?" said Hooley, quickly checking he hadn't missed this on his report. "Where did you get that from?"

"I found an online report that was part of a wider inquiry into corruption in Italy and allegation of Mafia involvement. The report said no evidence was found to implicate Ferrari and that it could have been an attempt to throw dirt to put her off her investigation."

Hooley was thinking rapidly. "So do you have the dates for this? We can do some proper digging and find out if there's a money trail."

Roper looked at him expectantly.

"As one of the section chiefs, I got an email a few minutes ago saying there was now a dedicated team of forensic accountants working with the MI5 team. I was going to tell you anyway — so the timing is perfect. That gives us all something to get stuck into."

Roper stood up. "Excellent news and perfect timing. We need to break off shortly to get you spinning, but I may also have something. I just need a little longer to let it come together."

The DCI's heart sank; he had managed to almost forget about it. He was honest enough to admit that Roper might have a point; he was losing his temper more easily, and that was something which worried him. In this job, you needed a cool head to make the right calls. Being bad-tempered was self-indulgent. He also acknowledged that his walking to work was not quite as beneficial as he imagined. He was supposed to maintain a brisk pace, but when Roper had accompanied him recently, he realised he was moving at little more than a comfortable stroll.

At the time, Roper had seemed to let it go — Hooley had even managed to convince himself that he wasn't going to pursue it — which was far from the truth. It was becoming clear that he had been plotting for a while.

With a sense of resignation, he stretched his arms above his head and looked at Roper with a thoughtful expression. "Do you think it would help if we had a chat with Tom Phillips? See what we can pick out of that rather clever mind of his?"

Roper looked very enthusiastic. "I should have thought of that; it's a great plan. I'd like to know if he agrees that one person could have planned all this."

Tom Phillips was a major with the SAS and had been seconded to work with Hooley and Roper on their most challenging investigations. They had formed a close bond over the years, most recently when the trio foiled a plot to detonate a dirty bomb in London.

After that case, the DCI had claimed his hair had gone grey — something which offended Roper's sense of right and wrong since he could see no difference in the DCI's normal salt-and-pepper hair colour.

Hooley put out a call to the major. To his disappointment, he quickly texted back and said he would be unavailable for a little while. The major was often on covert missions, so Hooley and Roper would just have to wait.

Soon, Roper started getting ready for the gym. As they were walking out, he had one more surprise. "I know I've just been saying it was the Ferrari attack which stood out," he began, "but what about Diamonds and Pearls? It is the only one that has no obvious individual target, or none that we know about. I think we're missing something."

CHAPTER 15

Face fixed in a rictus grin, sweat pouring from every pore of his body and taking in huge gulps of air, Brian Hooley was wondering if he was going to make it out of the gym alive. For some reason, Roper's observation that a gym was a reasonably good place to have a heart attack — "you've got well trained first aiders and a defibrillator on-site" — was not proving a comfort.

The instructor, a pretty, dark-haired woman, was looking at him closely. "Okay, Brian, that's the warm-up over. Catch your breath, take a drink of water, and when you're ready, we can move on. Remember — this is your first session. You go at the pace that's right for you. We can look at breaking records a little further down the line."

The DCI sat up and took a long swig from his water bottle. It had been a long time since he had been in a gym, and here he was sitting on a "spin" machine with Roper next to him. After the water, he grabbed his towel to dry his face, took some deep breaths and then leaned forward to place his hands on the handlebars to show the instructor he was ready.

"I think this time around we'll just get used to the machine. So, Brian, don't worry about your resistance just now. As for you, Jonathan, I want that resistance turned right up so you can feel it with every movement."

The DCI risked a glance and was dispirited to see that Roper was powering away, his legs a whirl of movement despite having to work extra hard.

The instructor said, "We'll have you doing that in no time at all. For now, give me a nice steady pedal and, in a minute, we'll try making it a little bit harder."

The rest of the session passed in a blur — but, to his surprise, Hooley kept going, and he experienced a sense of accomplishment when she called time on their workout.

"Little steps and we'll get you there in no time. Now, please stay in your seat while we do some breathing and stretching exercises. Then I'll tell you to get off your bike — but do it carefully and keep a hold of your bike until you're sure you've got your balance." She paused. "You did well today, but it's all a bit strange. Your bum hurts, and you don't know when it's going to end. The next session will be better, and so will the ones after that. At least you kept smiling."

Hooley shrugged, and a rueful expression crossed his face.

"To be honest, I think my face froze in fear."

She laughed. "We'll make a fitness convert out of you yet!"

After the warm-down, he tottered off to the showers. He did feel a little unsteady but underpinning that was a sense that he had done something worthwhile, and he had stopped feeling cross with Roper.

As they walked the short distance back to the office, Hooley was having a pleasant daydream about being fit enough to start running so missed what Roper had said to him.

"Sorry, Jonathan, would you mind repeating that?"

"I said, you have a good voice. I didn't realise you could sing."

Hooley had a horrible feeling he knew what was coming. "Was I singing along to the music in the spin class?"

"Yes, very loudly. It made everyone smile."

Hooley held his hands up in mock surrender. "She was playing a lot of stuff from my youth with all those eighties numbers. You forget how much those songs mean to you."

"You even knew all the lyrics, which was quite impressive."

"I did? What song was I singing along to?"

"It was 'Love Will Tear Us Apart' by Joy Division. The original version, written in August 1979 and released in June the following year. That's quite an iconic anthem."

Hooley tried to remember what he was doing in 1979. He knew he'd joined the police the following year but couldn't recall what he'd been up to. Then he thought about what Roper had just said.

"The stuff you carry about in your head! It's quite amazing, especially as I hadn't realised there were two versions of that song. Even I didn't know that, and I was singing it."

They arrived back at the office where Hooley was grateful to sit down. He could feel a slight tightness in his thighs, nothing too bad, but a caution that he had been working out. He resisted the urge to rub his legs and waited for Roper to sit down. He'd placed two cups of water on Hooley's desk with the instruction to drink both soon.

"Just before we left, you said you were going to tell me something about Diamonds and Pearls. Are you ready now?"

Roper nodded. "I'd pretty much made my mind up by then but wanted to make sure that nothing else occurred to me. As much as I have been saying the Ferrari murder didn't make sense, there is something about the attack on Diamonds and Pearls that's even stranger. You see, I don't understand why they targeted the shop rather than the owners. Of course, you could say they did try for both when they set off the bomb, but it was doubtful they would have caught one of the three partners there. That bomb went off at 10.02 a.m. The slightest bit of research would have turned up a dozen interviews with the owners saying they never got out of bed before midday."

Hooley was impressed but had questions. "Maybe they were lying about getting up? You know, to make themselves sound a bit different?"

Roper wasn't having that argument. "Not at all. You must have missed the interview the manager gave afterwards. He said the owners were never there before the afternoon."

"So maybe they just wanted to hit the shop and the customers?"

"No, no. There's more to it than that."

"All right, try me. What's your big theory?"

"I think it was done for two reasons. The first was for punishment, and the second was a warning."

Hooley rocked back in his chair. "Some punishment and one helluva warning. Assuming you're right, what on earth is it all about?"

Roper took his time answering.

"I can think of a couple of reasons. One is quite likely; the other is *very* likely."

CHAPTER 16

They'd made their way to Streatham by different routes; train, bus, Uber and even walking. Men like this couldn't risk being seen together — someone would call the police.

It wasn't just the shaven heads, well-defined muscles and tattoos; there was something about the way they moved which said, "We are your worst nightmare." They gave off an air of animal cunning and hidden weapons. They were exactly what they looked like. Killers.

They were all headed for a flat located off Streatham High Street, a bustling area of South London, lined with dozens of shops and restaurants and residential blocks built in the 1930s.

This flat was a brisk walk away from the bright lights of the main street and was currently home to six men, the type of people you'd cross the road to avoid. The flat was in the maze of streets where strangers didn't stand out. When they'd arrived, they'd found the property was stocked, as promised, with a week's supply of food and drink.

These were the men behind the attack on Valentina Ferrari. Forty-eight hours later, they were getting restless as they waited for their handler to turn up with their pay and details of how they were getting out of the country.

All the men had been flown in for the mission. Unknown to the British authorities, they were hoping that tonight would see them heading back to their homes in Chile.

Their leader was a scar-faced sociopath who scared even his fellow killers. They called him "El Serpiente" — the snake. For some reason, his DNA had given him eyes with yellow whites and browny-green pupils. It was a frightening combination, and even his own mother didn't like to make eye contact.

He was sitting in an armchair waiting patiently, the others close but not too close. There was total silence. El Serpiente had achieved this very simply. First, he snapped his fingers, once, very loudly.

He didn't wait to see if they had heard. He just placed his right index finger against his lips. Then he very slowly drew his little finger across his throat. There was no mistaking the message.

The waiting was becoming oppressive, but as restless as they felt, none of the other five made a sound. El Serpiente checked his watch. His mobile was in his lap, and now he very carefully rested it on one of the chair arms.

A few minutes later, it beeped with an incoming message. It seemed shockingly loud and everyone, except El Serpiente, jumped. He rechecked his watch. Then he opened the message. It was a six-digit code.

The right message at the right time. El Serpiente didn't move. Just because things looked right didn't mean they were. He glanced around, his strange eyes finally settling on one of the men, the youngest and least experienced.

He beckoned him over with his finger and pulled a photograph from his phone's memory. "If this man is standing outside the door," he said in a dry, raspy voice, courtesy of a taste for cheap cigars and raw native liquors, "let him in. If it's someone else, shoot them."

The man grabbed a Kalashnikov and swiftly, but quietly, made his way to the door. He realised he might be about to die but was phlegmatic. At least it would be quick.

Holding the gun down by his side, he opened the door. To his slight surprise, it was the man in the picture. He stepped back to allow the man inside.

John Palmer was through the door, carrying a large canvas bag. Upstairs, the rest of the gang were on their feet. The Snake stayed in his seat and Palmer paused in front of him, almost genuflecting as a mark of respect.

"Hello, my old friend. You and your men did well."

He held out his hand, which was totally ignored. Palmer kept it there for a moment, then pulled back, trying to hide his embarrassment.

"Let's get the money sorted. A reward for your excellent work."

Reaching into his bag, he produced a thick brick of notes; Euros as requested. He held it out, and the closest man greedily snatched it, holding it against his nose and grinning from ear to ear as the smell of money filled his nostrils.

The others quickly followed suit — until only El Serpiente was left. With a twirl of his finger, the others looked away. Palmer handed him two bricks of notes and a small bag to put them inside. Cash hidden, he snapped his fingers, and the other men relaxed again.

Each man had already received €25,000 as a down payment and a further €75,000 today. None expected to need to work for some time. No one felt the need to count the cash. They'd worked for this man many times — and they knew where to find him if there was a problem.

Short and going to seed, Palmer looked out of place among this group of lean, muscled killers. But being the paymaster won him acceptance. He rummaged around in the bottom of the bag. He didn't notice the increase in tension as everyone locked onto his movements. The younger man reached for the Kalashnikov.

With a surprising degree of theatricality, Palmer produced a bottle of Pisco, the Chilean national drink made from fermented grapes. They recognised the brand as one of the best and broke into gap-toothed smiles. Within minutes, a ragtag collection of shot glasses was brimming over with booze. Palmer raised his in salute, and they all knocked back their drinks.

All except Palmer.

Too late, El Serpiente noticed and tried to stop himself swallowing. By then, the damage was done; the drink was already halfway through his gullet.

Palmer watched in fascination as the six men started convulsing and calling out in Spanish. The only word he recognised was "Madre" — apparently, he mused, his victims wanted their mothers.

Within moments it was game over. They lay twitching and gurgling on the floor, blood pouring from their eyes, noses and mouths. It had been a nasty death, the poison reacting with their stomach contents to create a powerful acid that destroyed their insides.

The last to stop twitching was the man who had let him in, the agony he'd gone through leaving him with a reproachful look on his face. Quietly, Palmer backed out of the room. Apart from anything else, he was anxious to get away from the appalling smell. The police would find his fingerprints — but it would do them no good. He was a ghost, and all traces of his existence had been removed from official records.

The burner phone he supplied to El Serpiente was safely in his pocket. That would need disposing of properly.

Standing in the doorway, Palmer touched his forehead with the first two fingers of his right hand in a macabre salute. "Nothing personal, chaps. It's just there was a bigger plan this time. I'm afraid you were never meant to move forward."

His gaze lingered on the now-dead leader. "By the way, old chap, it's bad form not to shake hands."

If Palmer had a weakness, it was this addiction to melodrama, but this particular audience was in no position to complain.

He left, walking briskly to his car parked half a mile away. Before driving off, he sent a one-word text to a man in Paris. An hour later, this same man would send a text to the private number of the head of MI5. It would give them the address in Streatham. With digital hunters already starting to turn towards him, the man would abandon the mobile phone and slip away into the night. He had no time to waste.

By then, Palmer would have completed his second rendezvous of the evening, this time with two men in a small flat near Waterloo railway station. That would trigger a second text, this time from Berlin, followed by another dash into the night.

Palmer was working to a strict timetable. He wanted to be on his last train home from Waterloo, but he had left plenty of time to offer the next pair a toast as thanks for their work.

CHAPTER 17

Over cups of strong tea — it was going to be a long night — Hooley and Roper had a lengthy discussion about the relative merits of having the three owners of Diamonds and Pearls picked up tonight and brought to Victoria for questioning or leaving it to the morning.

In the end, they agreed to wait until the following day, but for different reasons.

The DCI was concerned the trio would be legally entitled to refuse a night-time interview and felt it would be better to start talking to them on their home turf — "You never know, it might mean they will let their guard down enough to give us something useful. If you're right about them, bringing them in will definitely make them clam-up" — while Roper argued for a delay since it would allow him to gain more data.

"The more I know in advance," he said, "the better it will be."

An hour later, Hooley looked up. He had been disturbed by a noise, and he quickly realised it was Roper, hunched over an iPad, swiping continuously. Roper kept his nails long, and they brushed against the screen with every swipe.

"I don't know how you get through information so fast."

Roper looked up. "It's only messages taken from their phones, and some emails. All short stuff and none of it very interesting so far. Not even the stuff on WhatsApp. Mostly going on about how brilliant their store is."

Hooley nodded and went back to his words. It took a few seconds, but then he did a double take.

"I thought WhatsApp was super encrypted, or something? Isn't it supposed to stop people like us reading it?"

"That's what everyone wants you to believe," said Roper, enigmatically. "If you think about it, no government wants you to know exactly what they are capable of. Even the so-called good ones."

Hooley was reminded, once again, that working with Roper was neither dull nor predictable. It wasn't so much that he was a conspiracy theorist; it was just that he seemed to know things other people didn't. And if he didn't know them himself, he knew people who did.

Roper's unpredictability kept Hooley on his toes — he often needed to remind the younger man of what they were trying to achieve — but he could understand why so many of his fellow senior officers found him near impossible to work with. Roper was extremely independent and was barely on nodding terms with the concept of a chain of command. But their loss was the DCI's gain. The critical thing was solving crimes, and on that score, Roper was in a league of his own.

"I hope you're making sure to keep what you're doing very discreet. And have you put in a formal request to access this data?"

Roper looked impatient. "I put the request in as soon as we got back from the gym. We know the answer will be yes, so why wait?"

A few hours later, Hooley was lost in a complicated report on organised crime when a loud crash made him start. He knocked a cup of water all over his trousers. Muttering angrily, he looked at the clock. It was almost 10 p.m. This only made him more irritable. He and Roper had been reading continuously since they had got back from the exercise class. No wonder he was getting an attack of the jitters. It had been a long time since they were on board the Eurostar.

Concentration well and truly broken, he became aware of voices just outside the door. One clearly belonged to a woman, and it sounded like she was apologising. He stuck his head outside and saw Fred, the night cleaner, trying to reload his trolley with various containers.

A woman with dyed blonde hair was trying to help. She seemed familiar, but Hooley couldn't quite place her. She kept dropping everything she picked up. Fred flapped his hands in her direction, nearly pleading. "Please. It's not a problem. Much easier if I do it myself."

The woman immediately stopped, her reaction suggesting that she was used to people telling her not to help. There was something about the resigned way she was behaving, as though this sort of thing happened all the time.

As she stepped away, she noticed Hooley and broke into a big smile which chased away all the deep worry lines on her forehead. Tentatively, he smiled back. Encouraged, she rushed towards him at an alarming rate, causing him to back-pedal rapidly, holding his hands out in a warding gesture.

"Detective Chief Inspector Brian Hooley," she said, pronouncing his name very carefully and demonstrating that she knew exactly who he was. Despite her size, barely five feet tall, she marched right up to him, craning her head to make eye contact.

He tried to make room by stepping back — but she followed him until he was pressed up against his desk and could go no further. She seemed entirely oblivious to his obvious discomfort at having his personal space so thoroughly invaded.

"My name is Susan Brooker. I came in to meet you nine months ago, but you don't remember me, do you? Wait, I have something that will help."

She produced her phone and started prodding the screen energetically, finally finding what she was looking for. She thrust the phone straight towards his face, so close that it made him cross-eyed. Placing his hand on the mobile, he gently pushed it away so that he could focus on the screen.

"I've changed my look since then, so this is how I was when you met me."

The photo was of an unsmiling woman with dark brown hair. Looking back at Brooker, he realised she was studying him in an intense, almost feverish way. He couldn't think of anything to say, but then the memory of the meeting floated suddenly to the front of his mind. She was the first person they'd spoken to when he and Roper were thinking about setting up the Odd Bods.

The DCI was surprised he had forgotten her as he now clearly remembered the way she had managed to walk straight into the corner of his desk. She'd nearly fallen, and he had winced in sympathy at how painful it must have been. Roper, he recalled, had been untroubled by this — and, after quizzing her in-depth, had announced she was perfect. It was agreed that she would be one of the first people called in if they got the chance to create the new team.

"I do remember you, Susan. You made quite an impact, in all senses of the word, if my memory serves right."

She looked solemn.

"It's my dyspraxia. I often find myself bumping into people or things." She jerked her thumb at the doorway. "Things like that trolley belonging to the night cleaner. Some people think I do it on purpose, but I don't. It's like I can't quite judge things. Anyway, Jonathan called me this evening and told me the Odd Bods were up and running. He said you'd be here really late, so I cleared my desk and got straight over here. I'm ready to get started."

Glancing back at the clock, Hooley said, "Your enthusiasm and work ethic can't be faulted, although I do try to make sure people don't overdo it. At least I do normally, but with three investigations, all of them urgent, normal rules have gone out of the window."

He gestured at the empty desks. "You're the first here, so choose where you want — but maybe that desk next to

Jonathan might be best." He paused, his memory filling in more gaps. "Am I right in saying you're a civilian worker attached to the records department at the Met's training centre in Hendon? Or at least you were until tonight?"

She nodded vigorously. "That's right. When one of the sergeants there heard that you might be setting up this new squad, he arranged for me to get an interview. I was the first person you two spoke to. After I spoke to Jonathan tonight, I told Sergeant Evans. He said the best thing was for me to get over here as quickly as I could — and that he would sort out all the paperwork."

Hooley hid a smile. He knew Sergeant Evans quite well and recalled that he had described Brooker as "very talented and very complicated".

He also knew that Evans would never have recommended her for such a high-profile post unless he thought she was up to the task. It was that which persuaded him to give her an opportunity to make her case.

Roper thought she was terrific, saying her skills at data analysis would help him fine-tune the way he used his Rainbow Spectrum. Hooley was impressed. He liked the idea that things could only get better.

Roper had helped Brooker settle in and had given her a password that would allow her temporary access to the system. Realising the pair were clearly intent on a few more hours' work brought into sharp focus just how hungry he was.

"I think we could all do with coffee and something to eat. How about pizza from that place around the corner? They're open until midnight. They also do a half-decent cup of coffee."

Brooker jumped up. "I'm happy to do that; just tell me where to go."

Hooley had an image of his food and drink ending up on the floor and waved her back into her seat. "No, it's my treat! Besides, I could do with stretching my legs. I can't keep going as long as you young people . . ."

There was a short delay while Roper agonised about whether to order double portions but was talked out of it by the DCI, who pointed out that the extra-large pepperoni he wanted was described on the menu as already being enough for three. Roper looked dubious but eventually relented.

When he left the building, Hooley was surprised at how many people were still around. Even after three atrocities, it was good to see Londoners were still out and about. He also reflected that tonight was a significant moment. The Odd Bods were up and running. He just hoped he hadn't taken on too much responsibility; he was beginning to suspect that being Chief Odd Bod was going to need a lot of thought.

Just after midnight, the three were getting ready to head home for some badly needed rest when Hooley's phone pinged. At this time of night, it could only be linked to the investigation. He grabbed his device and looked at the message.

He read it, sat down and wordlessly handed the phone to Roper.

CHAPTER 18

The dying agonies endured by the men were reflected in the grotesque way their faces were contorted by pain, their lips drawn back from their teeth in a macabre parody of laughter. Dark red blood mingled with vivid yellow bile to create a sinister orange colour.

As he looked around the dingy flat in Streatham, Hooley fought back a shudder. He knew the victims were most likely terrible men, but this was a lousy way to die. Whoever had done this was entirely without mercy.

If he'd felt weary earlier, this had driven the tiredness away. When he'd read the message, Hooley had needed thirty seconds to decide whether he would go to the crime scene. Roper had declined. It wasn't because of the bodies; it was because he wanted to get Susan Brooker up to speed.

The squad car had picked him and, with blue lights flashing, the journey had taken less than fifteen minutes. Now, at last, he had his "boots on the ground".

All the victims looked the same: relatively short at well under six foot, with muscular builds, powerful shoulders and big hands. One man was lying on his back by an armchair, his eyes wide open. The eyes themselves had a disturbing reptilian cast.

He looked up and spotted the duty inspector; it was a face he knew well. Hooley and Mike Bell had worked together on several occasions, and Hooley liked the man's quiet competence.

The two men shook hands and the DI nodded at the bodies. "South Americans, most likely from Chile. Tough little sods; they get flown in for specialist crimes, usually burglary. None of them has ever been arrested here, so they never show up on border controls. We've sent their details over to Chile, and I just know they'll come back with records as long as your arm. I wouldn't be at all surprised to find some have military service. Their Special Forces guys are said to be especially tough.

"So," he smiled at Hooley, "what brings the great DCI Hooley to our humble crime scene? I heard you did everything long-range nowadays, not wanting to get your shoes dirty."

His enormous grin showed he was just teasing, but it still stung.

"I spend too much time behind a desk. I missed the first three crime scenes because I was on a train." He held up his hands. "It's a long story. Anyway, I needed to get out to this one. Sitting indoors is an easy way to forget that murder is always nasty and smelly."

DI Bell nodded in sombre agreement. "Anything you need, just ask."

"Thanks. In fact, you've already been a fantastic help with the tip about South America. We've had a brilliant researcher join us today — tonight actually — so I can get her working on that straight away. Anything coming from door to door?"

Bell laughed. "Amazingly, everyone around here goes to bed early — at least that's what they told us — so no one saw anything. We'll be back first thing but, somehow, I doubt we're going to get very much more. Everyone keeps themselves to themselves."

"Anything from forensics, or medical?"

"Nope, nothing there either. There was a bottle of Pisco, a sort of Chilean firewater, so I'm led to believe. The lab boys have taken it. The smart money says it was laced with whatever the poison was since there are seven shot glasses and six victims."

"So there was one other person here. The poisoner? He — or she — must have been known to them, which makes all of this all the colder."

The DI nodded. "You can probably bet your mortgage it was a man who was here. Huge fingerprints apparently. There was also enough weaponry here to start a small war. We're obviously optimistic that the forensics match up with the attack on the Ferrari woman."

With nothing else to do, apart from get in the way, Hooley organised a lift back to Victoria. It would take a while for all the information to get into the system, so coming here had been a good call. Plus, it gave him a vital sense of engagement. Now it felt personal.

On the journey back, he thought back on all that he'd seen. Something was still bothering him: why — and *how* — had someone alerted senior figures at MI5, using contact details that were supposed to be highly classified? The whole thing was a mystery, in the same way that the group claiming responsibility for the earlier attacks had been able to access a protected email account belonging to Mayweather.

It was just after 1 a.m. when he walked back into the office. Roper and Brooker still looked as fresh as daisies and were eager to hear the details. Before long, Brooker was chasing up the South American angle, keen to contact any law-enforcement people who might know the guys.

Hooley had already given up on the idea of going home. He'd snatch a few hours' sleep at the office instead. They had day beds in a couple of unused rooms, and there was access to showers, plus he kept a change of clothes in his desk.

Best of all was that, when they pulled all-nighters, Roper had nominated himself the official bacon-sandwich provider.

He'd found a little place that made the best bacon sand-wiches he'd ever eaten. They made up for lost sleep.

In the event, Hooley managed four hours, and after a shower, he was feeling surprisingly chipper. Just after 6 a.m. he found Roper ordering breakfast and Susan Brooker still going strong.

"A couple of them were ex-Chilean Special Forces," she called out as he sat down. "I should be getting details soon. At least one of them has connections to the UK."

Roper was also looking pleased.

"I may have a picture of the back of the poisoner's head."

"Yay," was all Hooley could think to say.

"I've been checking CCTV in the area, and it's mostly out of action — but there are a couple of cameras operating. One of them has a man walking away from the street the flat's on at about the right time."

He tapped his phone and called up a picture. It was the back of someone's head. But it was very grainy and quite dark.

"Brilliant work, Jonathan, but I can't see a jury getting too worked up about that."

For some reason, this conversation filled him with renewed enthusiasm, and he surprised Roper by jumping up and purposefully pacing around their office. He stopped in front of Brooker's desk.

"Have you got what you need, Susan?"

"I'm fine, sir. Jonathan has got me all the access I need. I can get on to a load more databases than I could at Hendon. At the moment, I'm just looking for anything unusual or things that might connect all three incidents. We can refine that as you get more specific information."

"Great." He rubbed his hands together. "By the way, I'm banning the use of 'sir'; it makes me feel old. But that's all great — because Jonathan and I are going out in about an hour.

"We need to talk to the people behind Diamonds and Pearls. The main squad is going to be spending all of today either with the IMF people, the head of security at the O2 or at the two poisonings — so that gives us a small window to talk to the store owners."

Roper piped up. "That will be Mark and Julie Savage, brother and sister, and her friend Emily Wong. I think she put the money up for the initial investment."

"So, you're happy with the plan then?"

"I am. Something tells me these three are important. It's frustrating because I can't quite pin down why that is, but it is there." He looked intently at Hooley. "I know you're going to ask but, at the moment, my Rainbow Spectrum doesn't really help — we just don't have enough information. But I do feel that, if I keep adding data in, I will start to get somewhere."

Hooley powered off his terminal and rushed out of the door, before turning around and walking back in, nearly colliding with Roper who was rushing to catch up.

He looked at Brooker. "Sorry, Susan, with just me and Jonathan I've got out of the habit of being a team player. Can you hold the fort here and we'll stay in touch and let you know when we'll be back?" He shook his head. "I know this is going to make me sound like Jonathan, but I have the strongest sense that the clock is ticking, and we only have a small window to get the people behind these attacks."

CHAPTER 19

The Diamonds and Pearls store in Sloane Street was no more. Huge white painted boards completely covered the extensive damage to the front of the building. Inside, engineers were carefully stabilising the structure after an initial assessment had warned it was in danger of collapse.

Hooley and Roper had been directed to an office at Chelsea Harbour, an upmarket development of businesses, residential units and a five-star hotel, a couple of miles from Diamonds and Pearls.

They walked into a small reception area, identified themselves to the guard and watched as he picked up the phone.

"Police are 'ere," he mumbled.

Long minutes dragged by and a smiling woman, dressed in a severe black outfit, her blonde hair scraped back, arrived and asked to check their IDs. The DCI nodded at Roper.

After spending far too long studying their pictures, the woman finally handed them back. "I'm afraid security is very tight now. We can't take risks."

Hooley nodded, inwardly wishing the same level of security had somehow been present outside Diamonds and Pearls on the day of the bomb.

She led them to a rectangular shaped room dominated by a dark grey table with black leather chairs on either side. At one end of the room, floor to ceiling windows flooded the space with natural light and gave a distant view of the River Thames.

Waving them inside, the woman said, "The owners know you're here. They'll be with you shortly."

A few minutes later, the three showed up. They were about Roper's age, but here the similarities ended. These people were toned and buffed, beautifully dressed — and the women had a perfection that came only with expertly applied make-up, lots of money and plenty of time.

They trooped in, making no attempt to shake hands, and simply sat down on one side of the table. Soon they were followed in by a couple of men wearing black suits who placed their phones on the table — clearly intended to record the interview — and then took seats behind the three.

Everything was done in total silence. Hooley studied them for a long moment and then carefully placed his phone on the table, gesturing with his head for Roper to do the same. He recognised power games when he saw them, and he knew exactly what to do.

After letting the silence grow a moment, he started talking — using what his children said was his "Sergeant Major's" voice.

"Thank you for seeing us. At this stage, you are merely assisting our inquiry." His voice boomed out, and the trio flinched. "You should keep in mind this is an anti-terror investigation and, as such, the police have wide-ranging powers to question anyone of interest."

Now he had their attention. The threat of arrest, no matter how vague, tended to focus most people.

He studied them more closely. The brother and sister closely resembled each other and wore carefully matched trousers and tops, him in neutral colours, her in pale pinks and blue. Emily Wong favoured a slightly more casual look which the DCI guessed cost thousands.

Games over, he nodded at Roper to start the questions. He wasted no time, speaking fast but clearly. "Your shop was at the centre of a lot of controversies. Did you get threats or maybe hate mail?"

Mark Savage answered. "We get a pretty steady stream of hate mail. People saying what they'd like to do to us, to our customers and even to our staff. I used to throw it away — but for the last couple of years, we've employed security people to go through it, just in case we need to take some of it more seriously. A couple of months ago, Emily became convinced that someone was stalking her. Our security team put people on it and believed they managed to frighten someone off."

Hooley jumped in. "Did you inform the police?"

Savage shrugged helplessly.

Hooley tried a different tack. "Did your security people manage to get pictures, some sort of ID or even a description?"

Savage looked miserable. "Nothing beyond him being a white male, about five feet ten inches tall, wearing glasses and fit enough to outrun our people. To be honest, we thought it might have been someone trying to get Emily's attention. Rich and beautiful women can attract unwelcome approaches."

"We're going to need to speak to your security team," said Hooley. "We need every single detail, no matter how unimportant you might think it is."

Roper jumped in again. "But it would be right to say that a lot of people didn't like you."

Throughout the session, Julie Savage had been staring at the floor — but this seemed to attract her attention.

"That's rather direct of you, Mr Roper. Most people are little more circumspect — but why not call a spade a spade? A lot of people like us and a lot don't. Mark says we are like Marmite."

Roper looked puzzled.

"You know, Marmite! People either love it or hate it. There's no in-between. That's how people seem to react to us."

Hooley recognised the expression on Roper's face and decided to head him off before they got bogged down. "Let's talk about the Marmite reference later. For now, I'd like to get back to any concerns you may have had, anything that was bothering or maybe really worrying you."

Mark Savage, who was looking at Roper with an interested expression, managed to drag himself back into the conversation and switched his gaze to the older detective.

"I've been asking myself the same question, and I don't think there is. Yes, we get a lot of hate mail, but we knew we would get that when we opened our store. It was bound to polarise opinion, but we banked on that."

"You mean you were using hatred as part of your business plan?" Hooley thought he had heard it all now.

Savage showed some genuine enthusiasm. "Exactly!" he said, waving a finger in their direction. "Right from the beginning, we knew it was going to be a great marketing tool. We were all over the internet in the months before we opened."

"What about staff? Did you have any disgruntled employees?"

The brother and sister shared a look. Then, Mark spoke: "There was an issue, but I can't believe it would have led to this."

"Perhaps you'd better tell us and let us be the judge of that."

CHAPTER 20

Josephine Taggert was interviewed by two senior intelligence operatives, nominally assigned to GCHQ. For this interview, they'd opted to describe themselves as "working with Scotland Yard". Because Taggert was no fool, this made her assume they were members of the security services. Both sides left it unsaid. The relationship between big tech companies and domestic intelligence organisations was complicated, to say the least.

As the door closed, she put her head in her hands, exhausted by the non-stop roller coaster she'd been on since the attack on Ryder. Everyone she met had questions, to which she had very few answers.

It wasn't just the police and their "assistants" who wanted a piece of her. She needed to spend time reassuring anxious staff that the Ryder Corporation was worth sticking with. She knew rivals were already making approaches to her most valuable people.

Ryder had spent a lot of time in London, claiming it was his favourite location, but she knew he wasn't above telling the other regional chiefs the same thing. Not that it bothered her. John Ryder was one of those people you always looked forward to meeting. His energy was contagious and, even though he was a genius, he had a way of involving people that made them feel that, on their very best day, they were on his level. She feared he might prove irreplaceable.

Despite the mountainous work to be done in London, she had to free up time to travel to California. Yesterday she had plucked up the courage to ask the detectives if she could leave the country, causing furrowed brows and muttering that it was much too soon. But the two people who had just left had surprised her by arriving with a solution. She could go so long as she consented to be available for questions at any time and made sure there was someone in the UK who could cover the bases.

It was a reasonable request but left her with a dilemma. She usually took her assistant, Mary Lou Healy, on any significant trip. Healy had made herself indispensable over the last couple of years and had long outstripped her nominal role as a PA. She was Taggert's right-hand woman.

That made her the obvious choice to liaise with the police teams and keep a careful eye on the UK operation. By the same token, she would be invaluable in America, especially as the launch was undoubtedly the most critical in the organisation's history. Josephine was in danger of arguing herself into a standstill and needed to make the call. As Ryder always said, "Leaders, lead."

Decision made, she stood up and went into her outer office to find Healy. Seeing that her assistant was engrossed in preparing a report, she walked over to the coffee machine.

"Small black coffee, one sweetener?" she said, holding up a cup.

Healy laughed. "I'm wired enough as it is. One more shot of caffeine and my eyeballs will start revolving."

"Well, I'm going to risk it. I know what you mean — but, if I stop drinking coffee now, I won't be held responsible for the consequences. I'd put the crazy in crazy lady. When you're free, can you come in and we can talk about the launch?"

Five minutes later, she and Healy were sitting on the sofa. Even though her assistant was a few years younger,

Taggert thought it was amazing how fresh she looked. By contrast, Taggert was sure that she was showing the first signs of bags under her eyes.

"The police are saying that I can probably head over to California, but they'd prefer it if someone senior stayed here to help with any immediate inquiries. To be honest, you should be first on the list to come with me, but it might be better to leave you here. You know everything I know, which makes you the right person to deal with the police. What do you think?"

Healy didn't answer straight away but looked oddly embarrassed. "Normally I would bite your hand off to go on that trip, but I do have a problem . . ."

Taggert suddenly thought she knew why her assistant was embarrassed.

"Is there an issue with Miss Kitty?"

Miss Kitty was Healy's much-loved cat who repaid her owner's devotion with total disdain. This only seemed to make her love the cat more.

"Normally she stays with my neighbour — but she's in hospital at the moment and won't be up to looking after her for a couple of weeks. I'm not saying I can't go — there's an excellent cattery I can use. But she'll be grumpy with me for ages if I leave her there, so maybe this is serendipity."

Taggert smiled at her. "Well, I would hate to upset Miss Kitty. I'll talk to California today and explain that we're thinking of leaving you behind to run things here." A horrified expression flitted across her face. "Don't worry. Miss Kitty is our guilty secret. I'll explain what the police have said, and that should be fine. But thanks for being willing to send her off to the cattery. I could ask no more of you."

CHAPTER 21

Julie Savage sighed heavily and stared at the floor, unable to make eye contact. She remained this way for a long moment before she seemed to gather herself, puffing out her cheeks with an air of embarrassed resignation.

Addressing a point in the centre of the table, she said, "It's down to me — so I might as well tell you. I had an affair with one of the floor managers. I thought it was just a bit of fun, but he seemed to take it a lot more seriously. In the end, Mark had to step in."

On a personal level, Hooley hated this sort of thing, but as he often told Roper, it was their job to know everything that might be relevant, especially when people don't want to tell them. He knew they just had to treat it as detail — whether it's either useful or not.

"I'm afraid," he said now, "we'll need you to give us a more detailed account. I know it's not great, having to reveal personal information to people you don't know, but if it helps, just remember that this is a line of inquiry. It might hold the answer, or it might not, but either way, we will be discrete."

She nodded, apparently resigned to having to come clean, and gathered her emotions enough to finally look up.

"Jasper and I were together for almost three months. At first, we had lots of fun and just enjoyed our time together. But he suddenly started getting intense and jealous. He hated me talking to other men — so I realised he had to go. I let him down as gently as I could. Told him he was a great guy and it was all my fault that we couldn't develop the relationship. The truth is, I'm relationship phobic. I can't stand it when people come over all needy. I told him over drinks, and he reacted badly. Told me I needed protection from other men, and he was the one to provide it. I'm afraid I made a bad mistake and laughed at him for that. He became furious, threw his drink over me and stormed out." She shook her head.

"It was very embarrassing, and I do regret upsetting him, but he just disappeared after that, not even coming to work. I asked HR to send him a letter confirming he had now left our employ but, as a recognition of his work, we were giving him the equivalent of three months' salary."

Hooley worked hard to keep a poker face — but some sense of his discomfort at her last remarks must have filtered through because Julie Savage looked defensive.

"He wasn't actually entitled to anything, so three months was pretty generous. But it seemed to encourage him again because, after that, he started hanging around outside my house. In the end, he became such a nuisance I had to get Mark to talk to him."

"And this went okay? Did things get a little fraught for a while?"

"It was fine," said her brother. "I found Jasper waiting near Julie's flat and had a talk to him, man to man. There was no trouble at all. I thought he took it very well. After that, we never saw him again. The only reason we're mentioning it now is that there really is no other member of staff who might have had some sort of beef with us. Even so, it would be a stretch to imagine that Jasper might have taken it a bit further. At worst, he's guilty of a bit of stalking, and he put his hands up when I confronted him. There's no way he would have organised something like a bomb attack on the store. It just wasn't in his nature. We probably shouldn't have even mentioned him."

Roper had been silent during the latest exchanges but now interjected. "But you have raised him, and he is obviously a suspect. Do you happen to have an address, his full name and any personal details, like his parents, for instance? Who did he name as his next of kin on the work contract? Do you any pictures?"

Mark Savage rewarded him with another stare, before crossing to a small desk where he picked up the phone and dialled. After issuing his request, he came back to his chair.

"I'll have those details in just a moment, apart from the next of kin. Everyone has a standard contract put together by HR, but most people don't worry about the details. People are so keen to get working at Diamonds and Pearls on their CVs; I suspect most of them would turn up if we said they had to do it naked."

The way the man smirked at this riled Hooley, who hated that sort of arrogance. "That would be a sort of zero-hours contract you offer people. No guarantees or other protection, I suppose," he said, his tone showing he was becoming less and less impressed with the way the three did business.

Savage didn't bother to reply, just shrugged his shoulders. Before the DCI could say anything else, Mark's phone beeped with an incoming message. He checked his screen.

"I have those details and photo for you."

As he pinged them to Roper's phone, Hooley decided this was a good point to break off the interview; he'd had more than enough of these three for now, and they could always come back. He also wanted to check something with Roper.

The moment they were outside and safe from being overheard; Hooley spoke. "I know we've got a suspect now, but I was expecting you to raise those theories you mentioned last night."

Roper shrugged. "I thought it was a bit convenient that they offered up this guy, Jasper Fitzhenry, so I thought to get him out of the way first. His address isn't that far away. I would be surprised if it were him, but he might know something that can help us."

Hooley was frustrated, but there was no point arguing. Their police driver had been waiting for them, and they clambered into the back of the car. He put a call into the central control room; he wanted backup. While he shared Roper's scepticism that this was the man, he had no option but to take it seriously.

The driver took them east until they crossed the river at Lambeth and headed towards Stockwell, home to a large Portuguese population. The address they were looking for was at the Lambeth end of Stockwell and was off the main drag. It turned out to be a small white-fronted Victorian property in a small terrace of similar houses.

It was Fitzhenry himself who opened the door. He was slight with a darkly handsome face, a perfect match for his photo.

Hooley had already grabbed his ID but, before he could hold it up, Fitzhenry's expression switched from welcome to alarm and he slammed the door shut. Hooley cursed. He'd committed the absolute sin of not making sure he got his foot in the door.

Roper was looking amazed. "I'm pretty certain I heard him running to the back of the house. He must be going out the back way."

"Did you see him long enough to get a decent description of what he was wearing?" asked Hooley, who was already starting to dial Scotland Yard. "We need to get an urgent alert on this man. Maybe he's not as harmless as we've been led to believe."

"Yeah. He's five feet and eleven inches tall, lean build and was wearing blue jeans from Primark, a white t-shirt from Gap and black shoes from Sketchers. The picture is a good likeness, but he has changed his hair from a centre parting to slightly longer and parted on the right. He needs glasses, but he wasn't wearing them when he answered the door."

Hooley stared. "Are you sure about all that? I mean, the detail about where he got his stuff from — and the glasses? I missed pretty much all that . . ."

Roper looked puzzled to be asked. "Of course, I'm sure. When I walk to work, I like to practise by seeing what people are wearing and where they bought it from. I am also excellent at judging height and making allowance for the type of shoes they wear. Some heels are much higher than others. As for glasses, you could see the indentations on his nose."

Hooley shook his head, amazed. "You might have noticed indentations. All I saw was a bloke running away very fast."

The uniformed officers were already looking for a rear exit, and Hooley phoned in with the news and detailed description. They'd barely moved from the spot on the pavement, but now Roper went to lift the letterbox so he could peer inside.

Hooley grabbed him by the shoulder and pulled him back.

"Are you crazy? That man has just jumped to the top of the queue. Maybe he's left a little surprise for us too. You have no idea what might be wired to that letterbox, so don't go poking around! In fact, we'd better make a start on getting people out of the houses next door . . ."

CHAPTER 22

Even in the school photo, John Palmer was that kid right at the back with his face obscured by someone else's shoulder, and in his adult life, he had displayed the same skill at anonymity. He hated it, but there was nothing he could do about it.

He tried to be bitter and twisted, but people seemed to ignore him — so the best he could manage was a sullen silence which everyone ignored. Then, much to his surprise, he was noticed. And not just by anyone. The boss.

Tony Cross was the owner of the enormous warehouse where Palmer had ended up working in logistics. It was a busy site, but the big money came from his secret sale of drugs, as Cross fed a growing habit, targeting the towns and coastal villages of Devon and Cornwall.

These areas presented a uniquely complex challenge. During the peak holiday periods, they were jam-packed with people and customers. But at quiet times of the year, the area was significantly under-populated.

The problem was having the right number of boots on the ground at the right times. What Cross noticed was that when Palmer was running the legitimate side of the supply chain errors were at a bare minimum. Realising that a significant talent might be sitting right under his nose, Cross made him an offer. This is the profit, he explained, that I have been making for the last few years. Double it, and I will cut you in for a percentage. It turned out that all Palmer needed to bring was the right sort of motivation. Before long, the new approach was paying dividends. Profits went up by nearly fourfold, generating extra millions for Cross and a considerable bonus for Palmer.

In the past, their work might have gone unnoticed, but in the modern world of drug smuggling, the top-end players kept an eye out for innovation. Within a short space of time, word had spread that Cross and Palmer were the pair to turn to if you were working on complex problems with many moving parts. Between them, this pair could keep anything running smoothly.

Eventually, they attracted attention from those who lurked in the darkest corners of the dark web. Before long, they were contemplating offers that would pay fantastically well — but also drag them out of their comfort zones.

Which is when Palmer's genius for understatement came to the fore; the problem was murder. Both men were happy to deal in drugs that destroyed lives — but suggest that they should arrange a killing to order, and it got complicated.

Palmer's solution was simple. If you created a spreadsheet that showed murder as one of the key business tools, it sanitised the issue and made both men feel comfortable with what they were doing.

Within a few years, Palmer was thoroughly addicted to his lucrative lifestyle. He enjoyed a fantastic standard of living with minimal effort. He'd even got to the point where he could kill with ease; hence his lack of squeamishness with his direct part in the murders the night before.

Having got home late, today he was "working from home" and looking forward to using his new, ride-on lawn-mower. He lived in the exclusive Crown Estate, in Oxshott, Surrey, where he rubbed shoulders with millionaire lawyers, bankers and footballers. His was one of the biggest houses with eight bedrooms spread over three floors, a basement swimming pool and a vast expanse of lawn. For a while he tried cutting the grass with a conventional mower, claiming the exercise would do him good. But he was too idle to keep it up for long, first bringing in a gardener and then developing serious mower envy after his neighbour bought a top-of-the-range sit-on. Last week his machine had been delivered and set up. Today he was using it for the first time as a "reward" for his poisoning work.

Palmer had persuaded his wife to come and film him on her mobile phone, and she had been happy to play along. Wearing his gardening outfit, a pair of shorts, an oversized t-shirt, grubby baseball cap and raggedy shoes, he turned the ignition on.

The explosion ripped them both to shreds.

The blast shattered windows in nearby houses. The first police officers on the scene had no words to describe the mayhem. Where Palmer, his mower and his wife had been was now a smoking hole in the ground.

With all the resources being sucked in by the London terror investigation, the lab tests got pushed to the back of the queue — so it would be a few days before the results got sorted.

But, when they did, it would cause uproar.

CHAPTER 23

This was not turning out to be the best day of Jasper Fitzhenry's life. After slamming the front door he had run, panic-stricken, to the rear of the house intending to escape before realising that was a dead end. He decided he had no choice but risk his luck with the pair on the pavement.

Hooley and Roper were astonished to see the front door reopen, out of which shot a wild-eyed Fitzhenry. He ran full tilt at the DCI, clearly marking him down as the weakest link, which is where his bad luck struck again.

The DCI instinctively swayed to one side, leaving his left foot planted on the pavement. Fitzhenry managed to trip over the foot and went sprawling onto the ground, winding himself in the process. An elated Hooley, who couldn't entirely take in what he had just done, ordered Roper to sit on their suspect while he whistled up the two uniforms.

Now it was Roper's turn to look impressed. "That was amazing. You reacted so fast and then it was all over."

Hooley took a small bow. "I'd love to say it was all planned, but I doubt if I will ever be able to repeat it. I must admit though, that was a bit of dumb move on our bloke's part. I think he may turn out not to be our bombing mastermind."

* * *

Back at Victoria, Hooley and Roper got the first crack at him. Julie Mayweather had intervened on their behalf, arguing that it was their detective work that had got them so far in the first place.

Fitzhenry was handcuffed to a table in a secure interview room and, while the pressure was on to talk to him, the DCI had insisted that they wait a while in order to make him "sweat a bit more".

Roper and Hooley watched him through the camera system. New HD colour units gave a pretty good view, and the more he looked, the less convinced the DCI was becoming. Fitzhenry looked like a little boy and nothing like a terrorist.

"What do you think, Jonathan? Have we got our man? Or one of them?"

Roper shrugged. In some ways, he was very smart with body language and Hooley had recently learned this had come from his university training as a psychologist that enabled him to spot classic signs of people telling lies. This skill made it all the more puzzling that Roper couldn't read what Hooley thought of as "day to day" emotions, such as mild irritation, happiness or boredom.

The pair watched Fitzhenry drink a paper cup of tea with trembling hands and decided they might as well start, with the DCI leading and Roper following up any lines of inquiry that struck him as promising.

In the room, they sat down and introduced themselves, going through the formalities of an interview under caution. Fitzhenry turned down the chance of a lawyer, saying he wanted to get "on with it." In Hooley's mind, this lessened the possibility that he was guilty.

His opening question was the obvious one. "Why did you run?"

His answer was a surprise. "I just saw two blokes on the doorstep and thought the Savages had sent some more of their goons round." Pulling up his shirt, he showed them some bruises on the right side of his ribcage. "They did this to me a couple of weeks ago, and all because I ditched that mad, psycho-bitch sister. She won't take no for an answer and keeps telling me she's going to tie me up and keep me in her basement. I used to think she was just trash-talking, but lately, she's got a lot scarier. That demented brother of hers is in on it too. I don't know what sort of relationship they have, but it can't be healthy. This last beating, he turned up and watched while his people worked me over. They stuffed a gag in my mouth to stop me screaming. When they were finished, I was lying on the floor, and he pissed on me."

"Why didn't you report them to the police?" Hooley asked although he was guessing at the answer.

The incredulous look he got confirmed he had guessed right. "What, you lot are going to take my word against the 'Golden Trio'? Fat chance that was going to happen! A working-class snot like me, against a bunch of posh twats? I'd have had no chance at all. Besides, they're well out of control. I wouldn't like to think about what would have happened to me if I'd made a complaint." He paused. "The thing is, I can't help wondering about them. Even on a good day, they piss off a lot of people with their 'no entry' policy. There's a lot of rich people who get caught up in that as well, and some of them really don't like being told no. I can't help wondering if their beloved store got blown up because they managed to annoy the wrong people."

This last comment triggered an idea with Hooley, and he spent a moment mulling it over. Then, pushing his chair back, he told Roper, "I just want to check something out. Let's take a break for a minute."

Fitzhenry watched them leave, looking anxious.

Outside the interview room, Roper seized the moment to go on a coffee run. By the time he got back, the DCI was looking relaxed.

Roper handed over an Americano and said, "I'm guessing that you have just checked we are in the clear for picking those three up?"

Hooley jerked his thumb in the general direction of the interview room.

"I've got no idea whose version of events is right, but what he just told us in there could not be more different to what they're saying. We need to get the three of them in here and put them under pressure. What do you make of it?"

Roper said, "I was watching him very closely. He was giving off mixed signals."

"I noticed he kept looking up to the right when he answered questions. Isn't that some sort of signal he's telling lies or making things up as he goes along?"

Roper shook his head. "Not at all. People did believe that sort of thing for a while, but it has been shown to be total rubbish. If you want to read someone from their facial expression, you have to know them really well and understand how they react in different situations. Imagining you can tell if someone is lying by the way their eyes move is stupid."

He took a breath; the DCI could sense he was just getting into his stride and decided to intervene.

"Sorry, my mistake. Let's stick to what you have discovered."

"Yes, yes, of course," said Roper. He was used to Hooley guiding him and didn't get in a flap. "I really could do with more time to establish some baseline observations, but I also used my Rainbow Spectrum. That told me he is very anxious and definitely lying about something. He's not the bomber, so I'm sure it is something to do with his relationship with the sister. The Spectrum is telling me this, and at the moment I can't quite work out *why* he's lying."

Hooley frowned as a thought struck him. "Do you think he might have played her along a bit, spun her a yarn about being wildly in love and she was the only girl for him?"

Roper went silent for a moment while he processed this thought. When he refocused, he looked at Hooley.

"I think you are right. I re-ran the Rainbow Spectrum, and that suggested your analysis fits very well. How did you work that out?"

The DCI shrugged. "Because he wouldn't be the first bloke to whisper any old nonsense to get what he wanted. He probably saw her as a meal ticket for life."

Roper looked intrigued and clearly had many questions, but Hooley held him off with a double hands up, palms out. "Sorry, Jonathan, but there isn't enough time to explain the ins and out of that sort of thing. At least it means there's still room for a bit of old-fashioned police thinking." He hesitated before carrying on. "Is this any help in bringing up your theory, the one you're keeping to yourself at the moment?" He tried to keep his tone light, but he knew he hadn't quite managed it. He wanted to know.

Roper looked thoughtful. "I think the way they have dealt with Fitzhenry shows there is a dark side to those three."

The younger man frowned and was about to go on when Hooley's phone rang. The DCI was tempted to ignore it — at least until he saw who was on the line. It was the duty sergeant back at Victoria.

The sergeant only said a few words before Hooley snapped into action. "Make this a full alert. Right now, they're our number one suspects — check everywhere, airports, roads, stations and ports. It sounds like they're on the run so let's get them. Make sure every senior officer on the alert list is informed."

CHAPTER 24

The trio had taken off fast just after Hooley and Roper left.

CCTV footage showed them hurrying from the building just a few minutes behind the two detectives. Had they been any quicker, they might well have bumped into them in the lobby area.

The security guard claimed he'd seen them climbing into the back of a black cab. Their PA said they had given no clue as to where they had gone.

Attempts to reach them on their mobile phones resulted in calls ringing out. Location services appeared to be switched off — although MI5 experts said they had the technology to switch them back on and track them.

Within twenty minutes, the spooks had established that the phones were in the Piccadilly area and heading east. Half an hour after that, they were discovered abandoned in the black cab. The three had left their phones when they got dropped at South Kensington. The driver had decided to treat them as an extra payment.

Five hours after Hooley and Roper had last seen them, the trail ran cold. The cab driver couldn't help, claiming they had stood on the pavement watching until he was out of sight.

Reading the details of the latest findings, Roper grunted and leaned back with his eyes closed, keeping very still until he finally came out of his trance. "What if they are guilty of something, just not the bombings? They would be feeling intense pressure right now — and us turning up might have just tipped them over the edge."

Hooley flexed his fingers, a nervous habit when he was impatient. "I don't get it. By running, they might as well have told us they're guilty. But I agree — I can't see those three behind the attacks. They're certainly annoying and unpleasant, but that's not a crime in its own right. I wouldn't mind giving that brother a bit of a slap, but they don't strike me as cold-hearted killers, although I'm happy to keep an open mind. Murderers come in all shapes and sizes."

Roper said, "I've been doing some background research, and they went to the best schools. A few years ago, they were mixing with other rich people and celebrities."

"You mean they were A-listers?"

Roper — who took the view that only bona fide geniuses should be considered A-listers — ignored him. The mood was broken by Susan Brooker entering the office, carrying a large paper bag.

"I've got enough sandwiches for six people, so no one can complain about feeling hungry." She gave Roper a meaningful look, which he missed as he was already rooting through the options. Hooley joined him, extracting a ham and mustard. Suddenly hungry, he took an overlarge bite, making him choke.

Through his tears, he could see Roper approaching. Recovering his poise, he held up his hand. "Were you thinking about performing the Heimlich manoeuvre on me? There was something in your expression."

Roper inclined his head. "As you know, I have just been on the advanced first aid course, and it did cross my mind that you might be in trouble. You should have seen yourself. Your eyes were bulging, and you went very red."

The DCI decided to move on. He recalled that Roper had been on the brink of sharing a theory about Diamonds and Pearls but the news of the trio making a run for it had got in the way.

"So, what were you going to say before we got that message?"

Roper was quiet for a moment, obviously debating whether to talk about it. A deep frown appeared on his face, and the DCI hoped that it didn't mean Roper was getting cross.

"I have run it through my Rainbow Spectrum, and I think I have an answer. First of all, I do not believe they are the bombers. I know it looks bad now, but there is nothing that suggests they have the skills or contacts to organise three such attacks. It would take military expertise, and they do not possess that."

Hooley went to interrupt him, but Roper shook his head.

"I know what you're going to say, and they don't have any military contacts who could have fixed it for them." He paused again before continuing. "But there is something very interesting in their backgrounds."

He stopped and produced one of his enigmatic expressions. To his surprise, Hooley realised he had stopped breathing. Every now and again, Roper showed he could spin things with the best of them.

"Go on then," he urged.

"We've been assuming all along that the three of them are rich kids with access to lots of money. Well, the truth is they are, and they aren't. You see, they met up at the costly English public school, Millfield, but they had to leave before their A levels because both sets of their parents coincidentally lost their money at the same time. They were said to be angry and upset about losing their lifestyle. They dropped out of sight, then reappeared a few years later with Diamonds and Pearls. It looked like that lifestyle allowed them to mix with wealthy socialites who helped arrange funding."

"So, you're saying teenage trauma turned them into the nasty little gits they are today?"

If he noted the sarcasm, Roper wasn't biting. "There is that aspect, certainly. But I think it is most likely they were left uniquely vulnerable. I think someone worked out that all three of them could be lured into wrongdoing by the promise of restoring their former lives."

CHAPTER 25

Mary Lou Healy had a work ethic second to none. In a company notorious for the hours put in by its staff, she was a workaholic cliché: first in, last out. She always said her early starts gave her the chance to get ahead of any updates that arrived overnight from California. In practice that meant she was switching on the coffee machine at a time when most people still had a couple of hours in bed. Night security called her the "Dawn Ranger" and jokingly chided her if she was just a few minutes late.

Today the coffee maker was still cold because she realised there was trouble ahead. An urgent request had come in from Silicon Valley; it raised technical concerns about the new phones and their foldable screens. The problem was exacerbated by the way John Ryder worked. He might have been a genius at marketing, and the man who knew exactly what his customers wanted, but he kept his secrets close and always had. When he was around to ask that didn't matter, but now it did.

She was acutely aware that, with Ryder out of action, she didn't have a clue who to speak to about the development work, or even which continent it was being carried out on. Last year he had developed new software with an Indian company that no one else had known about until he produced the finished product. The year before he had teamed up with a Hungarian maverick who had approached him directly, having heard that Ryder was open to striking immediate deals with people who had "interesting" work. Not everything worked out, but it was the way he liked it, keeping things close until they were ready for launch, never mind how many people at his own company would suddenly find they had been out of the loop.

For years Healy had accepted that this was the price to be paid for working with such a brilliant man — but recently she felt he was ever more willing to go out on a limb, even when the odds weren't all that favourable.

She was no engineer, but she knew that the technology behind the supersized phone screen was complicated. People had been trying to crack it for years and, until a few days ago, she had heard nothing to suggest it was about to be fixed.

She also knew that Ryder had become increasingly obsessed with the progress a Chinese competitor was making, saying that they left his company grubbing around in the dirt.

Her gloomy thoughts were interrupted as Taggert walked in, her jaw set, radiating intense energy. She made a beeline for the coffee maker, exasperated that it was still in the process of warming up. Healy looked at her, waiting for her to say what was on her mind — but Taggert only stared at the machine, willing it to hurry up and get ready.

Finally, she dragged herself away and turned to Healy. "I guess it's true about watched pots never boiling. But I could really do with a cup of Java right now."

"It'll be five minutes at least, I'm afraid. I can make you a cup of instant coffee. I always keep some just in case of emergencies like this."

This produced a smile. "Thank you, Mary Lou, but I'll wait for the real stuff. It's just that I've spent most of the night talking to people in California and I need the caffeine."

She looked up to check the door was shut and then made her way over to Healy's desk, walking round to sit on the edge next to her assistant, she leaned in conspiratorially.

"That problem with the screens is proving much worse than we first thought. A few are okay, but a lot are hopeless, and some keep switching on and off. No one knows who made them so we can't find out how to fix it. Everyone thought that because John came over here for the launch, I would have all the answers. Since the early hours, I've been trying to tell people that I don't. I'd already told them everything I knew on that earlier conference call. I assume John was going to fill in all the details after the launch, but obviously, he never got the chance to do that. They've asked me to get over there and coordinate everything. In the meantime, our techs are looking to see if they can reverse engineer a solution."

She stopped talking and, for just a moment, her face showed how tired she was. She gently rubbed at her temples.

"I'm glad that you and Miss Kitty are going to be here, watching my back. I'm going to need you to see if we can work out who John was talking to, to get these handsets into production. They're sending one of the company planes over to pick me up from London City Airport. I need to be there in a couple of hours."

Healy patted her boss's hand. "At least the coffee should be ready by then. I noticed you didn't bring any bags in with you. Are you going to take the emergency kit from here?"

"I didn't want to waste time thinking about what I needed when I knew you had already prepared something for me."

Healy smiled. "You've got five days of clothes so, after that, get them cleaned or buy in new. I've added a small bottle of clothes wash just in case." She suddenly looked serious. "I do think it's bizarre that all these handsets have suddenly got problems. We both know that John isn't afraid of taking a risk, but I can't see him taking such a big one."

"I know. That's been bothering me as well. He gave no hint of any concerns, and it's really not like him to send out something with so many question marks over it. I can't help wondering if the attack, and now this, is somehow connected."

CHAPTER 26

Hooley thought Roper was overdoing the big reveal but kept his tone light.

"Okay. You've got my attention."

Roper gave a short nod, which seemed to suggest he had just run through what he was going to say. "I think Diamonds and Pearls are about drugs, money laundering or industrial espionage."

The DCI was taken aback. Whatever he'd been expecting, it wasn't this. Roper seemed oblivious to his surprise as he explained his thinking.

"If I am honest, the first two are probably the things that most people would suggest. I guess drugs would be the top choice because you have a lot of wealthy young people around, and money laundering would be an obvious concern because it is a business with a high turnover, a lot of it in cash.

"But I've had a chance to do some digging around Emily Wong and where her money comes from. Her father is described as an industrialist, and he is linked to various production sites in and around Hong Kong. It's only when you try to get a bit deeper that you run into difficulties with him. Some reports say he works in sensitive fields of Artificial

Intelligence and military operations, so I have to wonder if there is a link there.

"There's a lot of discussion on the net about China trying to get its hands on Western technology. Apparently they could be stealing all sorts of advances, especially in AI or machine learning. We know the Americans are furious about it. The trouble is, I don't really know much, apart from what I've read, so I can't say how true it is. The reality is probably that everyone is watching what everyone else is doing. So many developments are open-sourced now — so I suppose you could find out what is going on quite easily. But I think Diamonds and Pearls would make a perfect front for industrial espionage as it would allow people to come and go all the time without drawing attention to themselves."

As he listened, Hooley realised he was conflicted. The idea was fascinating, and a perfect demonstration of the way Roper's thought process was so different from everyone else. He might have gone for the drugs option, maybe money laundering — but never industrial espionage.

"Do you have anything to really stand this up, or is it more a sense you're getting through how your research stacks up in the Rainbow Spectrum?"

Roper steepled his hands again. "I do get a sense through the Spectrum, but I am going to have to talk to MI5 and MI6 about this. I thought I could also get Sam to talk to her sources in American intelligence. What I need is to be briefed by people with real knowledge."

Hooley nodded approvingly. "Good idea, especially talking to Sam. I bet she's itching to get more involved." Hooley had only met her a couple of times but had always been impressed by her self-confidence and energy. Before Roper could reply, he went on, "What do you make of the way they were able to vanish so quickly?"

"That's the easy bit. It shows that, whatever they were involved in, they were worried enough to have a plan for getting away in the event of things going wrong. To me, that makes espionage more likely." He stopped and looked rueful. "But that theory could apply to drugs or money laundering."

"I agree with you there. The more intelligent criminals do tend to think a few steps ahead, rather than assuming that everything is going to be all right. It's always the daft ones who get caught first."

He picked up a copy of the *London Evening Standard*. Although it was available online, he enjoyed the feel of the paper in his hands.

"People who get away with things for a long time start to think they're invincible," he continued. "Then something happens, and they realise they're not safe at all."

He glanced up. Roper was staring into the middle distance.

Hooley had seen this look many times. "So, what's going through that planet-sized brain of yours?"

This comment brought Roper back into the real world — and for a moment, he looked at Hooley in such a puzzled way that the DCI had to fight off an urge to laugh.

"How did you know I was thinking about something?"

Hooley grinned at him. "That would be telling, but let's just say it would be 'elementary, my dear Watson'."

Roper scowled. "I suppose you're making one of your Sherlock Holmes jokes. But you're right: the Rainbow Spectrum has suggested a possibility, and it could be that our three suspects may be smarter than we had thought."

CHAPTER 27

After making his announcement, Roper stood up and left the office. Hooley watched him go, being careful not to let his feelings get in the way. He'd seen Roper do this many times before. Faced with a difficult problem, he often went for a walk as he tried to resolve the issue.

This time it must have been extraordinarily complex as he was gone for more than fifteen minutes. But now he was back, and from his expression, he was working it out.

"I'm ready, I'm sitting down, and I don't need a drink," said Hooley. "Hit me with your theory."

Roper didn't need any further prompting. "What if everything they've said to us so far has been done to disguise the real operation and the fallout from it? As you said, it's hard to imagine those three getting involved in a murder. The last thing we would expect is for them to be involved in industrial espionage. That's the sort of thing that nation states get up to, not three young people somehow persuading their fellows to buy a load of over-priced produce. So I'm wondering if even that nonsense story they told us about the sister and the manager was just to buy them time. They'd know we'd check it out, but they could launch their getaway plan in the meantime."

Hooley was looking confused. "You seem to be making an awful lot of intuitive jumps today. Do you think you should rein things back in a little? I'm not sure if I'm following."

Roper was nodding vigorously. "I know, I know. The thing is, my Rainbow Spectrum has really jumped into life. It seems to be working flat-out at the moment. It's the clearest it's been on anything since I started." He paused. "I haven't wanted to say anything before, but I was getting worried about the idea that the spectrum might have been going dark. Maybe I had too much to think about and couldn't get things straight. But the chance to talk things through with you just now has made the difference."

Hooley leaned back in his chair. "I don't suppose your spectrum can tell us where they might go?"

Roper jumped up. "My spectrum may not be up to that, but I do have an idea. I think we should look at Paris."

Hooley took a deep breath. "Any reason for that theory? Apart from the fact that it was only a few days ago that you and I got as far as Gare du Nord? We didn't even get off the train, I might add . . ."

This was the type of comment that often flummoxed Roper. He looked anxious and said, "Is that some sort of joke? Have I just missed something?"

On another occasion, the pair could have explored that idea for some time, not today.

"No, it's not a joke," said Hooley. "Well, at least not a big joke. I was just making a point that we managed to get as far as a Parisian railway station and then had to come straight home. I don't suppose many people can say that."

The DCI knew that Roper had an eclectic range of knowledge and an eidetic memory to explore it with, but even he was surprised at what Roper said next.

"You would be surprised. While there are no official figures, we are definitely not the first people to arrive and go straight back to the UK. I read about it in a blog that came up when I was doing some research. It was fascinating, and I have to say . . ." He trailed off as Hooley held up both hands, palms out. It was his long-understood signal for Roper to stop talking.

"I don't think we have the time to go off-message just now. I'm not being rude, but you need to explain why you think Paris should be the main place we're looking at."

"I was doing some background research, and I noticed that Diamonds and Pearls sold a lot of items that were made in France. In a recent interview, the brother said that they had invested in an apartment in Paris. I don't know if they'll be staying in that apartment, but clearly, they know the city well — and it may be exactly the type of place they would feel safe in. At the last count, the population of the whole Paris region was 12,082,144. So easy to hide away."

Hooley, listening intently, nodded. "I'm happy to go along with this. We can put the request through the commissioner's office so that it comes with maximum authority."

Roper's expression became ever more boyish. He looked like he was about to burst into applause. "This is incredibly exciting," he said. "I've heard that the French have been working on a new piece of software which can search through thousands of hours of CCTV footage and find matches that other software misses. The point of difference is that the software can access even the cheapest home-surveillance system and enhance the pictures. If what I hear is accurate, we may not have to wait very long to find out if these three are in Paris. Then they can be picked up and brought back here."

Hooley reached for his phone and placed a speed dial to Julie Mayweather's private line, which he only used for the most urgent matters.

"The good news," he finally said, "is that, when it comes to terror attacks, the French don't mess about. If they do find them, there won't be any silly stuff about human rights. They'll be happy to send them straight back."

CHAPTER 28

Tony Cross was planning to disappear — and fast.

He'd always feared a day like this would come and his priority, now, was putting his escape plan into action.

Many years ago, without consulting Palmer, he had bought a remote cottage in northern Wales that would serve as an immediate bolthole in the event of emergencies. His priority had been choosing somewhere that was hidden from sight, and the two-bedroom property suited his purpose. The nearest neighbour was more than three miles away, and the house itself was tucked away in a little valley accessed by an unpromising looking track.

The house itself was little more than a sheep shelter that had been given a minimal makeover to allow it to be used for human habitation. It wasn't linked to any services, not even water — and certainly not electricity or telephone. It didn't even register on the local authority's council tax lists. For all intents and purposes, it was invisible.

He'd bought it through a shell company that couldn't be traced back to him, and he'd offered the seller, a taciturn Welsh sheep farmer, the option of taking the price in cash. This was the only time he had seen the man smile, albeit briefly.

It had cost him the same as buying a conventional property with all services, but he hadn't cared about that. He was paying for security — and in the farmer, he recognised that he had found a man who could put a price on discretion.

The other advantage of the property was that it wasn't far from Holyhead and the regular ferry services to Ireland. This was the second part of his escape plan, but something only to be triggered in the worst case. If the worst came to the worst, he would catch a ferry to Eire and disappear into an isolated spot in County Kerry. It offered the same deal as Wales but with the added sense of security that came with being further away from London.

He'd put his plan into action the moment he had found out what had happened to Palmer and his wife. Cross had been invited for afternoon drinks and arrived to discover stunned neighbours and the still-smoking hole in the ground. He didn't waste a moment, jumping straight back in his car and heading for his warehouse where he collected a small leather bag filled with cash, including both Euros and US dollars, and a selection of identity cards, credit cards, and passports.

In his line of work, he'd learned about the finest forgers and carefully cultivated them over the years. Today he intended to take advantage of his foresight. The only other things in the bag were toothpaste, a toothbrush and deodorant — the three ingredients he couldn't cope without.

As for his wife of twenty years and his two teenage children, he barely spared a thought beyond the idea that they could already be dead, or at the very least being held hostage by the same people who'd killed Palmer and his wife. Besides, he figured he owed them nothing. All three had enjoyed the benefits of the money he brought in; no one had thought to question where it came from, and now it was a case of every man for themselves. That was just the way of the world.

Cross drove carefully, not wanting to draw police attention. It was only as he arrived in the vicinity of the farmhouse that his sense of caution kicked in, causing him to park up in the shelter of a glade of trees near the top of a hill. From here, he had a clear line of sight to his property. He spent the remaining hours of daylight watching carefully to make sure it was deserted.

With the light fading fast, he approached the cottage and let himself in. Even though it was late spring, the place felt abandoned and was bitingly cold. He was glad that he had, on his last visit more than a year ago, laid in supplies. Soon, he had the wood burner blazing away.

Electricity came from his own generator, and that was well-stocked with fuel. He knew he could do nothing about the smoke from the chimney and the light in the windows — but he was willing to bank on the isolation to keep him safe.

He had bought several bottles of whisky and half a dozen packets of sandwiches from a service station almost half a day ago now. Suddenly hungry, he bolted down a rubbery cheese and tomato, followed by a stale ham and mustard. He didn't dwell on the poor quality. It filled a hole and gave him a lining for the whisky, which he drank straight from the bottle as he couldn't be bothered to switch on the pump that brought water to the property and would have let him clean a glass.

The potent drink did little to calm his nerves, but he was past being sensible. He drank on regardless, eventually falling into an alcoholic stupor as his head slumped forward and the wood burner died out.

He didn't hear the front door being opened just fifteen minutes after he had fallen into drunken oblivion. He didn't see the two men come in, each wearing a balaclava, and step silently toward him on their rubber-soled shoes.

Cross was a dead man the moment he walked into the cottage. He was picked up on the carefully hidden camera with a powerful transmitter that alerted the two men of his arrival. They watched him pass out and made their move. Once inside the property, they grabbed their target, hauling him to his feet, and holding him in a painful grip. At first, the effects of the booze made him think he was dreaming. Then, an animal sense kicked in. He was suddenly horribly sober. He had no doubts about what was about to happen.

Cross was neither proud nor brave. "Please don't kill me. I've got money, plenty of it. I can pay you far more than you have already received."

He would have dropped to his knees and begged, but they were holding his arms in a vice-like grip. He was hopelessly overmatched and wouldn't stand a chance once things got physical.

A wave of self-pity swept over him, and he burst into tears. Even now a tiny part of him was hoping this display would soften their resolve.

Not a chance.

His pleading didn't have any impact. Even through the balaclavas, he could see by their grim expressions that there would be no mercy here. This was his secret hiding place, and it had been invaded.

The man holding his right arm let go with one hand and produced a pistol from a holster under his armpit. The gun was placed in Cross's hand and lifted until the barrel was resting under his chin.

He made no effort to resist. All he could feel was a sense of immense loss. Cross was so terrified he wet himself and a large stain spread around his trousers. Yet, with death hovering so close, shame was the last of his worries. He thought of pleading again, but fatalistic calm came over him, and he slumped in the grip of his assailants.

As the man squeezed his finger against the trigger, he could only hope that the sensation would not be too painful. He knew it would only last for a moment.

Then it was all over.

He never heard the gun firing, nor felt the bullet lance into his brain.

The assassins didn't waste time studying the body; they'd had plenty of experience of death and took no pleasure from its finer details. Instead, they walked out, leaving the door ajar to encourage animals, and kept their balaclavas on until they reached the motorway heading for Manchester.

The traffic on the M56 was still heavy, despite the rush hour being long past — but the two men were unbothered and settled in for the drive home.

"I'm glad to be rid of that thing," said the passenger. "The material makes my head itch like the devil. I have to stop myself scratching at it — I don't want to be known as the 'itchy killer'."

The driver gave a harsh laugh, which came out as almost a bark. He glanced across at the passenger and said, "That went well. I prefer it when they don't scream too much. But why do they always think that money can buy them out of it? It's not like some guardian angel is going to appear."

The passenger was silent for a moment. "I wonder who he pissed off to have us come to visit? And how old do you think he was? I'd say about mid-fifties — but he could have been a lot younger. He hadn't taken care of himself."

They drove on for a little while before the driver asked, "Why are you asking about his age?"

The passenger kept his eyes on the road. "In our line of work, you need to know when it's time to get out. If you make it through your twenties, that is."

The silence went on for a while longer — until the driver could resist no longer.

"So . . . what's the answer then? How long is too long in this business?"

The driver shrugged. He wasn't a man much given to introspection. "When someone like us turns up, I suppose."

CHAPTER 29

Hooley was expounding on what he liked to call his "boots on the ground time out" and was explaining it to Susan Brooker.

"When I first started working with Jonathan, I was so impressed with the way he makes these intuitive leaps that I forgot to back things up with more formal police work. Gathering evidence, talking to witnesses and liaising with different agencies. So, when I say, 'boots on the ground,' I'm reminding myself to make sure all the bases are covered. When Jonathan talks about the father of Emily Wong, I need to make sure that the right people in MI5 and MI6 know what we think and can follow it up accurately." He paused for a moment. "Actually, do you want to take charge of that? Given you know Sam Tyler, you can cover the US end as well as the UK end. If you have any worries that you're not getting through to people, come back to me, and we can make sure they do listen."

Brooker nodded.

"Great," said Hooley, before ploughing on. "I also need to get some more of our people talking to all the serving staff from Diamonds and Pearls, and I want the accountancy specialists warned that they need to look very carefully at that business. To be quite honest it would be a great help if you took that under your wing as well."

Brooker smiled. "I'd be delighted. I thought you might keep me on the sidelines until you were more used to me."

"There was never a chance of that," said Hooley. "Once Jonathan said yes, you were always going to be involved. Mostly there's just the three of us, plus the detectives in the 'Research Room' whom I have managed to borrow for the time being."

He carried on talking to Susan for a few more minutes until he was happy he had things back under control. "It doesn't matter how smart your detective work is, without evidence that stands up in court, you can't win."

It was at this moment that Roper put in an appearance, saying immediately: "I've been thinking. We're not going to get very much free time now so we need to take advantage when we can."

The statement apparently concluded; Roper fell silent.

It was one of the problems you sometimes faced with Roper. His thought processes were so intense that he often forgot to share all the details. People who didn't know him thought he was doing it for effect, an attempt to look enigmatic, but in fact, he was just telling the story as he saw it at that moment.

The DCI went for the direct approach. "And your point is?"

For just a moment it looked as though Roper was fighting to keep some sort of expression off his face. *Is he trying to conceal something?* thought Hooley. *Surely not.*

Before he could pursue this, Roper said, "I have booked us in for another gym session. If we leave now, we will make it back long before we hear anything new from the investigation teams and it will be a day, at least, before the French talk to us."

Hooley couldn't help the hiss of irritation that emerged. Being relentless was what made Roper such an excellent investigator, but it also made him hard work to be around when he got the bit between his teeth.

Hooley held up an admonishing finger. "What makes you think that I'm going to get up from this desk, walk to the gym, get hot and sweaty, and walk back here?"

Roper had a range of shrugs that conveyed his thoughts very accurately. Right now, he produced the "that's exactly what I think" version. "I think you are in serious danger of becoming very unwell unless you take exercise. I wouldn't be suggesting it unless I had thought about it. I have been researching this and am sorry to tell you that you are in the 'at risk' category."

Hooley's father had suffered a severe heart attack in his fifties, so the same thing happening to him was one of his private dreads. He felt, as his mother might say, someone "walking over his grave". A slight wooziness came over him and, realising that he had been standing up as he admonished Roper, he sat back down, being very careful to disguise what had just happened.

"If you like," said Roper, "I can go through what's making me think that you have to get fitter, but I know you don't like me doing that so I thought I would just present you with the basic conclusions. That really is all you need to know."

Hooley was now feeling hot and sweaty — and without having gone to the gym at all. He took a deep breath. Tiny black spots had started dancing around in front of his eyes. He looked around for a drink of water, but when he reached out, his hands found only an empty cup.

Was this a panic attack? He wondered. Or maybe it was more?

"What are the symptoms of a heart attack?" he uttered. "I feel very thirsty suddenly."

"You look terrible. Do you really think you are having a heart attack now?"

The DCI was starting to wonder. "I don't know. Just tell me what the symptoms are."

"I'm not a doctor. We need a doctor for that."

"Jonathan, don't go wobbly on me now! I know you. You read about stuff like this for your bedtime relaxation. Now, what can you recall from what you've seen?"

"I need to warn you that I may get something wrong . . ."

Hooley cut him off. "Just do it now or ring for an ambulance! I can't wait."

"Okay. Are you having chest pains at all, especially in the middle of your chest?"

For a bizarre moment, the DCI couldn't decide. Then, finally, he answered:

"No."

"What about pains in your arms?"

"No."

"Anything in the rest of your body? Around your jaw, neck or maybe your abdomen?"

"No."

"Are you having trouble breathing?"

"I sort of was, but that's gone away."

"Do you know where you are?"

"Yes!" Hooley finally snapped. "I'm in an office with you, and I'm beginning to think you've given me a heart attack by telling me I'm at risk. You gave me a hell of a fright, just now!"

"I suppose that might explain why you suddenly looked all sweaty," said Roper, reluctant to totally abandon his new role as health overseer. "Getting hot and sweaty is one of the signs that I read about. There are a few more symptoms I could go through."

Hooley grumbled, "No, thanks. I think I've had quite enough of Dr Roper for now."

Roper's face screwed up with consternation. "I'm certainly no doctor. I hope I haven't given you the impression I've been studying medical matters."

His face was such a picture of misery that it made Hooley laugh. But at least the room was coming back into focus around him. At least all those tiny black dots in his eyes had danced away.

"I think it's a good job you're not a doctor. Your bedside manner would be the stuff of legend, and not in a good way. If you're determined to tell people about their health, you need to be kind and gentle. A little empathy goes a long way."

Roper looked indignant. Empathy was something he'd seen written in a book, not something he took much notice of. "I don't understand. If there is a problem then surely you would want to know about it, not have someone keeping things from you? Actually, I've just thought of the perfect example. Do you remember, a couple of weeks ago, I saved you from being killed by that bus?"

Hooley did. "You yelled 'BUS' right in my ear. You gave me a terrible fright. It was just after we'd eaten, and I was nearly sick in the street."

"You keep going on about that, but you can't deny that, if I hadn't stopped you stepping out, you'd have been crushed. I saved your life by letting you know there was a problem, not pretending it would go away."

There were times when Hooley recognised he wasn't going to win. If he got into this fight, Roper would refuse to give up until he had worn the DCI down. He gathered his dignity.

"I suppose now might be as good a time as any for us to take a break. So long as it doesn't take longer than forty-five minutes."

Roper didn't bother replying. He moved back to his desk, picked up his kitbag and led the way.

Hooley had cheered up by the time they reached the gym. As he walked out of the changing rooms, an instructor smiled at him kindly and then pointed at the spin cycles.

"We're going to do the same as before, no more and no less."

To his secret delight, Hooley enjoyed the warm-up session — it gave him a real boost, his confidence rising as he set off.

He threw himself into the first exercise at a rapid pace and, within minutes, was starting to worry he'd overstretched himself, so he slowed down a little and managed to keep going.

Ten minutes later, his session was over, and he headed off for a quick shower before the walk back to the office. He had to wait briefly for Roper — who remained behind to speak to the fitness instructor.

The walk back to the office seemed to last longer than expected, and the stairs made Hooley's legs ache, which he put down to the cycling. Downing a glass of water, he decided a couple of painkillers might not go amiss.

About half an hour later, he could feel the paracetamol start to kick in, bringing some welcome relief. He told himself that exercise was bound to be tough at first, but it would get easier. At that point, he got the most definite sense that Roper was looking at him. Glancing over, he realised that Roper was alternating between studying him intently and staring at something he had on his screen. This went on for several seconds.

Feeling worried, but wanting to sound authoritative, Hooley asked, "What on earth are you doing? This is the second time today you've put the wind up me. I can tell you now that it's not funny."

The answer rocked him.

"This is my fault," said Roper, "but I'm wondering if we should have gone to the gym at all. I'm not sure it's doing you any good at the moment, certainly not to look at you. You went a bit purple back then." Roper paused. Then he looked at Hooley with rising alarm. "There is no doubt about it. You need to see a cardiologist as soon as possible."

CHAPTER 30

Roper never delayed once he had decided to act.

"I've made the appointment," he declared. "And I've already paid for it."

Hooley looked up in amazement. "You don't need to do that. Anyway, I'm sure the union medical care will take care of it . . ."

"Yes, but what if they need time to process your claim?" said Roper. "And they might not pay all of it. With me paying you don't need to worry, and it gets it done faster. You know I can afford it, and you know I wouldn't offer unless that was the case."

Hooley looked at the determined expression on Roper's face and realised they would just go around in circles until he agreed.

"You win. So, tell me, where and when?"

"It's at a clinic in Harley Street, and you need to be there by 7 a.m."

Hooley did a double take. "Are you sure that's the right time? I was expecting a little later . . ."

Roper waved his hand in a dismissive gesture. "Of course, it's the right time. This man may be the best cardiologist in London. That means he's in high demand and is used to working with business leaders who hate wasting time, especially when it's about their health. He offered to see you an hour earlier, but I told him you would be grumpy if it was too early. If we get there at 7 a.m. we should be out in an hour and be here by 9 a.m."

Hooley rolled his eyes but didn't complain. He would have moaned about getting up any earlier. He'd also picked up on the "we". Evidently, Roper had every intention of being there too.

That night, despite feeling bone-weary, Hooley slept restlessly. For long hours, his night was punctuated by unsettling dreams that left him feeling washed out when his alarm clock went off at 5 a.m. Feeling sluggish, he spent an extra ten minutes under a hot shower to restore some sense of wellbeing.

By the time he reached the clinic on Harley Street, it was already 6:45 a.m., and there was Roper, draining the last of the extra-large cup of coffee he'd bought.

Handing Hooley a bottle of water, he said, "I'm not sure what you're allowed to have before the tests, so better safe than sorry. If you have a cup of coffee now, they may just cancel the tests today and make you come back tomorrow."

His words made Hooley feel a little shaky since they reminded him of the potential seriousness of what was about to happen. Without another word, he rang the bell — only to be greeted by a young man in his early thirties wearing jeans, a blue shirt, black shoes, and sporting a full beard.

"Mr Hooley, I'm Andy, your nurse today." At least he had a welcoming smile, and his manner was calming. "You're our first patient, so I thought I'd get you settled, then go off and prepare everything. I promise you — I'll have everything nicely warmed up in no time."

The DCI was anxious to look untroubled. "Do you work here all the time?" he asked, in what he hoped was a calm-sounding voice.

"Oh, no. I do this as a little extra on top of my NHS work. I don't mind working odd hours, so I'm perfect for this job. Then I do a normal shift just down the road."

At that point, a man appeared, radiating energy. His thick black hair was flecked with strands of grey. He had large brown eyes and a warm, reassuring smile that said, "You're in safe hands now."

He could have featured in an advert hailing the positive effects of healthy living — and, with his smooth skin, he was probably about forty years old. He was dressed in a sombre black business suit and dark blue shirt, but no necktie. Hooley decided he liked this touch of informality.

The doctor held out his hand. "Robert Turner," he began, "and I'm guessing you must be Jonathan's boss? I've heard so much about you. I just wish that the people who worked for me were so enthusiastic."

Andy laughed and walked off. "I'm going to make sure everything is ready," he said.

Dr Turner showed them into an office, and Hooley took what turned out to be a very comfortable seat in front of the desk, while Roper sat off to the side.

The doctor looked at them both and said, "Are you happy for Mr Roper to be in for this consultation?"

The DCI smiled and shrugged. "If it weren't for him, I wouldn't be seeing you in the first place, so why not?"

The doctor asked a series of questions, including how he was feeling. Hooley told him he wasn't sure. "There's nothing really obvious apart from feeling a bit tired, which I thought was normal for my age."

"What about any chest pains, or shortage of breath?"

"Nothing I've really noticed. I did struggle during spin cycling — but I thought that was normal. I certainly haven't felt any chest pain."

"What about going upstairs, or maybe getting into bed?"

The DCI thought for a moment and then pressed his hand to his chest. "Now you ask, yes, I do sometimes feel a bit short of breath. Nothing terrible, though."

Dr Turner asked Hooley to remove his shirt while he listened to his chest through a stethoscope. Soon, he seemed to spend a lot of time hovering over a small area on the front left-side.

Hooley had been around too many interview rooms and suspects keeping things to themselves not to recognise the signs.

"Find something, doc?"

"Maybe." The doctor's face gave nothing away. "I don't want to say anything more until we've done the echocardiogram we've lined up for you. I know that can sound alarming, but it will give us a clearer picture, and we may have to do some more tests. So, let's get you through to Andy. He's one of the best around, so you're in safe hands."

Hooley put on a brave face — but now he feared the worst. In the corner of his eye, Roper couldn't keep the anxiety off his face.

The doctor led him into a room with a bed and a medical machine with a large monitor. Here, Andy got him to lie on his left-hand side and rubbed a clear gel over the paddles before placing them on his chest.

Like the doctor, he zeroed in on the same area, while carefully studying the results on the screen.

"I suppose the good news is that I do indeed have a heart," said Hooley. His voice sounded a bit thin, and he was glad that it didn't break.

The nurse patted him gently and smiled. "Don't worry. I just need to go and talk to Dr Turner. Then he can tell you what he thinks is going on."

He watched the nurse go. For a moment he worried about Roper being left in the consulting room but thought it was too late to be concerned now. He rolled onto his back, stared at the ceiling and let his mind go blank.

After a short while the doctor reappeared, told Hooley to get dressed and follow him back to the consulting room. Moments later, he walked in, nodded at Roper — who didn't look as though he'd moved a muscle — and waited for the worst.

Dr Turner did not beat about the bush. "Okay, Brian, I can tell you that you have a problem with your mitral valve. I'm going to need to have another look, in more detail, at what is going on there. Now, I know that sounds quite frightening — but there is some good news. I can safely say that we have caught this in time. These things often show up after someone has had a heart attack, so at least it hasn't damaged your heart." He paused. "In other words, you seem to be in decent shape, and that is going to make a positive difference, whatever happens next. But I do need more information before we make any decisions."

Hooley was surprised by how calm he felt. He looked at Roper. "Good job he's here. I expect I'll need him later to remember everything you tell me."

Turner smiled. "I don't want you to think I'm rushing this because it's an emergency, but I could do one of the tests in a couple of hours. You mentioned you haven't eaten since midnight so what do you think? Shall we crack on?"

Hooley seemed uncertain.

"My guess is you're one of those people who needs answers. I'm proposing we give you an angiogram. It's a small camera inserted into an artery in your arm, and it allows me to look inside your heart.

"It's a well-tried and tested examination — so there's very little danger. Although I do have to warn you that some people can react badly to it. I'd suggest you take the rest of the day off, and I'll get you some information to read while you think about it."

Hooley knew sensible advice when he heard it. He didn't like to think through the implications of what he was being told, but it was clear the cardiologist was worried.

He looked at the doctor. "I want to get this done as soon as I can but, right now, we're in the middle of an investigation, and it may be that lives depend on us. I'm not saying it can't happen without me, but I need to make sure people are ready to pick up the reins." He hesitated before going on. "Do you have a private room Jonathan and I could borrow for a short while and make some phone calls?"

The doctor stood up. "This room can be all yours. I have another consulting room. I'll see my next patient, and we can talk again in about an hour, maybe less."

After he had gone, the DCI talked to Roper. "Get on to Susan and explain what's happening. Then I think you need to get back. We can't afford both of us here, and it looks like I have no choice. I'll ring Julie and tell her."

Roper didn't argue, just pulled out his mobile and tapped in a number from memory. A few minutes later, Hooley was explaining his situation to a shocked Julie Mayweather. She agreed to hang fire until he had more news.

Three hours later, with the procedure complete, he was back in the doctor's office. He felt oddly guilty at undergoing tests while Roper was back at Victoria pushing the investigation forward. The procedure hadn't been painful, but Hooley had disliked the sensation of the camera going into his body. It made him feel strangely vulnerable.

Taking a drink of water, he waited for the doctor to tell him what was going on. Again, when he returned, Turner was highly professional.

"You're going to need surgery, Mr Hooley, and if there is one surgeon I would recommend, without hesitation, it is Mr James Thomas. I've already sent in your details, and he's agreed he will see you. His team will go through what I've sent over, including all the video of the tests carried out, then get in touch with you to arrange an appointment for you to see Mr Thomas. Not only will you be under a great surgeon, but this is also an operation with a very high success rate. I know you haven't experienced any obvious sensations, but I predict you will feel a lot better."

Hooley sat very still. Every word was hitting home like a hammer blow, but he did his best to remain calm. "How long until I need the operation?"

"You need to determine that with the surgeon . . . but I don't think you're anywhere near a crisis so you may have a few weeks. As I say, it will be sooner rather than later, but you really should give Mr Thomas the final say."

With that, Hooley stood up, thanked Dr Turner and walked out into Harley Street. Suddenly, he felt totally alone and couldn't help thinking about his wife. She had always been the strong one where illness was concerned. He'd never known what to do when other people had health problems — now here he was with a heart condition that needed urgent treatment, and he didn't know what to think.

Had he brought this on himself? Too much stress, too much fatty food, too much alcohol, not enough sleep and heaven knows how many times he had ignored his wife's pleas to work less and lose weight. And why hadn't he asked more questions while he was with the doctor?

He started to choke up, gripped by an unfamiliar and unwelcome feeling — fear. Was this it? Was his time up? Angrily he pushed the panic away. What had the doctor said? It was very routine and treatable. He needed to remember that. And he must thank Roper for nagging him. What might have happened otherwise?

He switched his thoughts to the investigation. He wanted to stay on it, but the doctors might say otherwise. He hoped Roper would cope if he had to pull out.

In their new role, they hadn't operated as they might normally. This was all different, but yes, Roper was responding well to the new rules of engagement, coming up with a steady stream of ideas and theories.

With a sudden sense of self-awareness, he knew he was struggling to adapt to new ways of working. This insight relaxed him. He had never thought he was indispensable, and he knew he wasn't now.

He needed to put his trust in the new processes that he, Roper and Julie Mayweather had discussed at length. He laughed as he recalled one especially relevant comment from the commissioner. "You have to trust that other people will do their jobs," she had told him. "I want you and Jonathan making sure you're directing efforts in the right direction. Do that, and we'll win."

He was glad Roper had been there today. He might not be a conversationalist, but he was company.

He'd gone a short distance when he received a message.

It was from the surgical team. An appointment had been arranged for his consultation. In two days, he would find out if he was going to be taken out of action in what was proving their toughest case yet.

For now, he was going back to work. He intended to make the most of the time available.

CHAPTER 31

Mary Lou Healy was lying on her bed, beaded in sweat. Sleep was proving elusive tonight, and her fevered imagination was filling her mind with troubling thoughts. Even though she knew her brain was playing tricks, everything felt so real.

The strange thing was that, wearied by everything she'd been through that day, she had gone to sleep the moment her head had hit the pillow. But twenty minutes later, she was wide awake, trying unsuccessfully to slow her racing thoughts.

Miss Kitty was proving no help at all. Curled up at the end of the bed, she had briefly woken, stretched and gone back to sleep, not even sparing her mistress the faintest glance.

After a restless two hours, Healy could no longer stand it. Even the touch of the expensive cotton sheets was proving uncomfortable against her body. Giving up the fight, she decided she might as well go with the flow. What she needed was the comfort of a strong cup of tea — she was well past worrying about the stimulating effect of caffeine — and then try to distract herself with some early hours TV.

As she made the brew, she rattled a couple of tins to try and attract Miss Kitty's attention, but the cat was far too smart to fall for that one and carried on ignoring her.

After the tea was made, she found a channel re-running an old episode of CSI Miami and briefly wondered if the show was always on somewhere in the world. Then, holding her steaming mug in both hands, she did her best to relax.

To her surprise, the familiar programmes sucked her in, and she jumped when her regular alarm went off at 3.30 a.m. Reluctantly, she turned the TV off and hauled her body, aching all over, towards the shower.

Afterwards, she dried off, got dressed, and applied minimal make-up, mostly comprising of a touch of lipstick. With a final check in the mirror, she was ready to go. Her flat was walking distance to the office which was, in turn, close to Old Street Underground station and the famous Moorfields Eye Hospital. There, she was greeted by the security guards. Just seeing other people helped ease her tension.

Walking into her office, she fired up her computer and watched as message after message flashed up. They were all in the same vein: routine administrative tasks that were essential to the smooth running of the Ryder Corporation. It was a mountain of work and would keep her busy for hours, but this pleased her; it meant she could genuinely claim not to have time for anything else.

By midday, she had already completed what most people would view as a full working day and went for a walk. Despite not eating since the previous day, she had no appetite and marched past her favourite takeaway spots. As usual, the area felt like it was designed more for cars than it was for people, although the pavements were busy enough with pedestrians going about their lunchtime business.

Back at her desk, she tried to drag out the rest of the work, but by mid-afternoon, she had cleared the backlog of urgent business. For the first time since walking through the doors early that morning, she could no longer afford to ignore the problem that had so far cost her a night's sleep — and might prove a lot more damaging than that.

She put her head in her hands, trying desperately to think through the problem and come up with a different solution. Nothing presented itself that was more likely than what she already suspected. The realisation that she had no choice brought her close to tears. What cut her to the quick was a bitter irony. The only way she could find out if someone was betraying the organisation was by committing her own betrayal.

Checking the time, it was a little after 3 p.m., making it 7 a.m. in California, a perfectly reasonable time to ring Josephine Taggert. Reasoning that her boss would probably be expecting a call about now, she hit the speed dial.

The mobile had barely started to ring before it was answered. Taggert, it seemed, was ready to roll. "I'm so glad you called," she said. "I've been having a terrible time with jet lag, and I can't take any more American TV. The BBC may have its critics, but at least there aren't any adverts." She paused. "But enough about me. You never call without a reason, so give me the worst." The last was accompanied by a laugh.

The comments induced a bout of coughing, forcing Healy to take a drink of water. "Apologies for the choking fit," she said. "My throat went dry. Do you want me to carry on talking on this line or call you back for a video call?"

Taggert laughed even louder. "You must be joking! It's far too early for anyone to be looking at me, not even you, the person I trust most in all the world."

Healy couldn't stop herself stiffening at this remark. She was glad her boss couldn't see her.

"Fair comment! I don't feel that fragrant myself. Let's stick to the 'old ways.' As you requested, I've got calls out to everyone I can think of who could be behind the manufacture of the screens, but there's no joy yet. I haven't given up hope — only about a quarter of my contacts have got back to me — so you never know when we'll get an answer. It could be a few days before everyone replies."

She thought about what to say next and launched in at the same time as Taggert. After a burst of confusion, her boss insisted Healy go first.

"I think we need to turn the spotlight on ourselves. I hate to say it because it will disrupt and unsettle people, but the police have made some interesting points. They're especially keen on finding out who knew that John Ryder was here in London. I've tried explaining that he rarely kept us fully informed of his movements, but they're asking how we can be so sure that no one here knew anything. Once you think about it, that's a tough thought to shake. I think we need to pursue it."

There was a long pause before Taggert replied. "I agree; it has to be done. I only found out he was coming to London when he physically arrived, but he had detailed plans which strongly suggest he must have had some help. It's alarming, but not unreasonable, for the police to pose the question. Do you suppose that, if we find someone was helping him, we find his would-be killer? That's a disconcerting thought."

The comments made Healy's stomach turn acid. She felt a wave of nausea sweep over her. Not for the first time, she was grateful they were on a regular call.

Regaining her composure, she said, "I thought you might say that, so I've already lined up the right people. They're incredibly discreet and understand they need to move with the utmost sensitivity. I'll let you know the moment there's anything to report."

"Do that. I'd hate to think one of our people was involved — but, if they are, I'd be seriously tempted to fly back and harm them myself. I really mean that."

Healy ended the conversation and headed for the private bathroom. She wanted to freshen up a little, but when she checked herself in the mirror, all she could see was a traitor.

CHAPTER 32

Hooley had grabbed a couple of hours on a day bed and, after a quick shower, was heading back to his desk. It was just after 4 a.m. and the lights were on.

"Morning, Jonathan."

They'd had a brief row a few hours earlier, as Roper had insisted he get some rest. With so little progress on the case, Hooley had been starting to feel the pressure in an almost physical way. It was affecting his concentration, so he had to read things several times over just to make sense of them.

"You look a lot better for some rest," Roper said, studying him carefully. "Do you mind if we have a quick conversation first?"

Hooley waved his hand in what he hoped was an effortless manner. "Please, go ahead."

As usual, the younger man was straight to it. "You don't need to worry about me. I will be fine while you are in hospital so if they say you need to go in straight away, that will be good."

Hooley went to respond. "Look, I'm not worried about you. I know you."

He got no further because Roper cut him off. "I know you are concerned about it. I can tell by the way you have been looking at me and then trying to pretend you are not really looking at me. I will be fine. I have learned so much from you that it won't be like the last time I was on my own.

"I realise now that I pushed everyone too hard and made unfair demands on them. You have taught me to give people space and not hold them to my standards. I promise that every day I will make an effort to listen to people and answer their questions."

Hooley felt himself welling up. The trouble was, he really was worried about Roper. The young detective had no idea how many enemies he'd made at Scotland Yard. That was the problem with being the most honest person around — when people asked you questions, you told the truth.

He coughed to cover up his emotion.

"I know you'll be fine. You've got Julie on your side and Susan will make a difference. Anyway, with a bit of luck, you'll have me for a little while yet. We don't know what the surgeon will say until I see him tomorrow." Then he remembered that Julie Mayweather had called him at about 7 p.m. last night. It felt like days ago. "If she can find the time, Julie is coming in this morning, just a flying visit."

They went back to work, trying to ignore a sense of unease.

Surprisingly, it was the forensic accountants who helped ease the mood. Just after 6 a.m., Hooley took a call from the senior accountant, Roger Croxford. Hooley had never met the man but had heard he was famously relentless. He sounded excited.

"We're on to something, thanks to the steer from you guys."

Hooley felt his mood lighten immediately. "Can you give me a moment while I put this on speaker?"

Roper leapt up and perched on the edge of Hooley's desk. Hooley asked him to carry on as he placed the phone between them.

"You may be right about the role played by Emily Wong's father." Hooley flashed a thumbs-up at Roper, who was leaning towards the phone, listening intently. "I'll spare you the details because they've made it very complicated, but we found money in an offshore account that we could link back to a company controlled by her father . . ."

"That's fantastic to hear," Hooley replied. "Can you give me any guidance on where this might take us?"

"Well, it seems that, for the last couple of years, substantial sums of money have been traded back and forward between this account and another offshore account controlled by either Mark Savage or someone else at Diamonds and Pearls."

"Is this strong enough to hold up in court?" Hooley was eager to know.

"Maybe, but we do need more." There was a lengthy pause. "I hope that didn't sound too downbeat. Now that we know what we're looking at, we will get more. For now, what I can tell you is that it's a substantial sum of money. High six figures, maybe even seven. Too much to be explained away by regular payments for services. To me, it has all the hallmarks of money laundering. So our next step is making sure that we get the details that firm that up. I never like to get ahead of myself, but I reckon we'll find everything you need."

Hooley ended the call and leaned back in his seat.

"That is such good news and a massive relief. I feel like a proper detective."

This puzzled Roper. "You are a detective," he said.

"Of course. But we all need to be reminded from time to time."

At that moment a tired but determined-looking Julie Mayweather appeared. "I knew you two would be at your desks. I've got to be at Downing Street in an hour to brief the PM, but I wanted to catch up with you first."

Roper noticed the time. "That brilliant cafe will be open now. Who wants a bacon sandwich and coffee?"

He didn't wait for an answer — if there was anything left over, he would eat it — and Hooley and Mayweather watched him as he walked out.

"Is he going to be all right when you have to go into hospital?" Mayweather asked.

"Funny you should mention that. He told me a couple of hours ago that I wasn't to worry about him. He's certainly better equipped now than he was. People are starting to understand him better. It wasn't that long ago that they thought he was a bit of a prat, but a lot of them get him now and know to give him a bit of space."

She couldn't keep the worry from her face. "Jonathan and you are helping drive this investigation forward — even the head of MI5, a man not given to lavish praise, acknowledged yesterday that you two are 'pretty good'. I think he appreciates the way you can avoid the distractions and stay locked on to your targets."

Hooley smiled. "I bet he found that difficult to say."

"He did look like he was sucking a slice of lemon at the time." Mayweather shook her head. "Anyway, if you get ordered in for this op, how long will we have before Jonathan starts to miss you?"

"I think if we try to have him reporting to you every day, then he'll be fine for a few weeks — but the Rainbow Spectrum, it works best when he's not under pressure. I'm not saying he can't do it, but it makes it harder for him to get those amazing insights."

Mayweather pursed her lips. "The problem is we can all feel the pressure now, and it's not going to ease off. What would be your worst-case scenario?"

"If I'm really pessimistic, I think you should allow for a week and then hope for more. The problem is that he doesn't really trust any 'normal' people. Unfortunately, that makes me the one person he believes."

Mayweather nodded. "In that case, can you do us all a big favour and solve this before you go into hospital?"

At that moment, Roper returned with the food. The commissioner apologised and left them to it, leaving Roper with a bonus sandwich which he was delighted about.

On a roller-coaster day, more good news continued with a telephone update from MI6 chief Andy Fishlock, who called Hooley on his mobile.

"Very interesting about your Mr Wong. It seems he's something of a high wire merchant. We had him pegged as an archetypal party loyalist, but there's a bit more to him than that."

He paused, and Hooley realised the man was building the moment.

Fishlock carried on. "As I say, no surprise that he has connections to the Chinese Communist Party, but his contacts are very senior, so he's more important than we had realised. But we also found out he has serious links to the Triads as well. Now that is important because the Communist Party likes to avoid getting its hands dirty, and effectively sub-contracts the criminal gangs to do the things they can't be associated with.

"That can be anything from drug running, sex trafficking and even large-scale intimidation. If he's in the middle of that, then he is a much bigger player than we had given him credit for. In fact, we've been underestimating him for a few years so there will be plenty more to come from him."

Hooley nodded. "Just as well Jonathan zeroed in on him so quickly. I've said it before, but the faster you find things out, the better."

He ended the call, briefed Roper and Brooker, and felt as if a huge weight had been lifted off his shoulders. "Seems like this remote detective work is pretty effective."

Roper shrugged. "I was never worried."

Hooley turned his attention to Brooker. He used to think Roper could put in the hours at his computer terminal, but she was more than a match for him.

"Are you okay, Susan? It must feel like you've drawn the short straw with all the background reading you've been doing."

She smiled. "No problem at all, I enjoy doing this, and I'm good at it. That's not boasting; it's just that I never get bored with what I'm doing. Anyway, Jonathan and I had a long discussion about it, and it's the best way to use our resources."

Hooley hid his surprise. No one had involved him in this conversation, although he could hardly fault their logic.

It seemed the kids were more than all right!

CHAPTER 33

The surgeon's PA, Cheryl McConnaughey, was polite, understanding and adamant.

"Once he's assessed you, the doctor will decide when you'll need surgery. Then we'll fit you onto the most appropriate list. I understand what you're saying, but you really need to discuss it with him."

Hooley had always known that it was a long shot to try and dictate the day of his operation, but given the circumstances, he felt compelled to try. The thought of leaving Roper alone at such a difficult time was too difficult to bear.

If he was honest, part of him was hoping that the surgeon would say he wasn't that bad, that he could afford to wait. But it wasn't a thought that stood up to the most significant scrutiny.

He had placed the call to McConnaughey on the day he received the diagnosis, and now he was waiting to see the surgeon in his office at Guy's Hospital, a sprawling complex situated close to London Bridge and not far from the Bank of England.

He didn't have to wait for long. Soon, the surgeon, a big man with broad shoulders and surprisingly large hands, breezed in. His radiated good humour, and the DCI liked him instinctively; he would have made a great companion in the pub, he thought, before berating himself for thinking of alcohol at such a moment.

Turning in his seat, he checked Roper. This morning he'd found him waiting outside the two-bedroom flat in Pimlico that Hooley's brother, a successful property developer, had presented to him following his divorce. It had been a timely intervention; the DCI had been preparing himself for life in a grim bedsit.

"I suppose telling you you'd be better off in the office won't make any difference?"

Roper didn't reply.

The DCI shrugged. "Follow me then. I don't want to be late for the appointment."

Hooley was pulled back to the present as Dr Thomas sat down and smiled at both of them in turn, seemingly unconcerned by Roper's presence. He radiated such a powerful sense of positivity that it was impossible to imagine anything going wrong during one of his operations. Hooley instantly relaxed.

"I've been able to look at all the video and read the reports — and I can tell you there's nothing out of the ordinary about what we need to do. Your valve will accept surgical repair very well. You'll also need a double bypass — but, again, this is routine."

The man was so reassuring that Hooley just smiled back at him, all his questions disappearing. He even wondered if Thomas was disappointed that this operation wasn't going to be a real challenge of his skills.

The surgeon went on, "From reading your notes, I gather you haven't felt any symptoms, and it was your colleague here who got anxious on your behalf. Well, you did a good job, Mr Roper. But, Mr Hooley, have you found yourself struggling in the afternoons? I'm talking about feeling tired, even in need of going for a sleep?"

It dawned on Hooley that this was exactly what had been happening. He had marked it down as normal. "I just put it down to getting older and the pressure of work."

He was treated to that grin again.

"Probably not old age, at least not just yet. You're far too young. Hopefully, we can sort that out with the operation. Now, you'll need to be in the hospital between five and seven days — the actual amount of time you spend will depend on how quickly you recover from the operation. Everyone is slightly different, so don't think of it as a race. It's just about getting well." He paused and, for the first time, his expression was serious. "Now, I understand the two of you are in the front line of the search for the idiots behind these bombs — which means you, Mr Hooley, would like to delay the operation for a long as it is safe." Thomas turned to gaze out of the window, but he wasn't looking at the view, just deep in thought. "When you have a damaged heart valve, it isn't something you can just ignore and deal with at your leisure. Normally, I wouldn't allow anybody to set a date that suits them. But I do understand the vital importance of what you do to keep the rest of us safe. So . . ."

Hooley seemed to rise higher in his chair, eager for what the doctor had to say.

"I will give you two weeks. There are two conditions. First, if you have any change in symptoms, any pains in the chest, any pain anywhere for that matter, you let me know as a matter of urgency. I don't want either of you making judgements on the symptoms." For just a moment, his gaze lingered on Roper — who seemed to become uncomfortable in the face of scrutiny. "The second thing is that you agree to be regularly monitored during this period. This isn't to say you're in danger, but I want to remind you of how serious your condition is."

Hooley couldn't decide whether to be pleased or worried. He hadn't expected to be allowed to carry on at all, so he had mixed feelings.

Mr Thomas looked carefully between the two of them to see if there were any more questions — but even Roper had run out of things to say. At last, they shook hands and left, Hooley promising he would liaise with the PA over the actual date.

Back on the street, the DCI stopped to send a text message to Julie Mayweather to inform her that he had been granted a fortnight's reprieve. Her reply came within moments.

"Fabulous news all round. Don't underestimate how important you are to him."

A few hours later, following a celebratory coffee, Hooley felt like he wanted to get out and about. The news from France was making him think here was the perfect opportunity.

The French authorities were closing in on an address for the runaways. Yet another Roper tip was proving central to solving the case.

MI5 had forwarded a confidential report. Hooley read out the key points.

"They've found them in a flat not that far from Gare du Nord. According to the French surveillance team, they've only come out to use a brasserie opposite. Otherwise, they're sitting still." He paused. "They'd like to know if they should go in and get them. They don't think it's going to be difficult. But the excellent news is that MI5 has a fast helicopter standing by at Battersea and we can be in Paris and on-site in about ninety minutes. The French are happy to wait for us to get there."

Roper didn't need any prodding. "I think it will be okay. We need to be there because they need to see us. They, and Mark Savage, in particular, have been acting like they totally control this situation.

"My Rainbow Spectrum says they think that Paris is their little bolthole, where they will be safe from events and can ride out the investigation. They're about to get a very nasty surprise, and it's critical that they see us over there after it has happened. They need to know that everyone and every country are working on this and they have no escape."

Hooley rubbed his hands together. "And there I just wanted to see the little toerags get their comeuppance. As usual, you have raised the bar. Come on then, Tiger, let's go get 'em. I've got a squad car on the way. It may even be here by the time we get outside."

Roper needed no further invitation and vanished, at speed. The somewhat slower Hooley spoke into thin air. "Well, the car might be there by the time *I* get outside."

It turned out that getting them to Paris was a major priority and it wasn't just a car waiting, there were four motorbikes as well. They would be acting in pairs to open the traffic as they raced south. The journey passed in a blur; Hooley doubted he had ever driven through London so fast.

There was no hanging around at the Battersea Heliport. Waiting staff urged them towards a gleaming Augusta Westland 109 that was only waiting for them. With a top speed of 168 knots — nearly 200 mph — it would get them to Paris in about one hour and ten minutes.

With just the two of them, the space in the passenger compartment seemed huge. Hooley had been on a helicopter on a few occasions but never anything so luxurious. The craft lifted off the moment they strapped in.

The DCI loved helicopter rides, despite the noise, and he could tell by the way Roper was intently staring out of his window that he too was enjoying the flight.

It was always a thrill to watch the traffic on the roads and motorways while high above you swept effortlessly by. The helicopter flew over the Kent coast, crossing into French space close to Le Touquet before gliding up towards Versailles and the vast sprawl of Paris itself. It wasn't long before they left the French countryside behind and shot towards the heart of the French capital.

Landing in Paris, they were whisked towards the Gare du Nord without delay.

The DCI had never experienced a trip like it. His heart beat harder as he sensed that events were moving to an outcome. His biggest fear was of more bomb attacks in London, but Roper seemed reassuringly confident that that was not going to happen. He was insisting his Rainbow Spectrum was quite clear on the issue.

CHAPTER 34

As he surveyed the French hit squad, Hooley was reminded of the Duke of Wellington's famous comment when he observed a tough-looking bunch of his own soldiers: "I don't know what effect these men will have upon the enemy, but by God, they frighten me."

The assembled soldiers seemed to vary in size from massive to enormous. They were dressed in black fatigues and had ski masks to cover their faces. Large hands clutched an impressive array of small arms. He recognised Uzi submachine guns and Heckler & Koch MP5s among them. The DCI realised that there were a few women among the team . . . all of them bigger than he was.

Roper had assumed he would be going in with the hit team. That had been flatly rejected, and Hooley had not objected. Roper had many qualities; being a fighting man was not among them.

To his relief, they had been given the opportunity to stress that the trio needed to be confronted by the Scotland Yard detectives and it was agreed that once they were suitably restrained, that would happen. Roper and Hooley had been taken to the mobile command vehicle, a huge purpose-built van parked close to the apartment that was about to be stormed.

Roper had become quite cross at this, saying that he didn't want to be shut away. Eventually, a compromise had been reached where they were allowed to stand on a street corner, just out of sight. The moment the Diamonds and Pearls trio were safely restrained, they could run to join the action.

The whole operation was quite an exercise. Residents were moved from nearby apartments and the normally bustling streets were slowly becoming quieter and quieter as pedestrians were directed away and customers herded from bars and restaurants. No one thought there were explosives at the target, but neither did they want to take a chance. From their vantage point 100 metres away, Hooley and Roper watched the action from the livestream on Roper's tablet computer.

"The quality of surveillance kit nowadays is just fantastic," said the DCI.

Roper ignored him, staring intently at the image as the French hit squad prepared to move in. He had split his screen; on the left, a clear view of the gathering forces outside and, on the right, another image showing what was happening inside the apartment.

Emily Wong and Mark Savage were sitting on a settee, the woman apparently asleep and the man sitting forward, bouncing his leg up and down, clearly very agitated.

His sister, her previously sleek hair now a mess of tangles, was slumped in a chair, listlessly reading a book. To Roper, it appeared that she was going back over the same page again and again.

In the street, the camera showed the intrusion team using a battering ram to smash open the front door, before tossing in a flash bang for good measure.

The effect of the sudden explosion of sound and light was like something out of a silent movie. All three people jumped up, their mouths open, clearly screaming. They started running backwards and forwards, the two women colliding and hitting their heads. It was almost comical; if he had not seen it with his own eyes, Hooley would not have believed it.

The women fell to the floor, clutching their wounds, and missed the sight of Mark Savage being laid out by an enormous French soldier wearing full battle kit and a face mask.

Even among his fellow giants, he was a fearsome size, so it was probably a welcome relief for Savage that he was rendered unconscious almost straight away. At least he was spared making a fool of himself by trying to fight back.

As the French officers had predicted, the whole thing was over in a matter of moments. With the trio failing to put up any sort of fight, it was only a matter of a short time before they were being led out of the apartment.

Roper broke cover, ignoring Hooley's pleas for him to stay put. The DCI followed more cautiously as the younger man reached the entrance to the building, still ignoring Hooley's shouts to be careful.

Two soldiers in the backup team were guarding the door. Hearing the commotion they swung round, levelling their weapons at the onrushing Roper. For a terrible moment, Hooley feared the worst, but the French soldiers showed superb discipline, watching closely but not opening fire.

Even Roper started to realise what he was risking, coming to a halt and holding his hands out to show he was unarmed. There was a brief standoff, before he was allowed forward to wait just outside. A good minute later, Hooley moved up to join him, albeit more carefully and slowly.

At that moment two of the soldiers who had successfully breached the apartment appeared, carrying a now semi-conscious Savage between them. He was dumped unceremoniously onto a stretcher that and a few hundred metres away, a small crowd of Parisians broke into a ragged cheer. They might not have known what was happening, but they had already taken sides. After so many incidents in France, it seemed the crowd was delighted to see some "terrorists" getting their comeuppance.

With the situation under control, Hooley and Roper stepped over to the stretcher where Savage continued to groan. On catching sight of them, he went pale.

"Good to see you again, Mr Savage," said Hooley, icily polite. "We seem to have quite a bit of talking to do. We thought we'd pop over and fly back to London with you. Give ourselves a bit of a head start."

A few moments later, the two women appeared. Julie Savage looked sick, and Emily Wong resigned.

Addressing the three of them, Hooley added: "I'm pretty certain that you three are going to prison for a very long time. At the very least, you're facing charges of obstructing a terror investigation." He paused. "On the way back to London, you need to think about that — and start talking to us. Your only chance is if you cooperate with us fully."

Forty minutes later the group, plus French guards, were in a secure zone at Charles de Gaulle airport, as they waited for the private Lear jet that was going to take them back to London.

The plane touched down five minutes later, and French security handed the prisoners over to the British team that had flown out with the flight. Take-off was fast, and as they reached cruising altitude, Hooley had the two women placed out of earshot at the rear of the plane. They would be able to see Savage being quizzed, but the cabin noise would drown out the sound.

Strictly speaking, they should have done this formally, with everything recorded for use as evidence, but Hooley was worried about the possibility of there being more bombs.

Savage was handcuffed to a small, leather-clad settee running along the right wall. The two detectives took seats directly opposite him. The prisoner looked sullen and had a swelling on his jaw and the whole scene seemed incongruous being played out against the luxury of the private jet.

As the plane turned towards London, Roper took the lead.

"What can you tell me?" As questions go, it wasn't the best, but it was a start.

Savage surprised them both with a defiant response. "I can tell you that I'm going to sue you for every penny I can get. This is a wrongful arrest. You are carrying out an illegal rendition flying me back from France."

Roper was unfazed. He was beginning to think Savage was the ringleader. The two women might be able to get reduced sentences if he was the most culpable.

"I've got bad news for you," he said. "We are quite within our rights. You were picked up on a European arrest warrant. That gives full rights to the participating countries of which France and the UK are leading members. You're also being held under the revised Terrorism Act. This allows us to hold you without access to a solicitor. If we want to hold you for longer, we just need permission from a senior police officer — and trust me when I say there will be no shortage of senior officers available tonight."

This seemed to knock all the bravado out of Savage, and he said nothing, staring down at his feet. He stayed like that for almost a full minute — long enough to start irritating Roper.

Finally, he looked up. "I want a deal."

"What sort of deal?"

"I give you those other two, and you let me off with a slap on the wrist, or maybe a bit of time in one of those cushy open prisons."

CHAPTER 35

Savage had refused to budge from his position of demanding a deal, and before long they were heading into London City Airport where armed officers would take the three suspects to Victoria.

After such a long and emotionally draining day, even Roper needed a break, and they had agreed to grab four hours of sleep and then continue the interrogation. For Hooley, it was an easy call. They were too tired to think straight and needed to recharge. The DCI would grab some sleep in the office. Roper was going for a run. It would help settle his mind, which was in danger of "overloading".

He planned to walk home first. Depending on your point of view, his penthouse apartment was either austere and lacking personal touches or a temple to minimalism. Roper liked the lack of "stuff" and told Hooley that he found objects like flowerpots and paintings a distraction. He needed a clutter-free space to be able to relax fully.

Once he was home, he stepped out of his work outfit, carefully folded it and placed it in the designated dry-cleaning bin. Other bins were for the clothes he cleaned in the washing machine and were labelled "white", "dark", or "coloured" so that nothing got mixed up.

Roper couldn't abide any form of untidiness. At work, he had to constantly grit his teeth at the messy behaviour of colleagues — but at home, he took no prisoners. His apartment was a haven where his few possessions were arranged with geometric precision.

With two spare bedrooms, he was even able to afford the luxury of a dedicated "flapping room". This involved a comfortable chair and piles of good quality A4 printing paper. The make and size were important as he liked to sit in the chair while carefully flapping the paper in a way he found instantly soothing. He'd discovered the technique in childhood and had been refining it ever since.

Clothes for cleaning packed away, he decided he would double up on his "long shower" routine, taking one now and one after he had completed the run. This was a highly structured routine — he washed his hair and body to a precise formula — and it acted like a superior form of Valium, calming the stress that was never far away, but without the side effects.

First shower completed, he walked naked into the bedroom and carefully laid out his jogging outfit on the bed. Here it was thoroughly inspected to make sure it was clean and free of blemishes.

Satisfied, he put it on. Roper had never lost a passion for the sort of black plimsolls that no one ever wore outside school. They were paired with baggy black shorts and a roomy white t-shirt. The first time Hooley had seen him in his outfit, he had laughed for several minutes. An indignant Roper had asked him what was so funny, and in turn, Hooley had replied, "I don't know how to break the news to you, but with your white skin and you being so skinny, you look like a pipe-cleaner wearing a pair of black shorts."

Roper had treated the remark with the contempt it deserved — although he did add, "At least I can be bothered to take some exercise . . . which is more than can be said for you."

For reasons that were entirely beyond Roper, this reply had made the DCI laugh all the more, so he'd given up in disgust, using the run to ponder, not for the first time, why it was that he found people so unpredictable.

As Roper set out, the moonlight was making shadows merge as the darkness held sway. Roper set off on a looping path heading roughly east. His route took him past Southwark Cathedral and along the busy main roads towards Peckham Rye, a green space ringed by residential properties that had become more popular with the middle classes over the years.

Roper's running style was best described as "unusual", since it looked as though he had modelled it on a newborn calf, with legs, knees and feet pointing in multiple directions as he trotted along with his hands clasped in front of him. One wit had once announced that Roper was "praying he doesn't fall over".

Despite looking awkward, he could really move — as a would-be mugger discovered when he tried to ambush him, along one of the backroads that were taking him towards the green spaces of Dulwich. The would-be thief was a fit teen-ager, but his pursuit left him gasping for air and he gave up, telling himself there would be easier prey later.

But Roper was concentrating so hard on running that he was oblivious to it all.

He carried on in the direction of Tulse Hill before making a right into Dulwich village. Moving steadily, he was soon loping through Camberwell and decided to head for Waterloo. Here he could get onto the South Bank and jog the rest of the way home. Finally, back in his apartment, it was time for his second shower, followed by a double portion of microwaved food.

Despite regularly eating enough for two grown men, Roper never seemed to gain an ounce in weight. Sometimes he even needed to pile on extra calories — chocolate muffins were the current favourite — just to maintain the weight he had been since he was eighteen years old.

Demolishing his food, he dressed and headed back to Victoria. It was just after 4 a.m. when he walked into the office to find that Hooley was already there.

The DCI lifted a hand in greeting. "Susan has gone to get us all coffee from an all-night place." He rubbed his hands together in a way that said he was ready to go. "As soon as we've got our drinks, we can start. I've been thinking about the best way to handle this, and I think that this time we should both question them one at a time. Susan's going to watch everything from the observation rooms and get involved as she likes."

As if on cue, Brooker arrived with coffee and, from Roper's point of view, a very welcome bag of chocolate muffins.

All three agreed they should start with Emily Wong. Together, they spent a few minutes studying her through the two-way mirror. Alone in the cell, she was wearing a police-issue boiler suit which swamped her petite figure. Though she had lost the air of composure she'd had before, she still seemed alert, her eyes kept darting towards the cell door.

"What do you think?" said Hooley.

Roper was first to respond. "She is doing her best to appear calm, but you can tell she is quite close to breaking. She's breathing in a shallow way, and her forehead is quite shiny, suggesting she is sweating, even though it's not that hot in there."

"What about you, Susan?"

Brooker hesitated a moment as if having an internal conversation, then squared her shoulders.

"I've noticed she keeps looking at her nails. My guess is that they're badly chipped. She's wealthy and unused to being anything other than well-groomed — so that would be bothering her. It will make her feel more vulnerable than usual."

The DCI was impressed. "Well observed," he said. "I get the feeling she's ready to talk. But I've made the mistake of being overconfident in the past, so I've got an idea about how to approach this. If Susan keeps a close eye on things, she could come in after a few minutes with a hand-written note

157

and hand it to me, make it seem like it's really vital information." He stopped, to make sure both Roper and Brooker were taking this in. "I'm improvising here, but say I read it, nod, hand it to Jonathan — who does the same thing — and then leave. That would put some pressure on and make her think she needs to look out for herself."

Roper looked inscrutable. "We persuade her we have more information than we're letting on. Clever of you — it takes away the need for her to initiate the confession and makes her feel there is no choice."

The DCI blinked back his surprise at this unexpected praise and saw that Susan was giving him a thumbs-up.

"So that's both of you, backing my idea — I must be doing something right! To be honest, I expected you both to complain about the deception." He smiled but noted neither Brooker nor Roper were smiling back so he hastily continued. "Seriously, I do feel she's the best chance we have of finding out what's going on. So far, they've been spinning us pre-prepared stories. Nothing they've said can be taken at one hundred per cent face value, but each has enough of the truth in it to distract us, at the very least." He looked back at Emily Wong, still sitting there through the two-way mirror. "I want to impress on her that this needs to end. We need the truth, and we need it fast."

He went to go inside, then stopped with his hand on the door handle. "I nearly forgot. One of the custody officers who was with Mark Savage reports he has slash marks all over his torso. We might need to quiz her about that — but keep it up our sleeves for a moment. She might even come out with it."

CHAPTER 36

"Remember, I'm a good cop, and you're a good cop. There are no bad guys around here." Hooley was leading the way to the interview room. "When we get in there, let's play it very cool, like we already know everything there is to know. I want her believing that we might be the only real friends she has, and I don't want her thinking her best option is to start talking about whatever scam the three of them have come up with."

Stepping inside, he nodded at the uniformed officer standing against one wall and directed his first questions at him.

"Has Ms Wong had something to eat and drink? Has she asked for anything special?"

"She's twice declined the opportunity to have something to eat and just requested a cup of tea, which she hasn't really touched."

Hooley pursed his lips as if he found this information fascinating. Then he turned his attention to Emily Wong, making eye contact as he sat opposite her, and placed a set of printed documents on the table between them. From this pile, he carefully extracted a blank notepad. Taking his time, he wrote her name on the front page of the pad, adding the date, time, location and names of the others present.

He paused for a minute, seemingly fascinated by the camera lens in the ceiling, then muttered as he carefully wrote a couple of phrases — including "terror suspect" and "high-security prison", all the time making sure Wong could see the words he spelt out.

Wong had not moved a muscle throughout this performance, but her eyes had grown wider and wider as he continued to scribble at the notepaper.

She finally cracked. "Wait . . . what are you writing?" The tension was making her voice squeak.

Hooley put down his pen and looked up, his face a mask of surprise. "I'm sorry I didn't realise you hadn't understood what I explained in Paris. You and your friends are at the centre of a terror investigation. You're the only people in custody right now — and that's probably not a great position to be in. I know you want a lawyer, but we don't have to supply you with one just yet."

A single tear leaked from her eye and she let out a quiet groan. The DCI was pleased that Roper was unmoved by her reaction. In the past, he had really struggled when people turned on the waterworks. It never occurred to him that someone might try and make themselves cry to make others feel sorry for them.

As more tears flowed, Hooley remained impassive, until he judged it was the right moment to offer a tissue. She might be faking, but he did have some sympathy. He'd be crying in her situation.

After she had dried her tears, he urged her to drink some tea. With a shaking hand, Wong picked up the paper cup and took a small mouthful; then she put it down again, probably worried that in her state she would either knock it over or drop it.

"Before we get down to talking," Hooley went on, "I just need to pull some details together — because we know, or suspect, quite a lot already. Then we can move on to the more difficult things."

The tension, which was simmering nicely, boiled over as there was a frantic pounding on the door, as everyone spun to look, the door burst open and an excited Brooker steamed in, brandishing a piece of paper.

Even though Hooley had been expecting it, her dramatic appearance set his heart racing. He could only imagine what it was doing to the unprepared Wong.

"You were right, sir," Brooker said. "It was exactly as you said."

She handed him the sheet of paper and stood there looking expectant. Hooley kept it turned away while he read the words, then re-read it before giving it, carefully, to Roper. Roper kept the pretence going as he looked at the sheet of paper, then handed it back.

"Didn't I tell you that was going to be the case?" Hooley asked. Looking at the suspect, he made a "what can you do" gesture with his hands. "My colleague and I need to break off for a moment, but we'll be back as quickly as we can."

Together, Hooley and Roper stepped out to meet Brooker in the corridor. "Your idea worked brilliantly!" she whispered. "I was watching her the whole time, and she was desperately trying to make out what was on the paper. I thought her eyes were going to pop out of her head."

As she talked, Hooley glanced at Roper and saw that the expression about her eyes "popping out of her head" was about to be challenged by his ever-literal minded fellow detective.

"It's okay, Jonathan. It's just an expression. Like that conversation we had about people saying it's 'raining cats and dogs'. They just mean it's heavy rain." Roper clamped his mouth shut as he thought about this, but the DCI swiftly moved on. "It did seem to go well. Let's go and have a very early tea break, so she stews on it for a little while. When we get back in, we'll find out just how much it's stirred things up for Ms Wong . . ."

As they walked back in half an hour later, Wong stared at them, a resigned look on her face. Her shoulders had slumped, her hair was flat, and her face reflected the depths of her misery.

They sat down and waited. This was clearly a pivotal moment. What came next could make all the difference.

Wong started talking slowly. At first, she seemed reluctant to speak, but soon her words were getting faster and faster.

"Diamonds and Pearls was being used by a drug-smuggling gang. They gave us their dirty money, and we cleaned it up. We were naive and stupid because we never saw it coming. Or at least I didn't. Everything had been planned in advance. We were offered a lot of money to set the business up. It came from an associate of my father's. I was stupid — I really believed my father when he told me this man was a good investor. And, well, all three of us were desperate for money. We'd had to leave school because our parents got into trouble, but we still had the same friends, and none of them had money worries. I wanted my old life back so hard I never asked questions. It was just greed, really. I closed my eyes to what was going on. The store was a perfect vehicle for the gangs. It generated an enormous cash flow, and we had multiple large credit-card transactions every day."

As she spoke, she kept her gaze low, looking at a single spot on the table. Hooley and Roper were content to let her keep talking, secure in the knowledge that every single word was being captured on tape.

Pausing only to catch her breath, she carried on. "The plan was really simple. Almost childish, I thought. Invoices were created for goods that never existed. We pushed them through the system, and clean cash came out at the other end. When we first started the business, with the money my father's friend had given us, they never asked for anything. We thought we were really clever, that we were proving what great business people we were. But we soon got a taste of what was about to happen."

She broke down and began to cry again. Hooley guessed that some she was recalling some unpleasant memory.

"Are you ready to continue?" he asked, not unkindly but also briskly. He needed the information as quickly as possible. "Remember, we need everything. I'm sorry if it's a bad memory — but you do need to tell us."

She seemed to gather herself and started again. This time, her voice was quiet, and they had to listen more carefully.

"About eighteen months ago, someone asked us to run money through the accounts. They said they knew my father and it was okay. I had no idea who they were, and Mark was especially angry. He said we were a unique company with many influential friends, and they should be cautious.

"They came back a few days later, and there were a lot more of them. They tricked us into a meeting at our office at Chelsea Harbour." She looked away, trembling. Moments later, she managed to carry on, this time keeping her eyes closed as if this would hold the memory at bay. "Two of them grabbed Mark. They were really rough with him. He was crying out in pain. Another pair made sure his sister and I watched. If we looked away, they hurt us. Then they ripped his shirt off and slashed him all over his body.

"Once he was bleeding, they squeezed lemon juice into his wounds, making him cry out even more. It was too much for me, and I was sick. They hit me for that, walloped me and told me I was a 'soft little girl'." She paused, obviously trying to process the memory. "The leader was the most frightening of all. He had a pair of eyes tattooed on his upper eyelids. They were so lifelike." She shuddered. "He told us that next time would be worse. 'We'll slice him up good and bring some proper stuff to pour over him,' he said, and that'd we'd have to watch as his skin dissolves away . . ." Again, Wong paused, steeling herself at the recollection. "We actually begged to be allowed to help the money-laundering scam take place. It all went on quite smoothly, if any crime can be said to be smooth, until there was the bomb."

Wong told them that the three partners were convinced that the bomb attack was carried out by a rival drug gang, although they had no evidence for this.

"It was the only thing that made sense," she insisted. "We'd done exactly as the man with the eyes asked, so it had to be another gang. Maybe they wanted to take over."

She slowed down — so Hooley asked her what she could tell them about the men. "I speak a little Spanish, and they were talking Spanish for sure. At the time, I thought they were South American, but I don't know."

When Wong had been talking non-stop for half an hour, Hooley called a break. He wanted to pool their thoughts and decide where to go next. His sense that they were close to something important was getting stronger.

Back at the office, Roper took charge.

"Sorry to jump in, but my Rainbow Spectrum suggests that neither woman knows that much, or at least not the whole truth. It's all down to Mark Savage."

"And you're quite sure about this?" Hooley knew the answer but felt he had to ask.

"This is the strongest sense I have had yet."

"Okay. In that case, do we even bother with the sister and just go straight to her brother?"

CHAPTER 37

Healy was keeping herself busy. She'd spent the bulk of her day attempting to chase down any details about who John Ryder had involved in producing the new screens for the mobile handsets.

It was clear that his product was some way behind those of his rivals. In effect, it was still at the innovation stage. That would all change if the concept made it through development — then it would be about measuring output in the millions — but, for now, it would be strictly small batch. Healy had already started having waking nightmares about just how many small labs and production facilities there were in the world. Just to add to her problems, it was inevitable that Ryder would have signed his collaborators to non-disclosure agreements.

This wasn't the first time that she had tried to backtrack Ryder's footsteps and previous experience had taught her to work her way through each area in as much detail as she possibly could. So far, Healy had concentrated her inquiries in the Far East because that was where she had the most contacts — although, if she was honest, they were spread pitifully thin. As well as developing countries, she was even sniffing around California. The state was chock full of developers, engineers and designers.

As usual, she had been working since before dawn. Her eyes felt gritty and she'd been so busy that she'd barely noticed a steady stream of people leaving documents in her in-tray. Now she realised how big the pile of papers needing her attention had become.

Healy reached for the stack, then stopped with her hand in mid-air. She was pushing herself too hard. She needed to take a moment to review what she'd done so far and find out what was happening with the confidential search operation she'd commissioned.

She'd contacted a very expensive, and very discreet, firm of security consultants yesterday morning and they had promised they would be working on the problem within the hour. She had no idea how they went about their work, but Ryder himself had always insisted they were the only people to use.

The more she thought about it, the stronger the temptation to give them a call, but she resisted — partly because she didn't want to tempt fate, and partly because she knew they would be in touch the moment they had anything.

She had just picked up a document from the in-tray when her mobile rang. The noise set her heart racing, and her whole body felt clammy.

She answered, not quite able to keep her voice steady. "Mary Lou Healy."

"This is Mr Elliot." The man spoke clearly and quietly. She tensed for the second part of the message. "Your order is ready for collection."

This was it. The signal that the security consultants had something. This was the agreed procedure for contact. The call ended, and she put her phone down. As she did so, she heard the ping of an incoming text message. Hurriedly, she pulled her desk drawer open. Inside there were two small handsets in a bag which had been delivered earlier by courier.

She recalled her instructions. "You will receive two one-time-use phones. The first will receive a message containing a telephone number — but this will not happen until you hear from Mr Elliot to say the 'package is ready.' Get rid of the first phone and make the call on the second. Do not attempt to use it more than once."

She stood up and gulped in some air, needing to calm down before she made the call. Her palms were sweating so much she couldn't dry her hands, despite her best efforts to wipe them on her clothes. It wasn't an exaggeration that her future might be ruined by this next conversation.

Finally feeling calm enough now to make the call, she went ahead. It was answered on the third ring, as she had been told. She listened carefully, all the colour draining from her face. Her worst fear was coming true.

She made a last attempt at escaping the inevitable. "Is there any chance you might have made a mistake? Could you check again, just in case? Please." To her dismay, she heard herself pleading, before the voice at the other end killed off the tiny bit of hope she was holding onto.

"There is no chance of a mistake. We have checked and rechecked. The answer is still the same."

Healy was seized by the need to do something. Anything. She dug out her personal phone and entered a number from memory. It was nowhere near as secure as using the "burner", but she didn't care.

She thought the call was about to go through to the message system when it was answered.

"Mary Lou. What a pleasure to hear from you. To what do I owe the honour?"

She had once thought his voice was rich and gentle — but now she knew different. The underlying note of entitlement made her sick to her stomach. She was hit with a wave of anger so intense that it was a good job she was sitting down. With a supreme effort of will, she kept the rage under control.

"Something very urgent has come up. You need to know. Can we meet tonight at 8 p.m.?"

"Sounds fascinating, but you always were an interesting woman. I've got a bottle of something special I was hanging on to for the right occasion. Let's make a night of it. The usual place."

It wasn't a question.

CHAPTER 38

It was a considerably more chastened Mark Savage who looked at Hooley and Roper as they walked into the interrogation room. Last time around, he'd seemed almost bloated with self-importance. Now he was anxious to please.

He was smiling in an ingratiating manner, even standing up briefly and nodding in what he clearly thought was a mark of respect, one which actually made him look as though he was putting on a performance. It occurred to Hooley how disappointed Savage would be if he knew just what little impact his display was having on Roper, and he struggled to keep the smile off his face.

As before, he had brought a large pile of documents and files which he dropped on the desk with a loud thud that made Savage pull a face. Spotting the reaction, he decided to see if he could get under the man's skin.

It was now that Hooley went into his "old man" routine, huffing and puffing as he poked and prodded at the pile, slowly withdrawing items of interest and then reading them in a painstakingly slow manner.

Despite his little show at the beginning, Savage quickly demonstrated that he was far from a patient man. "Why have you brought that stuff in here to read now?" he demanded. "The last time we spoke was to discuss the deal. I'm willing to tell you everything I know. In return, you make my charges disappear."

A passing alien might have wondered who was in charge here, and Hooley seemed happy to stretch the moment out, reaching into his jacket and pulling out a pair of vintage half-eyeglasses. Roper, who had never seen them before, stared at him before shrugging, remembering that he was following the DCI's lead.

The older man balanced the glasses on his nose, studied Savage, then searched his pockets until he found a handkerchief to clean the lenses.

By the time he appeared happy with the result, Savage was close to boiling over, squirming in his seat and unable to keep the angry expression off his face.

Without warning, Hooley barked a question. "What more can you tell me about this drugs gang?"

While the swift change in tone, clearly shocked Savage, he quickly recovered, showing no surprise at the question itself.

"I just said I want to know about the deal. What are you going to do for me?"

Hooley ponderously removed the glasses and stared unblinking at Savage. For all his bluster, the DCI knew he wasn't dealing with a brave man. "We're not going to do anything for you until you give us some details about what you're offering. If you think this works any other way, then you're sadly mistaken. We hold all the cards here, so you need to start thinking hard about what's in your best interest."

Savage opened his mouth to respond when there was a hammering at the door, and Brooker burst in. Once again, she was brandishing a note.

Hooley took his time reading it before handing it to Roper who, by this stage, was getting into the swing of things, reading it attentively before handing it back. "That's a brilliant call, sir," he said. "It makes all the difference."

The DCI returned it to Brooker. "That's exactly what we wanted. Make sure a detective goes and picks it up straight away."

She left without a word, and Hooley said, "I think you were about to tell us something, Mr Savage?"

The man used many more words than Emily Wong — and it took nearly two hours longer trying to provide the same information. The big difference was in his account of being slashed. This was a direct and personal account.

"I couldn't believe it," he'd told the two detectives. "The men holding me were so strong I couldn't move. Then one of them produced a knife. You could tell he was enjoying himself. He was a seriously sick man. The first cut, his eyes never left mine, not once. He did it very slowly and deliberately. It was the worst pain I've ever experienced. He winked at me when he'd finished the first cut. The girls were screaming blue murder, begging him to stop, but he took no notice.

"When he'd finally finished, he stared at me, this weird expression on his face. Then he actually licked the blood off the knife." He shook his head, looking green. "Fortunately, the girls were making such a fuss they missed it. And just to cap it all, they poured lemon juice all over me. It made me feel like I was on fire. They said next time it would be acid."

Hooley winced. Whatever else was going on here, Savage was painting a compelling picture.

"I presume you needed medical attention. How did you explain your wounds at the hospital?"

Savage gave a bark of laughter that told of his bitterness.

"They brought someone with them who sewed me up. It was a real stitch-up job. Look, I'll show you."

He stood up, gripped the bottom of his t-shirt and pulled it quickly over his head. It was not a pretty sight. Jagged wounds covered his torso. In places they still looked red-raw, dull pink in others — and there was one with a large patch of red all around it.

"Their hygiene left a lot to be desired. The lemon was useless. It took three courses of antibiotics to get me right, and even now some of the wounds flare up and weep. I need to be careful. Fortunately, there's any number of private GPs around here who'll keep quiet for cash."

The DCI called a halt. "We need to assess your information." If he was impressed by the display, he wasn't saying.

They had barely got out of the door to the interview room before Roper started talking.

"My Rainbow Spectrum reacted to that and not in a good way. He was definitely putting on a performance in there. I think he was lying by omission. He has more important information. He's keeping it back." Roper paused to catch his breath. "When Susan interrupted us, he was watching you with a calculated expression. It made me think he might have worked out what was going on and was thinking about how to use it to his own advantage. Emily Wong certainly didn't look like that at any stage . . ."

When they arrived back at the office, the DCI got him to repeat his observations to Brooker who was fascinated. "What else did you get?"

"He was almost tripping over himself to get his words out about the drugs cartel. It sounded as though he had rehearsed every word, and he was doing his best to look as relaxed as possible. I think he is trying to distract us."

Hooley nodded thoughtfully. "Anything else?"

"I still think that industrial espionage has some sort of role to play in this. Admittedly, this has a lot to do with what my Rainbow Spectrum is telling me, rather than any facts — but it does feel as though there is something in it." He paused and took a drink of water.

"What did you make of him telling us about being slashed?" Hooley aimed the question at Brooker.

"Even watching it over the video link you could feel his pain, but I definitely got a feeling he was putting on a show. I'm not saying it didn't hurt, but it felt staged."

Roper was animated. "Exactly right and that is the most important thing."

They both looked at him quizzically.

"When he was telling us about the slashing, he showed plenty of pain and even anger, but there was one thing missing. Although he talked about feeling fear, he never once showed it in his retelling. Yet anyone else would have been terrified. You saw how Emily Wong reacted when she had to describe it. That tells us something important." Roper began to pace.

"I think he was a willing victim in his own attack. It would have been hard for him but not impossible. He's obviously convinced the two women it was true. That tells us he is definitely using the drugs thing as a distraction for something else." Roper paused, taking his colleagues in one final time. "It also tells us that there is someone out there who really scares him. Far more than us."

CHAPTER 39

Mary Lou Healy's anger hadn't exactly subsided, but she was grappling with a realisation that was making her feel uncomfortable. She tried turning the thought away, but she was too honest to block it out effectively.

The idea had crept up on her like a thief in the night. One moment it hadn't been there and the next it had ripped away her self-protective veneer.

If she was honest, she preferred it when she was filled with righteous anger. At least, then, everything was black and white. It was all his fault, and he had duped her, taking advantage of her devotion in a cynical act of betrayal.

Unfortunately, her traitorous brain was getting in on the act. It was almost like there was a conversation going on inside her head, and she had no control of it. She shuddered. Was this going to be the start of hearing voices?

This was the argument going on inside her head. "He's evil and manipulative. I never had a chance against his dominant personality. He made me do it."

Then the second voice chimed in. "But is that true? You always knew you were playing with fire. Maybe you were a willing victim, always happy to look the other way. He'd never have done it if you hadn't wanted him to."

The argument, in various guises, had been running for an hour or more before she was able to shut it down. She realised that she was suffering some sort of victim syndrome. While she might be willing to admit she had been a bit naive, surely she didn't deserve to be blamed?

She puffed her cheeks out. She needed to hold herself together, or the meeting tonight would go badly.

Suddenly the day was over, and she experienced a sensation like getting off a moving walkway. The clock was showing just after 6 p.m., and staff were starting to pack up. A few stopped by her office, but she put them off until the following day.

Healy had always had strong feelings about the man she would be meeting in just a few hours. At first, it had been admiration, then love, and finally, if she was totally honest, fear. She knew she really should have contacted the police and left it to them. But her sense of guilt disguised a more deep-seated fear that she was more to blame than she was willing to admit. She was desperate to see him and find out if she needed to be concerned.

Out of nowhere came a memory of him touching her naked body; the recollection was so vivid that she only just made it to the bathroom and hunched over the toilet bowl to vomit, painfully and repeatedly. When the waves of nausea finally passed, she slumped back to the floor. As she lay there, her body covered in an unpleasant cold sweat, she shivered so violently her teeth chattered.

Seven p.m. was fast approaching. The destination was a short walk away — and, knowing that she needed to do something physical to release the nervous energy that had been building up inside her, she decided to set off early.

She doubted that he would be early. She had never known him to be punctual. He was the sort of man who believed that forcing others to wait made him the top dog; someone who should never be questioned; someone whose demands were met instantly.

The destination was a penthouse apartment in a compact three-storey building which boasted a roof that was shaped to look like a wave. It was supposed to add a nautical look and the developers of the property, which possessed ten apartments altogether, had called it the Old Ship. Local teenagers delighted in replacing the P with a T.

The walk took her along the always busy City Road, to the edge of Islington and by the time she arrived, she felt she had her nerves under control. She would go in, find out what he knew, work out if she was genuinely in trouble, then call the police. Promising this to herself made her feel better.

Now she stood on the pavement, looking up. As she had expected, all the penthouse lights were off, and the apartment was in darkness. Steeling herself, she walked to a side entrance and entered a six-digit code on the keypad.

This particular building came with some key advantages. First and foremost was an underground car park, from which the penthouse could be accessed via a private lift. This ensured the occupants could come and go with a minimal amount of observation. To Healy's lover, this had been the most important thing. Once their clandestine affair had begun, he had been determined that they should never enter the flat by the usual front entrance. It would only bring them under the scrutiny of the twenty-four-hour porter system — and this was something he was adamant could not be allowed to happen.

The metal security door rattled upwards, and she stepped into the dark space. It had been a while since she was last here and it took a second to make sure she was heading in the right direction for the lift.

As she traversed the space, it grew darker. Her shoes made a soft slapping sound on the cold concrete.

Sensing someone else close by, she slowed down and looked around.

It was very dark, and she could barely see her hand. She went to take another step.

Then she froze.

What looked like a pair of glowing green eyes were rushing towards her. She was being tracked by someone using night-vision goggles.

She turned to run, but she felt something like a wasp bite on the back of her neck. Her hand reached around instinctively, but she was already falling unconscious, collapsing into the arms of the man who had been waiting for her.

He was powerful and had no trouble carrying her over to a dark blue van. As a minor concession to her comfort, she was tossed onto a dirty mattress, followed by the military-grade night-vision goggles which landed next to her head.

The man walked over to the entrance ramp to get a signal and called his boss. "Just as you predicted. She turned up early and came in through the garage, so no one will have seen what happened."

The man on the other end grunted. He never used two words, where one would do. "That little potion you've given her will keep her under for a couple of hours. Get her here. I have some questions for her."

CHAPTER 40

Hooley sensed that they were getting closer to the truth. He knew it was imperative they set out the critical markers before restarting the interviews.

"I think there are three big things that are in play. The biggest of them all, is this — are the Savage pair, and Emily Wong, going to lead us to the people behind all three attacks? If they're not, then we're wasting time."

He checked to see if either of Roper or Brooker were about to object and was pleased to see they seemed to agree with this.

"If we do think we're on the right track, then who is the person Mark Savage is so frightened of? Frightened enough to risk lying to police investigating a triple terror attack . . ." He broke off briefly. "My last big question and I stress this is all down to you two and the way you're driving things, is this. Do we believe that Mark Savage has, for whatever reason, dragged the two women into a complicated deception?"

While this sort of "catch-up session" was sensible in any investigation, what he didn't add was that he wanted everyone clear on the goals and objectives in case he was suddenly pulled out of the fray. He'd been granted a little extra time, and he didn't want to squander a minute. He already knew how brilliant Roper could be and suspected Brooker was similar, but clear signposting could make the difference between success and failure.

To his relief, neither of them showed any signs of dissent.

Roper chipped in. "If we find the person dealing with Mark Savage, that will point us at the person behind all the attacks. I would add in one extra thing. I would like to know more about Emily Wong's father. My Rainbow Spectrum is telling me that there is still more about him than we have yet to learn." He paused. "You know I have an idea that industrial espionage is somehow involved in this. Well, I think that will involve Mr Wong — and since we now know he has both the Communist Party and Triad connections, I am more convinced than ever."

The DCI gently punched the palm of his left hand with his right fist. "I won't pretend that I can follow your thinking, but it's not the first time you've spotted something the rest of us have missed. So good for you." He looked over at Brooker. "Anything you'd like to add, Susan?"

He couldn't help thinking that, in many ways, her involvement in a massive case like this was the most remarkable of all. Barely twelve months ago, she'd been working on data collection with a big firm of paralegals. By a stroke of luck, her boss had recognised she was far too skilled at the job and had contacted a mate at the Met who was involved in building up the force's data management system. Within weeks, she had switched careers. It wasn't much longer before Roper's mystery group knew all about her skills.

Brooker nodded. "I wouldn't mind hearing what Julie Savage has got to say. I think we can leave her brother to stew a little while longer. He's the one who's been covering things up, so he'll be desperately hoping we aren't onto him."

Roper, who had been sitting on the edge of his desk, leapt up. "I completely agree. I think she was a bit scared of him. Or worried that she might say something wrong and he would get cross with her."

"Sounds like we have a plan," said Hooley. "We'll talk to Julie Savage and see where that takes us. Then we need to start thinking about putting the right kind of pressure on her brother."

As the trio walked into the interview room, Julie Savage jumped to her feet and bobbed up and down. She could not have looked more obviously obsequious and anxious to please.

All three sat down, and Hooley jumped straight in.

"Have you allowed Diamonds and Pearls to be used as a front for drug smugglers?"

She looked stricken. "Yes, it's true. But we had no choice; they were going to hurt Mark — they'd already attacked him once. They were threatening to do worse. We were terrified." She covered her face in her hands.

Hooley slammed his hands on the table, so hard that it made his pen bounce up in the air. On the other side of the table, Julie Savage sat up, startled.

"You can spare us the waterworks," said Hooley, looking angrier than Roper had ever seen him. "You have the nerve to sit there feeling sorry for yourself when what you were doing allowed drug dealers to hide their profits." He jabbed his finger at her in emphasis. "It's not just about the drugs anymore. They traffic *human beings*. A young woman like you would've been a top target. So, are you seriously going to tell me that you had no idea what was going on?" He glared at her, his eyes narrowing. "And before you try to insist that you didn't, let me assure you that claiming ignorance is absolutely no protection under the law." Hooley guessed she was close to cracking now and pressed on. "I'm going to give you one chance, and that one chance is now. We need to know everything. That's the only way you're going to get anything out of this mess." He stood up. "You've got five minutes to decide your future." He headed for the door, followed by the other two.

Outside, he turned to Roper and Brooker. "Why don't you two take charge of the interrogation while I watch from the observation room? Now I've roughed her up; it might be best if I wasn't there. But she's ready to talk."

179

Roper and Brooker nodded.

"Jonathan's got quite a bit of experience now so let him have the lead," he continued, "but, Susan, you've already proved you're a shrewd observer so if you think something important needs pursuing then dive in."

He knew he was putting a lot on them but, even as he'd been talking, his doubts had diminished. They were smart, resourceful, and what they lacked in experience was balanced by determination. It was also vital they got used to working without him, just in case he couldn't be around.

Inside the interview room, things were about to hot up. Roper was determined to get to the truth.

He hadn't even sat down when he flung the comments at her.

"We know you're not telling us something. You think you've been clever hiding it, but I'm afraid you haven't done a very good job."

She rocked back in her chair, looking stricken. Hooley, who had only just made it to the observation room in time to watch, was impressed. He willed Roper to succeed.

Julie Savage attempted recovery. "I honestly don't know what you mean. I've told you everything that I know. I'm not lying about anything."

With her eyes rimmed red, and her face tight with anxiety, she looked a picture of misery. For the first time, Brooker noticed what big eyes she had and right now they were looking at Roper imploringly. She hid a smile.

"Is that really true? Even now, with all that's at stake here, are you seriously trying to pretend you don't have any idea what I'm talking about?"

The blood had drained from her face, leaving her looking pale to the point of illness. She raised a hand to her face to rub at her cheek and Brooker could see that she was trembling.

Roper was not willing to show a trace of mercy. There wasn't enough time. They needed answers.

He rapped his knuckles on the table.

"Look at me; look directly at me." He waited until her fearful gaze had locked onto his. "I can be your best friend or your worst enemy. But you need to decide right here, right now."

The watching Hooley almost gave him a round of applause. This was good.

"What do you want to know?"

"We want to know everything. But I'll give you some clues to get you started."

Julie Savage couldn't draw her eyes away from him. She just nodded once. Even one step removed, Hooley could tell that all resistance had gone. It was remarkable; Roper had only been in there for a few minutes.

"I want you to think very carefully about the story you told us about Mark being slashed with a knife. I know most of what you told us is true, but there was something else, something you're not telling us."

She was silent for a long time before she started speaking — so quietly at first that he had to ask her to speak up and start again.

"I knew there was something wrong about it. I mean what happened with the men. It took me a long time to work it out, but then I realised — he wasn't frightened of them. Not really. They hurt him, but he was cross, not scared, and that's not like him. You see, I know my brother well, and he's a real coward at heart. I know he acts all tough, but he isn't. I'm afraid my father used to beat him, and he's never really got over it. If something gets tough, he crumbles."

Roper and Brooker shared a glance and Roper inclined his head to say she should step in.

"That all sounds very odd . . . are you saying you thought the slashing was just them acting out? Why would that happen?"

"Greed," she shrugged as if the answer was obvious. "Once I realised there something posed about the attack, I realised he must have been involved in planning it. There's only one thing that would make him willing to undergo pain — and that's money. I guess you know we had to leave Millfield when dad's business got into trouble?" She didn't wait for a reply. "Well, Mark's always been stupid about money. He used to say that being rich made us better than other people. But once we had financial problems, he got worse. He obsessed about money to the point where I didn't speak to him for a year. It was only when this Diamonds and Pearls opportunity came up, and he needed me, that I was put on board to provide the glamour."

Brooker raised a questioning eyebrow.

"Sorry, that sounds like I'm boasting — but when we were at school, we had the nickname, Beauty and the Beast. That was tough on him, but there's no way you'd bring him on board because of his looks."

She was on safer, more familiar ground, and it showed in her body posture. She stopped sagging in her chair, sitting a little straighter.

"Emily and I were given a lot of spin about us having the 'perfect look' and representing the 'rich and cultured'. It was all nonsense, but I admit it was flattering . . ." She stopped and looked embarrassed. "Sorry, you don't need to hear all that stuff. The point I was trying to make was that I think he would do anything for money. Literally anything."

"Including lying to his sister?" said Roper.

She nodded.

"Do you think he would kill for money?"

She said "no", but very quietly and not before a telling hesitation.

Roper and Brooker both stared at her, their arms folded, their faces impassive.

Julie Savage looked at the table. "No . . . I mean, I don't think so, I certainly hope not." Then she placed her head in her hands and bowed her head.

Roper gave her a moment, but that was all. He had one more question he needed answering.

"I know you've told us of your doubts about what happened when he was slashed in front of you, but did you ever see him being threatened on any other occasion?"

She didn't even have to think before answering. "Yes. And I remember it vividly because there was something about it that reminded me of the way he used to act with my father. It was at Chelsea Harbour, in the underground carpark. I'd come down to collect my car and saw him off at the far end. He was with a huge man. I could tell because he dwarfed Mark, and he's not exactly small. The thing is, Mark was in front of him, his head hanging down and his arms at his side, it was exactly like he used to do when he was in trouble at home. You could see where the expression 'hangdog' comes from. That's exactly what he looked like."

Roper was excited. "Could you catch any details about what they were talking about?"

She shrugged. "Not really. It was too far away. I got the impression the other man was talking, and Mark was listening, but as I've told you it reminded me of when he was about to get beaten by our father."

"Can you give me any details about what this man looked like, or was wearing?"

"He was tall, probably six foot four? Maybe a bit more. He was big all over, big shoulders, and big arms. I think he had dark hair and dark stubble, but that may have been shadows."

Roper looked at Brooker, who made a sweeping gesture with her hands to say she had nothing else to say. Then he stood up and made for the door, turning just before he reached for the handle.

"Please keep thinking about that man. He might be crucial."

Outside, Hooley was waiting.

"Well done," he said, genuinely impressed. "So what do we do now?"

Brooker piped up.

"I read somewhere that they kept a few staff at Chelsea Harbour. Let's get over and see if anyone is around and saw our big man. I have a feeling we'll find something."

CHAPTER 41

Mary Lou opened her eyes. She couldn't see a thing. It was blackout dark, made all the more frightening because it let her imagination run riot, wondering who, or what was out there.

If that wasn't enough, she had a blinding headache, a raging thirst — and her brain felt like it was full of holes. It didn't take a genius to work out that she'd been drugged. This sluggishness was just part of the side effects.

Slowly, she grew accustomed to her surroundings. She was lying on her back on a narrow bed, bound in a way that prevented her from sitting up. In the dark, it was hard to be sure what was holding her, but it felt like some sort of strong tape.

She did have free movement of her hands, so she fumbled around in the desperate hope that there was a glass of water within reach. There was — but, with a frustration that made her scream out, she only became aware of this when she knocked it over.

She struggled wildly against the restraints but quickly gave up. The thrashing around was making her see flashing lights and, coupled with the head pain, they only induced a sense of nausea. She lay back panting and tried to soothe her terror.

A series of questions were floating in her mind. How had she you got here? Where was here? Did she have a chance of surviving?

She knew her situation was bleak. She already suspected her former lover was capable of murder — and what would one more victim add to his tally? She hadn't been brought here to talk over old times.

Her sense of terror was slowly being replaced by self-recrimination. Yet again, she had allowed her emotions for this man to get in the way of common sense, and detailed planning.

These were the character traits she was known for. Everyone at her office knew Healy never acted without careful thought. Yet here she was, bound and captured after rushing off to confront him, acting so fast she hadn't told anyone where she was going.

Then, without warning, the space was filled with shockingly bright light, forcing her to cover her eyes. When she finally felt safe enough to open them, a man made of shadows was looming over her. She felt a shock, as though she had been punched in the stomach.

There he was: Peter Street. Grinning like the irritating narcissist he was. She couldn't believe she had once found that smile charming. Now she could see through it to the real man beneath, a man who had nothing but contempt for the rest of humanity.

Despite being in his mid-forties, he dressed in the hipster fashion of someone twenty years younger. A well-trimmed beard. Short, well below average height, and he used shoe lifts to disguise it. Even now, he was extremely skinny. She'd never minded anything about the way he dressed, thinking it was perfectly reasonable to try and stay young at heart — but now she could see, along with the shoes, that it was one of the ways he tried to deceive people.

To her eternal shame, she had once thought he was the intellectual equal of John Ryder. Too late, she had learned she was wrong. Ryder was a mathematical prodigy and brilliant entrepreneur. Street was nothing but a marketing man with a colossal ego. His success owed more to native cunning than serious brainpower.

She glared at him in hatred.

He sneered back at her. "If looks could kill, my dear, then I would have died a long time ago. But glare away, it won't make one iota of difference. I'm in charge, and you are my little victim."

He'd deliberately emphasised the phrase "my dear", knowing it was something she found incredibly patronising. It was a measure of the man that he was bothering with such things, even when he was the one holding all the power.

He pantomimed looking at his watch. "I'd love to spend time chatting and catching up," he leered, "but time is pressing. I had to cancel a couple of important appointments just to come and see you this evening, so I really don't want to waste any more time than I have to."

The door opened, and a giant of a man — the one who'd snatched her in the car park — walked in. His shoulders were so broad he had to navigate carefully to get through the door frame. As if his size wasn't intimidating enough, he was also wearing a terrifying mask. It reminded Healy of a documentary she had once seen about voodoo, made out of wood with white lines painted on it.

Street's sneering had given way to a sly smile as he noted the impact this frightening figure was having on his former conquest.

"I'm not going to pretend," he said. "This is going to hurt, and it's going to hurt a lot. If you want my advice, and you really should take it, then I would answer some questions and maybe buy yourself a little time."

His cold eyes flitted over her body, and she fought the urge to shiver, not wanting to give him any advantage. He smiled maliciously as he said, "You really are getting a little bit too old, aren't you? I think I may well have had the best of you."

To her horror, she started to cry. The cruelty of that last remark had brought home to her just how helpless she was.

The stress was too much, and now she had crumpled in front of him, increasing her self-loathing.

"You can blubber as much as you like. No one's coming to your rescue. You're quite alone, and you need to get ready because very soon, my man here—" he gestured at the giant, — "will give you a little taste of what to expect."

He paused once more if only to appraise her.

"We learned some time ago that people take advantage if we don't do things properly. You'd be amazed at how a little bit of torture helps most people become focused and helpful. I'm afraid that means you need to experience some discomfort before you start answering my questions. It's the only way I can guarantee you tell me the truth. You need to be afraid of the pain starting again to make sure you are fully incentivised."

He bent down close to her face, pretending to stroke her cheek in a comforting fashion. But his real intentions were laid bare when he pinched her cheek, making her cry out.

"Just a little taste of what's to come. I'll leave you to get better acquainted — and then, when I come back, I'll have some questions. Any delays in answering, any prevarication, any obvious lies, and we go back to the punishment."

He abruptly stood, closing the door behind him and extinguishing the neon light, plunging the room back into darkness. Then, for what seemed like a long time, nothing happened. Healy simply chewed her lower lip as she waited in the dark. She felt as though her heart might burst out of her chest.

As the silence grew, her ragged breathing sounded loud in her ears. But, as the moments stretched on, she became aware of the steady breathing of the man who was going to hurt her.

A sudden wash of sour breath made her flinch; she knew he was getting closer. Something cold and sharp pressed against her cheek.

She opened her mouth to scream.

A blade pressed against her skin.

CHAPTER 42

Roper and Brooker were champing at the bit to get to Chelsea Harbour, and Hooley was pleased to see them go. While he wanted to get back to Mark Savage, it wouldn't hurt to leave the man to stew a little while longer; the "big man" was an important clue because it added to the sense that Roper was on the right track.

As they set off, he picked up the phone — this was also an excellent opportunity to update Julie Mayweather.

An unmarked car was waiting outside the building when Roper and Brooker made it outside. As they clambered into the back, the driver turned around. "Might be best if we turn on the lights. This area, and as far as the Kings Road, is pretty badly locked up."

Even with the flashing blue lights and judicious use of the siren, it still took more than twenty minutes to arrive at their destination.

"Where do you want to start?" asked Brooker as they stood on the pavement looking over to the administrative HQ for Diamonds and Pearls.

Roper craned his head towards the entrance. "Let's start there with the security guard. Maybe he saw something."

Walking over to the locked glass doors they held up their ID cards, and the security guard glanced at them both and then back at Roper's, before opening the door.

"I remember you from last time," he told Roper. "You found those three yet?"

Roper ignored the man's question and came up with his own. "This might sound a bit strange, but we're looking for a man who had dealings with Mark Savage. He came here a few times."

"What did he look like?"

"Big. The kind of a guy you might remember."

The man thought deeply.

"There *was* a feller. Enormous he was. I saw him a couple of months ago. Pulled up in a Range Rover right where you just got dropped off. You know how big those cars are, right? Well, this bloke was struggling to get out of the door. Huge shoulders, like a heavyweight boxer. He was massive."

Brooker was pleased. It seemed the man wasn't just big he was incredibly, memorably large — which meant there was more chance they could track him down. They were tempted to get back immediately but might as well finish off first.

"Anyone from the company around today?" Roper asked.

"Sure, there are a few people. Upstairs and in the offices." He pointed at the lifts. "Third floor. Knock yourselves out."

Thirty minutes later, the pair had drawn a blank and were back with the security guard.

"I don't suppose you've managed to remember any more about our big man, have you?"

The guard looked pleased with himself. "Yes. I saw the big guy a couple more times. Each time Mr Savage was waiting for him."

Brooker asked. "Did Mr Savage seem scared of him at all? Maybe nervous at meeting him?"

The guard shook his head. "Not at all. If anything, they seemed quite pally, shaking hands and that."

Roper and Brooker thanked him and walked away.

"That's classic control," said Roper. "One minute our big guy is threatening Mark Savage, the next he's being nice to him — making sure he never knows what's going to happen."

* * *

Hooley was delighted with the new information.

"You've proved he exists, improved the description, and discovered something about the relationship. Well done."

He had a spring in his step as he led them back to the interview rooms to talk to Mark Savage.

"Let's get to it," he said and opened the door.

All three walked in. Savage was sitting at one side of a rectangular table, with chairs either side of him. Roper and Brooker took the facing chairs, and Hooley sat at the end to create a little space of his own.

Savage nodded politely. "How can I be of assistance, gentlemen and lady?"

The three detectives ignored him as they sat down.

"You know what assistance you can give us," Hooley began. "If you give us the right information, including names and dates, then we can talk about a deal."

Savage flushed with anger. "Stop messing me around. I've already told you that I'm willing to talk, and you know what my price is. I want to walk out of here at the end of the day, free to go wherever I want."

Hooley let out a snort of derision. "I know what you want — and I'm here to tell you that you are this far from getting it." He spread his arms wide to emphasise the point. "Let me explain how this will work. You tell us things and if you tell us enough, and the information is useful, then we can start to think about a deal."

Savage jumped to his feet. "Are you taking me for a fool? This is a stitch-up! I'm offering to help you, and you're just slinging it back in my face!"

"Sit down," Hooley said, his tone commanding. "You really don't listen, do you? Why should we hand out free passes to any spiv who wants one?"

The barb hit home harder than intended. "Don't call me a spiv. I'm a serious businessman. I made more money last month than all three of you will make in a year." The words were spat out as he remained standing, leaning on the edge of the table, panting with anger.

Hooley was pleased to note that Roper and Brooker were looking unimpressed by his bizarre diatribe. Making a soothing gesture with his hands, he went on, "We all want the same thing here, it's just the way we go about it. If you give me a moment, perhaps I can reassure you that we're doing everything we can to give you what you asked for."

Savage didn't reply, sitting down with surly ill grace.

"This may surprise you," the DCI said, "but I'm inclined to believe that you have something useful for us. Because you have already admitted to serious offences, I can't overlook those, but I can make recommendations."

He leaned back in his chair, folded his arms and stared at Savage.

"There's no chance you'll be walking out of here tonight. We may be able to do a deal, we may even agree the terms of a deal, but we'll need to see results first before you go waltzing off."

Savage tried to look as though he was offended by this, but couldn't hide the faintest trace of a smile. "Where would you like me to start?"

Without looking at his boss, Roper stepped in. "The beginning will be just fine," he said as he and Brooker prepared to start taking notes.

Savage stared down at the ground for almost a minute — but the three detectives were determined to wait. Eventually, he took a breath, placed his hands on the table, and began.

"I'm guessing that by now, you probably know about how we got started. A couple of years after we left school, I was approached by a man who had connections to Emily's father. He said Emily's dad wanted to set up a business which would involve all three of us. He said the girls were vital as they would create the right image for Diamonds and Pearls. He had a simple business plan which meant we had to hand over forty per cent of the profits, not turnover, so it seemed like a great deal. If I'm honest, I didn't think too hard about it."

He stopped, puffing out his cheeks and tugging his ear. Hooley knew they were heading for the real stuff.

"At first, things went well, and I was sure we were onto a winner. But I was wrong. The intermediary came back and, this time, it was no longer all smiles and nice words. He was insistent that a new deal was needed. Back then, I was still under the impression that he could be negotiated with. I twice told him, no, but he kept coming back. This time he claimed he was offering ten million quid for just ten per cent of the company.

"I was played like a piano," Savage said, shaking his head. "They knew which notes to strike. I got it into my head that I could make a lot more money than they were offering." He paused again. He had gone pale, and there was a thin sheen of sweat on his face.

Hooley, sensing this was the moment to remind him what was at stake, leaned forward. "I can see this is hard for you, but you need to explain why you have been a victim in this."

Savage sniffed loudly and cleared his throat before continuing. "I was told I needed to meet the money man at a flat near Harrods, that it was all a done deal with just a few loose ends to tie up. But I turned up, and it went wrong, very badly wrong. The moment the front door shut, I was grabbed. All I can remember was being jumped by two men. One had my arms. The other punched me in the stomach. I don't really know how many people were there. I got the impression about half a dozen, but one man was clearly in charge."

"Who was he?" asked Roper. "Had you seen him before?"

Savage shrugged. "I'd never met him. He was huge, far taller than me, and I'm six foot one. The other thing which stood out were his shoulders. They were massive, really broad. I had this ridiculous thought that he must have struggled to get clothes that fitted him. And he just started punching me. I've never been hit so hard in my life. Afterwards, I couldn't help wondering if he'd been a boxer. I put his age at about forty, but he could have been younger."

Savage looked between them. At last, his words were tumbling out. "The beating seemed to go on for ages. I don't really know how long. The only reason I didn't fall over was that I was being held up by either arm. When they let me go, I collapsed."

He turned his head away, clearly wanting to stop talking. Roper leaned forward, too. "You need to tell us everything."

"I soiled myself," Savage whispered. "It was incredibly humiliating, but I was terrified. They told me to go and wash. I used a downstairs shower, rinsing out my trousers. My clothes were wet — but at least they were clean. By now, I was desperate to get away, but the big man laughed at me and told me they were just getting started. I had one chance, and one chance only. I had to agree to do whatever they said — and then they would give me a week to prove myself. If I failed, they would kill me."

He looked down again, this time looking as though telling the story was hurting him.

Brooker stepped in to keep him going. "What happened next?"

"They told me they'd be sending a man to make sure I understood what needed to happen. Basically, they were going to launder a lot of cash through our accounts. My job was to find a way of hiding it. I could barely take it in. I was just desperate to get out of there."

"Why did they attack you in front of your sister and Emily Wong? Why did they do that if they'd already broken you?" Brooker was giving him her most intense scrutiny.

"That was the big man again. He said it was a good reminder to me what might happen, and it would let the women know what they were up against. I think he's the type of man who likes hurting people. He told me what he was going to do and warned me to cooperate."

At this point Hooley took a break. He was pleased to get out; something was irritating about the way Savage was telling the story. The DCI thought he probably was telling the truth, but he was making the most of it, to make sure he looked like a victim. For the next forty-five minutes, he watched from the observation room as the other two took down a lot of details about how the money laundering was done.

Hooley was sure Savage was talking up his fear to disguise how closely he was working with the big man, but this didn't stop him trusting the broad thrust of his confession. People told lies all the time; it was picking out the important ones that counted.

Finally, it looked like Savage was running out of steam, so Hooley walked back in.

"That's it," Mark Savage concluded, "that's everything I have — at least everything I can think of." He gave them a broad smile while trying to look as open and honest as possible.

Hooley returned the smile with one of his own. "I have one question for you."

Savage looked expectant.

"Do you think all policemen are idiots? Or is it just the three of us?"

Savage's reaction was almost comical. His mouth opened, and his jaw dropped. He tried to speak but could only stammer, "I, I . . ."

Hooley wasn't going to let him settle. "That was all terribly sad about you getting beaten up. We all really felt for you. And I do believe what you said, every word. You were obviously scared out of your mind, except you weren't."

Savage started looking desperate, but the DCI kept rolling.

"We have a credible eyewitness that tells us you and the big guy were best friends. Now, why would you tell us he was torturing you? I think you're trying the old three-card trick on us. You want us to concentrate on what you're doing with your right hand, so we don't notice what's going on with your left. If you're going to all this trouble, then that tells me that whatever you're hiding is the most important thing of all. So," he went on, "here's what's going to happen. While we leave you to have a little break, I want you to do some serious thinking. When we get back, you need to share those thoughts with us. If you don't, there is no chance of a deal. At all."

Hooley led his fellow detectives into the observation room. As they studied the clearly shocked Mark Savage, the DCI said, "I had the strongest sense that he was holding something big back. What did you make of it, Jonathan?"

"You beat me to it. He was telling the truth but only to try and stop us asking questions."

"Good, that's good," said Hooley. "I would have hated to misread that. I think we're edging closer to the truth."

CHAPTER 43

Healy pressed her fingers against her face. Somehow, she could feel no injuries. How this had happened, she had no idea. She could have sworn she felt something slicing into her face.

As the harsh neon light was switched back on, she looked at the man she thought had attacked her. He'd done away with the mask, and he had a mocking smile — but all he held up was a dessert spoon.

How could this be? she wondered. She had been attacked with what felt like a blade. It was so bizarre she could feel a sense of hysteria building.

Then Street appeared, looking smug. "Did you forget everything I ever told you about the power of the mind? How, if you set things up properly, you can make people believe anything? You thought my man was going to wound you; your brain did the rest."

She was filled with an intense fury, thrashing against her restraints as she tried to lunge at her former lover. The straps bit into the flesh around her shoulders. She started to bleed, ironically causing the sort of damage she'd been imagining.

Healy fell back onto the cot, all her energies spent. The day was taking a brutal toll.

"You need to calm down, Mary Lou. You're not helping yourself with all this thrashing around. It would help if you did what you do best — think. Because, if this carries on for much longer, you will get hurt — and this time for real."

He leaned forward and patted her on the cheek, at the spot where she thought she had been cut.

"If you're mad enough to try and hold out, this will get deeply unpleasant — and you really will end up with damage that will spoil your looks. Now, why would you want that? At the end of the day, Mary Lou, you're going to talk, so just get it over with. That little demonstration just then should really help you along. All you have to do is tell me the truth. You could choose not to cooperate, but, as I said, that would be pointless."

As he spoke, she felt her resolve melt. She tried to zone him out, but he was getting through; she knew she would work with him. Even though it was her only option, she felt awful. Even now, she couldn't escape the sense that she was betraying everyone.

Somehow, he seemed to read her mind. "You're probably feeling bad right now because you've made the right decision. If it's any consolation, you'll eventually realise it was your only rational choice. Personally, I'm already feeling a lot better, knowing that we won't have to hurt you. I won't lie, I was willing to take this as far as necessary, so it's a real bonus this won't get all messy, and you can live to fight another day."

Mary Lou Healy seriously doubted she was coming out of this alive, but his terrifying demonstration had broken her will to resist. She also knew that this was her only chance to find out what was compelling him to go to this much trouble.

By the end of their relationship, she had learned one thing about Street: he never got involved in anything unless he had a direct personal stake in it. Even quite significant company business was effectively ignored if it was deemed to be just part of a process.

She lay back on her cot, staring up at the ceiling. "You win," she uttered. "Ask me what you want to know, and I'll do my best to answer." She summoned up what strength she still had inside her and finally added, "I do, however, have two requests."

Street showed no reaction. "State your wishes. If it's in my power, I shall grant them."

This comment was topped off with another of those irritating little smirks that she wished she could wipe off his face. She kept that thought to herself, something to savour on her own.

"I really need a drink. Water will do, especially if you want me to do a lot of talking. Whatever your man gave me has left me feeling dehydrated. The other thing is, could you release me from these restraints, or at least loosen them?"

"I knew you'd see sense," Street replied. "I have some water right outside. And yes, we can release you now. It was always overkill — because you aren't getting out of this room unless I say so. Remember, though: if you mess up, you get tied up again."

They left her sitting on the bed with two half-litre bottles of water for company and the promise that they would be back in ten minutes. Unable to hold back, she drank the first bottle in one, barely pausing as she swallowed it. The second bottle, she saved.

Leaning against the wall, she closed her eyes; she felt sure she was getting a migraine, something she hadn't had for a while.

Moments later, she was shaken awake.

"Sorry to disturb you, my dear, but I'm ready to ask you those questions now. So, let's be sharp." Street came into focus, hanging above her, evil personified. "My first question is: how did you find the connection to me? I have my own thoughts on this so it will be interesting to hear what you have to say."

Healy sighed, "I used the security people that John recommended. He spoke highly of them and said their discretion was guaranteed. I gave them permission to access everywhere, including my personal files.

"They came back with details about when my private diary was accessed. I don't use it for work. It's there as a confidential backup to anything we need to be really discreet about, but I guess that you had a long, hard look at it. That was where you made a rare mistake. You opened it at a time when I was out of the office, taking Miss Kitty to the vet. She'd been injured in a catfight and needed urgent attention. It happened so suddenly that I never logged out of the main system — so you must have thought I was in the office. Well, as soon as I saw the diary had been opened, I knew it had to be you. The incident with Miss Kitty is still fresh in my mind, so I didn't even have to check to know that that was a day I spent most of the morning at the vets."

Street was still staring at her; his eyes fixed upon hers.

Somehow, Healy found the strength to go on. "I had the strongest sense you'd somehow accessed my diary. Then, after the three incidents, I recalled something. When we met for the first time, I found you messing around with my laptop. Do you remember?"

He nodded. "I most certainly do. I made up something about wanting to check the news. I wondered at the time if you would see through it, but you seemed to accept my explanation."

"I didn't want to not believe you. It was only when it came back to me that I realised it was a silly excuse. I presume you used some sort of software that allowed you to access my personal files?"

He bowed his head like an actor accepting an accolade. "Quite a clever bit of software actually. It hid itself away, only coming to life when you went into your personal areas. Then it taught itself what you were doing and piggybacked off your wi-fi to make a report."

She nodded as if that explained a puzzle. "The other reason I knew it had to be you was that you read the details about John Ryder; when he was coming over, where he was staying and his appearance in Greenwich. But if you don't mind me asking, how did you know to look in my files for those details? I'm part of the UK team. I don't have any involvement in his office set-up. It's run from the States."

"That was a bit of luck, mixed with brains. I like to keep a close watch on my rivals and often used to marvel at the way Ryder was always able to turn up in places where he wasn't expected. It struck me that he had to be having help with that. So I thought about it from his perspective. I asked myself who Ryder would trust with his personal secrets, and it came to me: you. After that, it was just about getting close enough to check."

With a sinking sensation, Healy realised the implications of what he was saying.

"You targeted me because you suspected I was the way to get to him. You were never interested in me at all."

He shrugged. "You're pretty enough, so it was no hardship. Now, while we're being frank, did he use you because you slept with him?"

She knew this was a far more loaded question than he was making out. Underneath his relaxed demeanour, she knew he was insanely — and she used the word advisedly — jealous of Ryder. In fact, he was obsessed with everything about him.

"It was strictly business," she said. "He's not the sort of man to take advantage of his staff. As you surmised, he couldn't just fly around without some planning. I used to book hotels and the like, under a false name, for the dates he wanted."

He pulled a face that suggested he wasn't convinced — but all she could do was tell him the truth.

Before Street could go on, the huge man turned up again with a bag full of convenience-store sandwiches, more water and three large coffees.

"We'll take another break now," said Street, "and leave you in peace for a little while. My advice is to get some sleep — because the next thing you're going to do is star in a little online movie. Well, we want you looking your best, don't we, Mary Lou? You'll be delivering an important message. It might just be the most important message of your life . . ."

CHAPTER 44

Hooley rechecked the time. They'd left Mark Savage to his thoughts for the best part of an hour — and, observing him through the CCTV cameras, they could see that he'd spent most of that time with his eyes shut. He was worried at how quickly time was flashing by. It had been hours since Hooley and Brooker had come back from Chelsea Harbour, but it felt like just a short time ago.

"Is he as relaxed as he looks?" Roper interrupted his thoughts. "Or is he actually tired?"

Hooley himself wasn't sure. "I think he's ready to talk sense. He's lost that swagger. He's gone very still. I think we can get back in there and find out what he's not telling us."

He looked at the other two. Though they looked bright and cheerful, ready to go on for hours, Hooley didn't need a mirror to know he wasn't looking the same. He tried to imagine his heart fighting his tiredness, or what Dr Turner might have said at seeing him standing here. Maybe it was time to call it a day. And yet . . .

"He's going to want reassurance. We need to offer to look after him."

He'd give it another go. If Savage wasn't cooperating, he'd call it for the night and insist they all grab some rest before a 6 a.m. start.

It turned out he wasn't the only one thinking along those lines. "You look knackered," said Roper. As usual, he did not attempt to play things down. He simply said it as he saw it.

"Thanks for telling me what I already know," muttered Hooley. "We'll have one more go at him tonight. If he's talking, we'll get everything out of him. But, if he still wants to play silly buggers, he can have the night to reflect on the error of his ways."

When the interview room door opened, Savage looked up. The three detectives entered silently and arrayed themselves around him, all looking down. By the weariness on his face, it was clear that Savage was ready to talk. He looked as though a huge weight had been lifted from him as he watched them take their seats opposite.

He held up both hands. "You're quite right," he breathed. "I was holding something back. But as I sat here, I realised I needed this to be over. I almost don't care what happens to me; I just want this to finish and have my life back."

"Go on," instructed Hooley.

"The first thing you need to know is that yes, I did put on an act of being best friends with the big guy, but that was it . . . an act. He ordered me to do it. Told me I was 'his bitch' and he could make me do whatever he wanted. I wasn't his friend; I was terrified of him.

"The second thing you need to know is these people have interests everywhere. What I told you about the money laundering was true, but I soon discovered there was more to it. Among their legitimate interests, is property development. I was told to visit the big guy at a site they're developing near Euston railway station. I had no idea what to expect; I just knew I had to be there." He paused for a moment, shaking his head as he thought about what he was going to say next. "It was like something out of a horror movie. The site was closed off by boards — but, just a few feet away, you could hear the sounds of people going about their lives.

"Inside, it was very different. That's where the big guy and his goons were. They didn't say anything — they just waited. A few minutes later, some poor bloke was dragged in. The monster picked him up, wrapped his enormous hands around his neck and strangled him, right in front of me. Then he tossed the body in a hole, and they poured concrete over him. The only consolation was that the man was so far gone I don't think he realised what was happening.

"How I didn't throw up was amazing, but I managed to just about hold it together. The big guy nodded at his goons, who started working me over. Not as bad as last time, and after a few hard slaps, they left me alone. Then the big guy looked at me like I was dirt on his shoe. He told me he would kill me the same way if I ever went against his orders. I didn't need telling twice. I got the message."

There was something about the way Savage's voice trembled that told Hooley he was telling the truth. "You keep referring to him as the 'big guy'. Do you have any idea what his name is? Even his first name will do if that's all you have . . ."

Savage shook his head. "They never used names. I realised how careful they were about that and I wasn't about to ask."

"I thought you might say that," said Hooley. "Please, carry on."

"Well, a week later, I got a summons to the building site. I dropped everything and made my way there. For once I didn't get beaten up — which made a nice change — and the big guy was there with one of our special mobile phones." He looked at them expectantly and could tell only Roper knew what he was talking about. "We make a lot of money out of selling people stuff they want, rather than the stuff they need. One of our biggest money-makers is mobile phones. Basically, all high-end models are pretty similar. For most people, it's about which manufacturer they prefer. If people are looking for something different, they come to us for our custom designs. You can have a phone made out of gold, encrusted with jewels and special carry cases. The sky's the limit. They're expensive to make — but we can charge even more . . ." He looked at Hooley. "I can tell from your expression that you don't approve. Well, if I'm honest, neither do I. These custom phones can easily cost seven figures; I just don't see the point myself, but plenty do."

Roper wanted to ask a question and almost put his hand in the air as if he was back in the classroom.

"Why would an international drugs cartel be worried about you ordering custom mobiles? From what you say, they make good profits — so to go to all that trouble, including murdering someone? It seems out of proportion."

"That's the million-dollar question," Savage agreed. "It took me a while to figure out what it was about. Our custom phones are made by an outfit in Cambodia. It turns out, they're an off-shoot of the company that currently makes all of the phones for the Ryder Corporation."

He could see that Roper was beginning to piece it together.

"They were using you to get access to a main Ryder production facility. Of course," Roper breathed, "now it makes sense."

Hooley cleared his throat. "It would be nice if you helped it make sense for the older members of the team."

"I think I can see where you're going, Jonathan," said Brooker. "Is this where your theory about industrial espionage comes into play?"

He nodded, and she turned to the DCI. "If a rival company could get hold of the production schedule for the Ryder phones, that would be massive. At the moment, the best way one company can gain an advantage over another is through some sort of innovation in production that will win them new sales. Then the other side catches up again, and so on." She paused, allowing Hooley to catch up. "But if you could find out early what was going on, it might save you tens of millions in sales. If, say, a rival found out Ryder was working on bendy phones, then they could know how far he'd got by finding out how the production line was being tooled up."

Roper interjected, "With so much money at stake, it would save having to go through a laborious process to launder cash. Just present an invoice for ten, twenty or thirty million pounds — and you're on to a winner . . ."

The information gave Hooley a bit of a lift. "This is good — if it's true . . . We'll be checking the location you've given us for the body. We can't leave the poor man there."

He looked at Savage, who was vigorously nodding his head. "It's all true, DCI Hooley. Every word of it. I just wish I had more information on who the man is. All I can say is that's he's white and speaks English like a native."

Hooley's looked at the clock hanging on the wall above Savage's head. It was already coming up to midnight. Telling Savage they would wrap it up, for now, he led Roper and Brooker out of the interview room.

"You two really need to think about getting some rest." He paused. "I'm going to be out all morning. It's Barry Asmus's funeral service. His wife has asked me to read a poem, which I'm not looking forward to, given that it will be at St Paul's. I'll have TV cameras on me, so I need my beauty sleep tonight."

Roper was worried. "That will put you under a lot of extra strain. Are you sure you should be doing this, especially in your condition?"

Hooley gave Roper his best enigmatic look, then wondered why he was bothering. He wouldn't notice.

"If I keel over at St Paul's, they'll probably give me a medal. If you're anxious, it all starts at 11 a.m. — so you can watch on TV while you and Susan search for the rest of the clues that break this case." Before he left, he turned back. "I'm wondering about this 'big guy'. He's new to us, but he hasn't just appeared out of nowhere.

"A man that size may have been in sport, like boxing, or rugby. Or maybe he's one of those guys who came up through the illegal fighting world. That can be a savage place, and you hear that people get badly hurt, or even killed. It sounds like our man would fit in well there."

Brooker perked up. "I think we might just do a bit of digging before we go anywhere . . ."

CHAPTER 45

Brian Hooley woke up and rolled over onto his back. He'd forgotten to draw the curtains when he'd fallen, exhausted, into his bed last night — so his room was full of light. Turning his head to check the clock, it was just after 6 a.m. He'd been asleep for five hours.

Staring at the ceiling, he began to remember Barry Asmus and the times they'd spent together. He remembered their triumphs, and there were many; he remembered their failures, and there were quite a few of those too.

Most of all, he remembered the laughter. The shared humour that had got them through the times when they'd endured too much of the darker side of human nature.

But there was plenty of laughter that came from enjoying the simple things as well, the little practical jokes that life would play on the unwary. Like the time Barry Asmus had taken a bite out of one end of a bread roll and the contents had shot out of the other. As a potent mix of egg, tomato and mayonnaise had landed messily on his desk, the look of total dismay on Barry's face had made Hooley laugh until he thought he would be sick. Even now, his shoulders started shaking as the memory washed over him.

When the terrible news broke that the explosion at the O2 had killed him, Hooley had not been surprised when details emerged about Asmus clearing the building and saving countless lives. It was a type of bravery that came naturally to Asmus. When people talked about the police service having a duty to serve and protect, that was one of the most important things which appealed to him. Asmus had always said it was a privilege to wear the uniform, to carry the badge and be in a position to protect people who might not be able to defend themselves. Given a chance to do it again, Asmus would have unflinchingly walked back into that building.

Hooley felt himself getting emotional, and that wouldn't do. His friend would have hated that. Indeed, he'd have pointed out that the DCI had his own duty today, helping the family in whatever way he could. Failure would see him haunted for the rest of his life.

Hooley sat up, then finally lurched to his feet and went through to the kitchen for his vital first cup of tea, without which he would continue to feel out of sorts. Leaving it to brew, he went to collect the post he'd ignored when he walked into the flat just a few hours ago.

Out of six letters, he picked up the only one which was directly addressed to him. It looked like a bank statement. The others were all direct mail advertising, ranging from charity requests to offers on bulk buying vitamins.

He tossed all but the bank statement straight into the bin. He almost held back the vitamin offer, but it was a bit late for supplements now. He'd see what the surgeon thought after the operation.

By now, the tea had been brewing for nearly five minutes. It was nice and strong, just the way he liked it. He took out the tea bag, added milk and turned on the TV.

He was watching the news without really taking it in, when suddenly a picture of Asmus appeared, jolting him back to reality. They were previewing the service due to take place in a few hours' time, and Hooley watched with a new intensity. According to the reporter, the queen had personally offered to have the coffin rest overnight in the Chapel of St Mary Undercroft in the Palace of Westminster. It was a great honour, and Hooley knew that Barry's wife, Linda, would have been deeply moved.

The reporter also said that it was anticipated that the two-mile route along the Victoria Embankment, from the Chapel to St Paul's Cathedral, would be lined by up to five thousand police officers and other members of the emergency services.

It was anticipated that police helicopters would perform a fly by, and the coffin would be accompanied by the family, the Met Colour Party and the Black Escort from the Mounted Division. The Last Post would be sounded by a bugler from the Royal Honourable Artillery Corps.

The top brass was sparing nothing, and Hooley couldn't help smiling. Barry would have pretended it was too much fuss — but, secretly, he would have loved it. When they were having a drink and complaining about the state of the police force, Barry would often say, "If the worst happens, the Old Bill do like to give you a good send-off." Well, he was certainly getting that send-off today.

After finishing his tea, Hooley found himself in a curious state where adrenaline was fighting a reluctance to see this day end. The Clash lyrics, "Should I Stay or Should I Go Now?" were on a repeat loop in his brain.

He made himself move. Sitting here wasn't going to change anything. It was still early, so he decided to take a leaf out of Roper's book and treat himself to an extra-long shower and shave. He wasn't one for pampering, but today was special.

An hour later, he was all fingers and thumbs as he tried, for the third time, to fasten his black tie. He was making a total hash of it. Suddenly, he was struck by an image of his wife: she'd have had him sorted out by now.

Thinking of her, he recalled their conversation after Barry had died. It had been one of the rare occasions where their animosities had been suspended. She would be there today, along with their children — and they had agreed to sit as a family. At least for the service.

Finally, he got his tie sorted out, put on his dress uniform jacket, his officer's hat and shoes. They'd already been polished to the point of shiny perfection. It was Roper who'd done it. A stickler for polished shoes, he'd made the offer and the DCI was more than happy to accept.

There was still another hour before the police driver was due, so it was time for more tea. Had he not had such a central role to play, he might have gone for a shot of nerve-steadying scotch, but he didn't dare — and, besides, he could imagine the disapproval of his heart surgeon.

* * *

Hooley jumped out of a cab close to the Central Criminal Court, the Old Bailey as it was widely known, and another of London's many notable landmarks. He'd spent many a long hour waiting to give evidence at the court.

As he headed east, he hoped the walk would help calm him down. Only now, as he got closer to St Paul's Cathedral, did he appreciate how much the surrounding area had been developed over the years. At least, he reflected, it still had a feeling of space — helped by the wide pavements which were busy with pedestrians.

Thirty minutes later, he was with his family inside the cathedral. It was the first time they'd been together in months, and yet they all looked as familiar as if he'd seen them only yesterday. He couldn't help noting, as always, that his two kids took their looks from their mother, better than the other way around.

His 23-year-old daughter, who was training to be a doctor, smiled sympathetically at him and held his hand for a moment. His son, two years younger and working with Hooley's brother as a property developer, was more reserved but still spared him a brief hug.

The last time he'd seen his children was for a meal just before Christmas. They'd been polite but withdrawn, clearly still taking their mother's view that he'd sacrificed his family for his career. That was also the last time he'd seen his ex-wife. Then she'd been cold and aloof, and the stiff way she'd carried herself was a warning that her rage was merely out of sight and could reboot at any moment.

Today there was none of that; all four briefly united in grief and his estranged family recognising the loss he had suffered from losing his friend. For that brief moment, all was as it had been. Not for the first time Hooley wished he could turn back the clock.

CHAPTER 46

If it was anyone other than Mary Lou Healy, Josephine Taggert wouldn't have been so concerned, but she'd heard nothing from her assistant for hours. Constantly refreshing her email wasn't helping, so she decided to get herself a coffee.

She was halfway out of her seat when an incoming message pinged onto her phone. It was from Mary Lou, finally.

Wow, she thought, the "going for a coffee" trick had really worked this time.

Sitting back down, she opened the message and then the attachment. The contents shocked her to the core. Was this some terrible practical joke? Surely Mary Lou wouldn't do something like that? Yet there she was, live on screen.

A powerful wave of emotion slammed through Taggert, threatening to derail her. She gripped her hands as tight as she could. No, she thought, she would not give in to despair.

She forced herself to be calm, fighting back a primal urge to panic. She felt cold and shivery as she pressed the play button again. This time she knew what to expect, and there was no doubt at all. This wasn't a joke. Her friend and colleague was in trouble, deep, deep trouble. Despite the temptation to scream and shout, she needed to think hard.

She had to react the right way. She was going to have to watch the video again and again until she had a handle on it.

The clip opened with a close-up shot of Mary Lou, but not as Taggert was used to seeing her. Instead of the composed woman that she knew, she looked dishevelled and had clearly been crying. Her eyelids were red and raw, and her face was swollen and blotchy. Her normally immaculate hair was standing on end; she was dirty, and she had thick black tape over her mouth.

But it was her eyes that were most shocking. Taggert always thought that Mary Lou had the most beautiful big green eyes which constantly sparkled with good humour. This woman's eyes could not be more different. They were dull and frightened. And there was something else there: helplessness and fear.

Over the hateful pictures, a digitally disguised voice was repeating the same short message.

"This is the Cohort," it announced. "Stay tuned if you want this woman back alive. Do not contact the police."

Taggert was over the initial shock, and now she responded. For the next few minutes, she was going to limit the people who knew about this. She would call them by phone and get them to her office. Each one would be told it was vital to say nothing. The half dozen most senior executives, including the head of security, would do in the first instance. More could and would be added.

She gave the warning about the police a moment's thought and then decided to ignore it. The police had to know; she just needed to think who to send it to. She checked a briefing note she'd been sent — and it was there that she saw the name: Brian Hooley.

She remembered him, an older man who hadn't known much about technology but certainly wasn't letting that get in his way. His attitude suggested that, while bad guys might wear different clothes nowadays, they were still only interested in one thing: the money. He had only spent a short time with them, but it was clear he had a lot of authority within the investigation.

Then she recalled the younger guy who'd been with him. Tall, skinny and intense, he'd said nothing and looked at everything. She employed a lot of people like that, but it was surprising to find him working with the police rather than a tech company.

She checked the time. Though it was mid-morning here, it was early evening in the UK. Urgently, she reached for a phone and called Hooley's number. It rang several times before he answered. Wherever he was, it was incredibly noisy. At first, he couldn't follow what she was saying, but he got enough to suddenly become all businesslike.

"Hang on. I'm going outside where it's quieter. If you lose me, call back." There was a short delay and then she heard his voice more clearly. "Can we start at the beginning again?"

Taggert didn't hesitate, explaining who she was and why she was calling. In a clear voice, she described the images in detail, told him what the message said and then let him hear it over the phone.

Hooley was immediately efficient.

"Make sure you impress on the people you tell that Mary Lou's life is in the balance here," he said, quickly. "It is vital this does not get out to the media, or I fear she will be killed instantly. I've got a lot of people to call, and I'm going to start with my colleague Jonathan Roper."

"I remember him from your visit to the London HQ. My security people have checked the email and say there's no sign of any tricks so I can forward this on to you."

"That would be great — but the best person to send this to is Jonathan. I'll give you his email address and his number. Call him as soon as we finish and repeat our conversation. Tell him I'm on my way in." He hesitated before going on. "I'm going to call my boss, Julie Mayweather, the commissioner, and bring her up to speed. Then the office can brief all the units involved. I'm going to need you glued to that phone for the next few hours. I'm not being rude — but no personal calls."

As soon as he cut the connection, she forwarded the email to Roper before calling his mobile number.

Roper answered straight away. "One moment. I'm just about to watch the video."

It was only while she was waiting that she wondered how he had known she was on the phone. Before she had time to think about it, he was back.

"Is that it?" he demanded. "Is there any more?" It was the first of a series of questions he fired at her.

"What do your security people say?"

"Have they been able to identify where it's come from?"

"When did you open this?"

"Did you get any warning?"

"How long has Mary Lou been missing?"

"Is she trustworthy?"

"Could she be involved in this?"

"Can your people track Mary Lou's last movements inside the London office?"

"Have you organised a check of her email and phone logs?

"Is there anyone in London she might have spoken to?"

"What is her home address?"

The bombardment left her reeling.

"Mr Roper, please slow down. I can't keep up. What I can tell you is that I received the email eighteen minutes ago, and I do not believe for a moment that Mary Lou is anything other than a victim in this."

Roper offered no apology. "Would you like me to repeat the questions?"

"Yes please, but slow down. I'm going to make a list."

"OK, make your list, but first give me her address. I need to get there as quickly as possible. I'll come back to you in a moment."

She breathed a sigh of relief that she could provide the information. As soon as he had the address, he broke the connection without a word. She had never spoken to someone so intense, but she suspected he might be the perfect person to save Mary Lou.

* * *

While Roper was firing questions at Josephine Taggert, Hooley was extracting himself from the wake.

The news he'd received from Taggert might have been grave, but at least he had just the excuse he needed to leave the group of close friends and colleagues who were seeing Asmus out on a tide of alcohol. Hooley had remained determinedly sober, and word had quickly got around that he was not drinking because catching the killer, or killers, was his key priority.

Leaving, however, took a little time. Hooley was treated to hugs and teary-eyed encouragement before he was able to swap the overheated atmosphere for some fresh air. Anyone who believed that middle-aged men didn't know how to get in touch with their feelings had never met this lot after a few pints. Hooley expected that more than a few would be paying a heavy price tomorrow.

The wake had ended up in the downstairs bar of the Coal Hole, a classic Victorian pub on the Strand. Hooley emerged into daylight and headed east towards Charing Cross, debating on the way whether to go by car or Tube. Given it was peak rush hour, he reckoned a car journey would be painfully slow — so he decided to jump on the District Line service from Embankment station. It was just a few stops up to Victoria and from there a short stroll to the office.

CHAPTER 47

Mary Lou Healy had been left alone with her thoughts, and it wasn't a happy experience, veering between fear and self-recrimination. What made it even worse was that she had no way of judging the passage of time. The light was either blindingly bright or totally extinguished when her captors came and went, but the rest of the time it was always on low. Currently, a dim glow emanated from a single bulb hanging from the ceiling.

Examining the door, she ruled out any chance of escape. It was made of solid wood with large hinges and a heavy-duty lock. It wasn't sophisticated, but it worked. At least Street had kept his word about removing her restraints. She also had a supply of sandwiches — but there was cold comfort to be had in choosing between tuna or ham.

At some point, Street had appeared and stared at her for a long time, saying nothing. It was a profoundly unpleasant experience which made her feel as if he had somehow stripped her naked.

Finally, he spoke. "Are you sure there's nothing else you need to tell me? Something that might have slipped your mind? I know I'm repeating myself, but it won't go well for you if I discover you've been hiding things."

He needn't have bothered. She was an extraordinarily pragmatic woman and had already decided she was not going to suffer if she didn't have to. Oddly, the thought of death didn't unduly trouble her, but the prospect of cruelty did.

"You really don't have to worry. I've gone over our conversation so far, and I can't add any further information. At least not anything that jumps out. If that changes, I promise I'll tell you."

He stared at her again and then licked his lips. She held back a shudder, vividly recollecting documentary footage of a Komodo Dragon tasting the air with its tongue.

"What can you tell me about the new 'bendy phone'?" As he spoke, he mimed quotation marks in the air with his fingers.

She thought hard. He would know more about that than her. He was one of the more successful players. Not in John Ryder's league — something that always annoyed him — but Street's was a well-known brand none the less.

"I don't know much at all. I booked the hotel room he was staying in — but all he'd given me were the dates he wanted. No details about why he was coming, other than it was part of a global marketing exercise. There was nothing out of the ordinary about that. All our marketing tends to be global. I wondered if he might announce price cuts because there's been a lot of stuff about 'price fatigue' at the top of the market. As for the O2 . . . Well, the booking was made by someone in the marketing team, so nothing was surprising there. I did get a slight warning that morning but again, no details. Since then, we've done nothing but try to find out more. The whole company has been involved in that. But with John so severely injured, we didn't know where to look. At the time you grabbed me, my contacts hadn't come up with anything."

She noticed he was looking at her in an extraordinarily intense manner. His forehead had gone shiny, and there was a trace of sweat on his lower lip. His eyes looked bright, almost feverish.

Healy had never seen him like this before. He usually had supreme physical control, so this was totally out of character. She tried to think what it was about the bendy phones that might have triggered the response.

She couldn't come up with much. A Chinese company had shocked John Ryder by demonstrating their own technology and showing that they were way ahead of the pack. The models Ryder himself had produced so far were quite poor — but, even so, Mary Lou had total confidence in his ability. Before the bomb attack, she would have said he was sure to deliver, even if there were a few setbacks along the way.

Now she wasn't so sure. Privately she wondered if he'd been rushing at it. With the 5G rollout due very soon, many experts were claiming it was the perfect time to introduce new models that could be converted from a phone to a tablet with a flick of the wrist. Some analysts had even predicted that companies like the Ryder Corp would be in trouble if they got left behind by new and more nimble rivals. Mary Lou found that hard to believe — but it had hit the stock price.

Even then, her faith in John Ryder was such that she hadn't given it a lot more thought. She knew he would have an answer to the problem, and they just had to wait for him to reveal it. He'd never let them down.

But everything had changed with that bomb attack. Even if he lived, he might not be the same man. It forced her to confront the thought that the company had allowed itself to be overtaken by new competitors. If a week was "a long time in politics," people should try spending a morning working at the cutting edge of new technology.

She snapped out of her reverie to see that Street was still staring at her. What was making him act so weirdly? He clearly wanted to know what she was thinking — but was it because he needed information, or was it because he wanted to check her knowledge against something he already had?

She looked at Street closely. Then it hit her. She sucked in a gulp of air as she suddenly put two and two together.

"You're responsible for trying to kill John Ryder!" She knew she'd been avoiding this reality because her own feelings of guilt made her feel culpable in some way. Out of nowhere self-doubt turned to hatred. Her rage was back, and that little voice in the back of her head — telling her to be cautious — was quickly overruled. "He's a far better man than you will ever be. More intelligent, more popular, a better leader. You aren't worth the ground he walks on, so you tried to bring him down to your level. Is that what this all about? Your jealousy?"

He seemed not to react to her words, his face appeared quite still — but, as she looked into his eyes, she could glimpse madness.

Another thought struck her and recklessly she ploughed on: "It was you behind those other attacks as well. Why? Why did you have to kill so many innocent people? What do you possibly hope to gain? You may have ruined John's life; maybe you've even killed him, but there's no way — absolutely no way! — you get to just walk away from this!"

Street still said nothing. Then he leaned over and kissed her on the head. There was no emotion in it. His lips were cold, and it felt like an assault.

"I'm going to let you think for a bit," he whispered. "But, when I come back, I need you to tell me all you can about Jonathan Roper."

Then he stood and left the room, his silence an eloquent answer to her questions.

CHAPTER 48

Mary Lou's apartment was a short walk from Liverpool Street station, part of a concrete and glass building that wouldn't win any design prizes but did the job.

Roper decided to walk up the steps rather than take the lift to the fifth-floor apartment. He hadn't done enough exercise recently. He didn't rate the workouts with Hooley.

The apartment was compact; an open-plan area housed a functional kitchen, an oval-shaped glass table that served multiple purposes, and at the other end of the space were two, small, brown leather sofas placed at right angles to each other. A pile of cushions on one suggested where Mary Lou sat to watch the large flat-screen TV hanging on the wall.

The flat also boasted two double bedrooms and two bathrooms. The biggest bedroom was obviously Mary Lou's and the second seemed to be more of a storeroom with an exercise bike. The colour scheme was beige, brown and cream. Roper approved. It wasn't as minimalist as his own apartment — the DCI had called it "bleak" on his last visit — but it came quite close.

There was one thing he didn't approve of: the cat sitting in a basket under the table. Cat fur made his nose and eyes itch. He was glad Taggert had warned him. He made a mental note that they needed to get the RSPCA involved to take care of it.

A team had arrived ahead of him, including a security specialist who bypassed the alarm system. The forensics team were busy doing their job. The CSIs had already found plenty of fingerprints but they were all the same, suggesting they were Mary Lou's.

Roper looked around the room and realised she was probably quite similar to him. Her home had few possessions, and everything was in its place. He often disliked other people's houses because they were too cluttered.

He sat on the settee and thought some more. If she was similar to him, she probably had trouble making friends, maybe spending her time buried under piles of work. He noted she had just one picture on display, a smiling older version of herself who he guessed was her mother. No father though — they might need to look into that.

He carried on with his careful check, and in her bedroom, he registered the small pile of books by her bedside table. Most of her generation used digital downloads unless it was for topics of particular interest.

The books were nearly all biographies of the so-called Tech Titans. Among them, work on John Ryder, Charles Lim the Chinese billionaire and the Brit, Peter Street. The only exception was a sign language manual. He flicked through it — the Makaton system for use with young children. He wondered why she had it; maybe she was a volunteer working with children? Or perhaps she was more like him than he had realised. During her own school days, had she also needed alternative ways of communicating? It was another thing to check out.

He replaced the manual and finished off his careful check of the flat, finally satisfied that it had given up its small haul of clues. He was glad he'd come. The visit was allowing him to create a detailed portrait of Mary Lou, and in the long run that might prove critical.

* * *

Back at Victoria, Brooker and Hooley were comparing notes. The DCI was keen to know if they'd had any luck with the CCTV footage.

"All being looked at right now." She tapped her fingers on her desk to emphasise the point. "Because everyone must swipe out, we know what time she left the Ryder building. There are loads of street cameras around the area, so we're working to track her route."

"And we're doing the same where she lives?"

"Of course," said Brooker. "Both places are getting equal attention, but Jonathan and I agree that work looks the best bet."

"What makes you feel that?"

"We're working on the theory that she went from work to the place where she was grabbed."

"That argument does not totally convince me," said Hooley. "But I'm happy to go with your gut feelings . . ."

Brooker smiled. "You should also know that Jonathan and I are approaching the algorithm in a different way."

Hooley never liked this type of discussion because he found himself saying things he didn't really understand. "So, what changes did you make?"

"We went back to the beginning and tried to put ourselves into the minds of the people behind these attacks. We know that it involved trained military personnel and we assume the person doing the hiring must be seriously wealthy. Whoever set this up will have needed somewhere to store a lot of equipment, even people, and do it very quietly. That would need something like a warehouse facility on an industrial estate, where no one's worried about who comes and goes.

"We also wanted to try and build in some factors around motive. Jonathan said that, if you'd been here, you'd have told us to follow the money, so we made that our first point. Who would have benefitted? We couldn't find anything that linked all three attacks, at least not that we've found yet, so we took each incident separately."

As this mini briefing unfolded, Hooley was increasingly impressed by the way Brooker was laying out the information. She had a good communication style which allowed her to make the point without over complicating it.

"The attack on John Ryder was the easiest to build an argument for," she went on. "He's the driving force at Ryder Corporation so we have several rivals who would benefit from him being taken out. But we were also able to put an argument together about an ambitious colleague wanting to take his job. Again, it was surprising how many names that gave us — but none that we could point at as the favourite."

"When you look at Valentina Ferrari from the same perspective, you do get some possibilities. She was seen as an influential politician, especially with her attacks on the big social media companies. Jonathan put forward the idea that the same person who attacked John Ryder would have also killed her because they might have benefitted from losing such an outspoken critic of the business. To be fair, we don't think that's very likely, but I suppose we must keep it in mind until we can prove otherwise. Plus, we're waiting for the accountants to report on her finances.

"But, when we come to Diamonds and Pearls, it gets kind of interesting. You can see they have lots of enemies — there are plenty of people on Twitter making all sorts of threatening remarks — but why attack Ryder and Ferrari as well? Again, it could be something we don't know yet, so we'll leave it as a possibility.

"So, then we looked at Jonathan's theory about industrial espionage, and you can see a connection. If Diamonds and Pearls give you access to what rivals are up to, then suddenly you can make an argument linking all three attacks."

Hooley smiled and said, "It feels like you two haven't missed me at all. Good briefing. I need to touch base with the chief and by then hopefully, Jonathan will be back."

Mayweather was tight for time, so his conversation was short. When Hooley put the phone down he asked Brooker, "I should have asked this already — what do we know about the victims' private lives? Love interests, gambling, drugs . . . the usual suspects?"

At that point, Roper walked back in and effortlessly picked up the conversation. "MI5 and MI6 are in charge of all that. I don't think they've dug anything up, but they weren't keen on talking to me. I kept getting put on to different people. At first, they even denied they were investigating anything at all. I had to get quite cross — but finally, I was given a very brief outline. Ferrari is spotless, which is why she could risk getting a big media profile. Ryder's not married and doesn't currently have a partner — but he does have a good reputation for behaving properly towards women. The actual phrase they used was, 'He's no powerful Hollywood producer.' As to Diamonds and Pearls, they didn't have anything to tell me. But it does worry me that MI5 and MI6 were so difficult to extract anything from, they might be hiding something."

Hooley sighed. "I'll ask Julie to lean on them. That's the trouble with spooks; they do love their secrets. I think they worry they'll lose their power if they have to talk about them." He tugged at his earlobe as he put his thoughts in order. "You both have covered a lot of ground in a very short period of time, and I like the sound of what you've been thinking about, especially being able to make a link to all three attacks. So, I guess the big question is — has all your theorising thrown up any leads yet?"

They both spoke simultaneously. "We might have found the first mistake they've made."

CHAPTER 49

Mary Lou Healy felt like banging her head against the wall. She normally boasted an excellent memory but was struggling to remember who Jonathan Roper was. She guessed her short-term memory was being affected by a combination of stress and the drugs they'd given her. She could feel the information she sought floating just beyond her reach.

"Think, think," she told herself. If Street was that interested, he must be either a rival or part of the police team. Impatiently, she tapped her head — but still, she felt nothing. She took a swig of water.

Suddenly she had it. There had been two detectives, one older than the other. The older man was one of those people you liked straight away; he had an open manner. She smiled as she recalled that she had thought he had that "sexy older dad" thing going on, in a charming way.

His partner, however, was quite different, giving nothing away about himself. He had said little but listened intently. He didn't make any notes, and she had guessed he had a good memory.

To her relief, their names came back to her. Brian Hooley and Jonathan Roper. Well, now she had the name

— but it wasn't going to do her much good if Street thought she had *War and Peace* on the man.

She could recall what he looked like: tall, very skinny and pale with thick curly black hair. She also remembered his outfit, a close-fitting black suit and white shirt combo.

Then there were his shoes, excellent quality and polished to a shine. It was the sort of thing, she reflected, that you might expect from a former military man. He was one of those silent types who observe everything and say nothing.

Well, it was more information than she'd had a few minutes ago — but she doubted it was enough to make Street happy when he came back.

As she sat on the edge of her bed, waiting for the door to open, she flicked through the bag of sandwiches. They still had some residual coolness from the chiller cabinet they'd been stored in — so she decided a ham salad would be safe enough to eat.

For some reason, fear was making her hungry, which was annoying. In the normal course of life, she avoided pre-prepared food of any kind, but she needed to keep her strength up. So far, she hadn't seen any opportunities for escape — but, if something did come up, she would have to be quick.

She was halfway through her sandwich, which didn't seem to have any taste at all when the door finally opened. Street was back. That unpleasant smile he was so good at was still plastered on his face.

The big man was with him. Perhaps Street was concerned that she might try and attack him. He wasn't the biggest man around, and she recalled that this was something he was very sensitive about.

With or without his sidekick, she would be sorely tempted to knee him in the "unmentionables" — as her mother liked to refer to them — if the opportunity presented itself. The thought of her mum made her smile; she would have had no hesitation in giving Street a piece of her mind.

"You find this amusing?" Street seethed, his unpleasant smile vanishing. "Care to share the joke with the rest of us?"

Healy shrugged, giving him a defiant stare. "I just thought that my mum wouldn't have taken any nonsense from you two."

Street looked at blankly for a moment.

He surprised her when he burst out laughing. It wasn't a warm laugh, more an unpleasant gurgle. Tears came to his eyes, which he wiped away with the back of his hand. It was a troubling performance, not helped by the big man remaining impassive throughout.

Either he'd decided Street was so mad there was nothing to be gained by worrying about it, or it was an act to get under her skin. She wondered why he was going to so much trouble. She'd already rolled over and promised she would help.

The big man had brought the video camera with him again. It looked like the kind of thing professional filmmakers would use. The last time around, he'd just taken some footage of her sitting on the bed. She wondered what he was going to do this time.

He interrupted her thoughts. "So. Jonathan Roper. What can you tell me?"

Her mouth went dry. "Not a lot, I'm afraid. He came to the office with another, older detective. I didn't speak to him. In fact, I don't recall him speaking at all. I can tell you what he was wearing if you like. He had very shiny shoes."

"Good job I'm not relying on you for information then." Street's voice was cold. "It turns out that Mr Roper is quite the man at Scotland Yard. He's different, but he gets results. This older man you mentioned. Was that Brian Hooley?"

She nodded.

"It seems they're the dream team. Well, I'm going to be their worst nightmare." He finished the sentence with a little snort, obviously thrilled with his own wit. Then he handed her a sheet of paper with words printed on it.

"I've got a message for Jonathan Roper. You can read it out for the camera."

CHAPTER 50

Brooker spoke the names carefully. "John Palmer and Tony Cross. They might be the first major clues our people have left."

That grabbed the DCI's attention. He waited patiently, taking a careful mouthful of coffee as he leaned back in his chair. He had a feeling he was going to enjoy listening to this explanation. Brooker and Roper were both clearly delighted at what they had found.

"Palmer and Cross?" Hooley looked from one to the other. "I can't say that those names leap out at me. All I can think of are the biscuit manufacturers, Huntley and Palmer." His attempt at comedy was ignored.

Roper took the lead. "The first thing to tell you is that it was thanks to Susan's algorithm tweaks that all this was picked up so quickly."

Hooley smiled at Brooker and was also impressed at Roper taking the time to acknowledging his colleague's work — in the past he might just have jumped straight into his explanation.

"John Palmer died after his ride-on-mower exploded," Roper continued. "Someone attached a bomb to it, killed him and his wife. The irony is that it took a few days to

229

confirm it was a bomb because everything's been so focused on these three attacks. At first, it was quite low priority, but Susan's algorithm still flagged it. That link gained in importance with another discovery yesterday."

"Is this where Tony Cross comes in?"

"Yes. His body was found in a remote cottage in Wales. At first, it was treated as suicide — it appeared as if he'd killed himself with a pistol shot to the head, and the situation wasn't helped because the body had been got at by wild animals. In the end, it was a local farmer who raised the alarm. He saw a large flock of crows at the house so feared the worst. He went to investigate and found Cross with the gun at his side." Roper paused. "It was information provided by his brother that made all the difference. Tony Cross was left-handed, you see, but it appeared the gun was fired with his right. That meant it had to be a set-up.

"Cross operated a warehouse, out near Heathrow. When the police reported his death locally, Susan's algorithm started making multiple links — and from that, we learned that the guy killed on the lawnmower also worked for Cross as his head of logistics.

"Even though the owner is dead, along with Cross, the warehouse is still operating with a team of managers staffing the place. There's enough work backed up in the system to keep it running for a few weeks."

Roper paused and looked over at Brooker.

"It's a 24-hour operation, so Susan and I were thinking of going down there just to see what there is to see. It could be the workers there have also seen this 'big man' — maybe he's been caught on CCTV. A place like that will be loaded with cameras."

Hooley was delighted. "That's all great work. And it would help if you got down there. I'll need to alert the commissioner and the other teams working on this but no reason why you two shouldn't go. I'll liaise with everyone else and arrange for a CSI team to follow you down."

* * *

Brooker was gripping her hands as the police driver executed yet another brilliantly skilful overtaking manoeuvre. This was the first time she had been driven at such speed, and she was both scared and elated. Next to her, Roper was a picture of relaxation. He'd done this many times before.

They were in the back of a dark blue Jaguar saloon, being driven by a petite female officer who handled the vehicle with an ease that Brooker could only admire. It was equipped with a siren and blue lights built into the front grille. Both had been used almost continuously since leaving Victoria.

The driver spoke over her shoulder.

"We're less than five minutes out. Local officers are on scene waiting for you before they do anything else." She had been fed the information through a discreet earpiece in her right ear. The entire journey was going to take less than forty minutes — frankly miraculous since they had had to contend with the rush hour traffic.

A few miles out of London, they turned off the M4 and completed the journey to the industrial estate through suburban roads. The warehouse was big: a vast grey and green oblong constructed from corrugated metal. Mostly functional, it had a massive loading bay at one end and offices at the other end that looked as if they'd been tacked on, almost as an afterthought.

Local police officers stood at both ends and around the perimeter. They had been given one instruction: "No one leaves until the London team gives permission."

The car dropped them outside the office area. Moments later, a uniformed sergeant approached them.

"We've been here for almost two hours and have stopped anyone leaving." He jerked his thumb in the direction of some large, glass double doors, which were directly behind him. "Can you see the bald man in there?"

They both spotted the man anxiously looking out at them and nodded.

"Well, he's the day manager, and he's been badgering me to be allowed to leave. I've told him he has to wait — but, just to warn you, he's persistent."

Thanking him, they headed towards the man who rushed out of the doors as they got close.

"It's my wife's birthday. I need to get home now."

Brooker smiled at him while narrowing her eyes. "I'm afraid we'll be a little while yet. This is a terrorism investigation, and we need you to cooperate. Otherwise, we'll have to assume you're trying to obstruct us and that would see you in a world of trouble."

He paled and backed away. "I'll ring my wife and tell her." The sergeant having a hard time keeping the smile off his face.

With the aid of the now-helpful manger, Roper established that there was a total of six staff on duty, working the 6 p.m. to 8 a.m. shift. It was also soon apparent that everyone present was working quite legitimately and that the owner and Cross were keeping the illegal part of their work under wraps. Everyone's story would need double-checking, but Roper was convinced there was nothing below board here.

The mournful-looking manager was the last to be quizzed. Like with everyone else, he had nothing to add — until they asked about the big man.

"There was a man who fits that description. He turned up here one morning in one of those huge SUVs."

"Was it a Range Rover?" Brooker asked.

He shrugged. "It might have been. It had blacked-out windows. I was on a break and saw it arrive. The man who got out was huge, much taller than the car. Mr Cross was outside waiting for him. He'd got about halfway to the car when the other man started jabbing his finger at him. Mr Cross looked really worried. Scared even. I'd never seen him like that before. The big man was shouting. Eventually, he drove off, leaving Mr Cross standing there."

"Does CCTV cover that front area?" asked Roper.

The manager nodded.

"I can let you have the footage, no problem. I can remember perfectly because it was my birthday. All CCTV is backed up on the computer and kept for twelve months. I'll go and get what you need."

Ten minutes later he was back, looking flustered.

"I don't understand this — but there's no footage from that day. I've checked a couple of days either side, and there's nothing there either."

Roper was frustrated. This was an ominous sign. "We'll need to get our experts to double-check that."

They travelled back to Central London in silence. As they hurtled back through the traffic, Roper seemed especially lost in his thoughts. Even returning to Victoria didn't immediately snap him out of it.

Finally, when Roper had returned from wherever he'd gone, he looked carefully at both Hooley and Brooker as though he wasn't sure who they were then took a breath and nodded.

"I think our target has given us a clue."

CHAPTER 51

Healy had once sat in on an advertising shoot. It had been hard, monotonous work which required huge concentration, enlivened only by interventions from the director. Now, that experience was being repeated, as Street and the big man tried to set up the perfect shot. So far, she'd been "filmed" from a variety of angles before it was decided that the original position sitting on the bed worked best.

She'd sat patiently throughout, and the preparations appeared to have relaxed Street a little — just enough for her to risk trying a conversation that would give her a chance to judge his frame of mind.

"Where is this place?" she asked.

For some reason, this seemed to please him. His face lit up, and he became far more expressive.

"What do you think? Maybe this is underground, part of a cellar?"

Her shrug showed he was right. That was exactly what she thought.

"Well, you'd be wrong. You're at ground level — and this isn't the first time you've been here." He swept his arm around. "Not that it looked like this, to be fair. But you do know this space."

She looked puzzled. She couldn't think of anywhere that might have been like this.

"I have no idea where we are. My guess is you've brought me out of London."

"Top marks. Do you remember when we drove out to Surrey one afternoon, and I showed you that house, the one my parents used to live in?"

It was a large, wooded plot, near Leatherhead. It had been a beautiful day when they'd visited. He'd been in a good mood, talking about how much he'd enjoyed living there as a child.

"I remember you saying great location, shame about the house."

"I had it rebuilt, and it was finished a few months ago. You're actually in my safe room or, I should say, safe rooms. They're the same size and built side by side. This is the scruffy one, I'm afraid. They're concealed behind a wall in the living room. The house is so big that it was easy enough to conceal two rooms within it. That feeling you have of being underground is the result of soundproofed walls."

She thought he seemed in the mood to talk, so maybe she could try another question.

"What is it you want with me and all these videos? You seem to be keeping me alive for some reason."

He gave her that peculiar look again. "I'll tell you what. You behave while we shoot this video and I'll explain all." He clapped his hands together. "Why don't you do a read through first . . . and then it's for real. Get this right, and maybe it will help you to walk out of here."

For some reason, the impending activity triggered an idea. It was a long shot, but it might just work. It was going to take a lot of luck — and the first thing she needed was to find a distraction that wasn't too obvious. She made her mind up. She would give it a go.

She picked up her "script" and started reading through. As she thought about reading it out loud, she looked apologetic and asked if she could have a drink.

Street handed her a water bottle, and she drank thirstily. She had an idea — maybe she was holding the answer in her hand. She coughed a couple of times. "I've got a bit of tickle in my throat, nothing too serious. I'll be fine to read out your message. But maybe I can keep the water to hand?"

To emphasise the point, she coughed, raising her hand to pat the top of her chest. She was just going to have to try and get away with it when they switched the camera on.

Street told her to practice the run through. She read the message slowly and clearly.

"I suppose I should be flattered that the great Jonathan Roper is on the case. It strikes me that you may not be as good as they say. Are you running out of time?"

She thought it was a strange message but kept that to herself. Street, who had been watching closely, patted her arm. "Well done. We're going to do this like we mean it . . ." He'd always been pompous and having a captive audience only made him worse. She really couldn't imagine what she'd ever seen in him.

Street checked with his underling, who was acting as the cameraman and received a thumbs-up. Then, he turned back to Healy, pointed at her, and slowly started the countdown.

"Three, two, one . . . ACTION!"

Healy took a breath and coughed gently, quickly patting herself as she did. Not looking to check their reactions, she launched straight into it. It didn't take long to read.

The two men bent over the camera as they watched the playback, their expressions intent as they replayed it twice more.

Finally, Street spoke, "What about the cough and those hands?" Before the big guy could reply, he answered his own question. "Nah, don't worry. I reckon it makes the whole thing a bit more real."

Healy hadn't dared look at them. She realised, now, that she'd been holding her breath throughout the process — but the relief flooded through her body, making her cough for real.

Street loomed over her. "Don't let it be said that I don't keep my promises," he jeered. "Do you want to know what your role is? Well, you'll be pleased to know you have become quite significant. My original plan was to kill Ryder and then pick off his key employees by giving them jobs with me. It would make sure he was dead and buried while giving me the talent to move my company to the top spot. But it turns out that the people at your company seem to suffer from a misplaced loyalty. Acting through third parties, I approached the best of your people and offered them colossal sums, but they all said they would wait to see whether John Ryder recovered and what happened next. I was amazed." He reached forward and softly stroked her cheek, but his face was cold and devoid of affection. "Then you came along, all prying eyes, and I realised you were a loose end that needed to be tied up."

Despite her best efforts, she shivered at the implications.

"Sorry about this, but yes, the original plan was to terminate you and chuck your body in the Thames. But I realised that it would be a wasted opportunity. If I used you to torment Ryder Corp, I could cause real problems. Instead of killing you straight away, I suggesting that they might save you. Imagine the impact when they discover that they . . . can't. It will cause a lot of distress. Then wait until they get the warning from the Cohort! 'You will be one of many. It will only stop when Ryder Corp shuts down'."

She thought he looked quite mad. He was shaking and sweating, and scratching at his body. But the trouble was that there was an insane logic to his plan.

"What about the attack on Diamonds and Pearls and that Italian politician? Surely they don't have any links to you?"

"You'd be surprised." He was back in control of his emotions, at least for now. "That Ferrari woman was making a real nuisance of herself. She was giving herself new powers to break up big tech companies. Well, I couldn't stand idly by. Not with all the effort I put into getting rid of John Ryder and taking over his position as the biggest of them all.

When I discovered she was coming over to London, it was the perfect opportunity."

To her horror, she could see how his mind had worked. "But what about Diamonds and Pearls? Why did you need to blow them up?"

The crazy look was back.

"Like you — they were another loose end. And they were hardly innocents." He gave an enigmatic shrug.

At that moment, she knew there was nothing more she could do. A curious sense of calm washed over her. In impossible circumstances, she'd fought back in the only way she could. Now she just had to hope that the video was watched by someone with the skills to understand the message.

CHAPTER 52

Roper had their full attention, and for once, he didn't waste time on building the tension.

"I've been thinking about why they snatched Mary Lou, rather than someone else. It's her relationship with Josephine Taggert that is important. On the face of it, she's a PA, a very senior PA, but that's not her true role. From what we picked up from the company, she is like the second-in-command of the UK office. It's just that no one has got around to doing anything about her title, so they don't actually list her as that."

Hooley was frowning. "Hang on. I don't get that at all. If she's the deputy, then that should mean more money, pension and all the little extras that come with promotions. Take me. As a chief inspector, I earn more than an inspector, so the rank does matter."

"Not necessarily, or not anymore," said Roper. "I spoke to one of the Human Resources people, and she said it was quite common for top staff to get more money without having to change their status."

Hooley held his hands up. "To old ears like mine that sounds like a recipe for disaster — but maybe you should just ignore me. Sorry; I interrupted you telling us why our killer has made a mistake."

Roper practically bobbed up and down. "I am going to do that — but first of all, I was wondering if Mary Lou was sort of a double bluff. They were hoping that the fact they kidnapped her was making us think that it couldn't be that obvious. But really . . . it was."

Hooley held his head in his hands and groaned theatrically.

"What are you talking about? You're making my head hurt."

"The person who grabbed Mary Lou has made the mistake of thinking that we wouldn't realise how vital she is to the running of the company. They'll be assuming we keep looking at her as a senior PA, but not the effective number two."

Hooley was peering between his fingers. "This helps us how? And try to remember — I'm not supposed to be putting a strain on my heart, or what's left of it . . ."

"That's made a mistake in misleading us."

"You just told us that. How about sharing what the mistake is? I hope it's not listening to you . . ."

If Roper heard the last comment, he didn't show it. "It's obvious when you think about it. I am quite sure it means the person behind all this is also in the business because they know how important she is. It means that it must be someone who has dealings with the company. I am very confident, ninety-nine per cent, that it is someone from a rival company. We have to accept a one per cent chance that it is someone in the Ryder UK team — but I've checked and, apart from Taggert and Healy, everyone is accounted for." Roper paused. "It's like you're always telling me. If you want to mangle a big company, just interfere with the chain of command."

Hooley sat up. "As ever, you present a compelling case. So, what does that mean in terms of next steps?"

Roper closed his eyes and sat very still; his face screwed up in concentration. "We need the major. If it's possible to pull him out of whatever he's doing, then we need to do it."

Hooley leaned right back in his chair. "That's brilliant! Obvious, but brilliant!"

Brooker was looking between the two men, a quizzical expression on her face.

The DCI explained. "The major in question is Major Tom Phillips. Currently with the SAS. He knows everything there is to know about elite soldiers and mercenaries."

Her face lit up. "So, if the big man is an ex-soldier, then this Major Phillips might know who he is . . ."

Roper finished the thought. "And since we can be sure that the man he is working for is currently UK based, we should get both the names we need."

Hooley put the call in immediately and was told to wait for a response. It wasn't long in coming. Thirty minutes later his phone beeped with a message: "On my way. Thanks for getting me out of the world's most boring mission debrief."

He was showing the message to the other two when his phone started ringing. He almost dropped it in surprise.

It was Taggert: "I've got another email. It's for Mr Roper this time."

Minutes later, they were watching the video of Mary Lou.

Despite the desperate circumstances, she looked calm.

Looking directly at the camera, she spoke slowly and clearly, like it was something she did every day.

"I suppose I should be flattered that the great Jonathan Roper is on the case. It strikes me that you may not be as good as they say. Are you running out of time?"

All three leaned closer to the screen as they heard Roper's name, Roper looking as though he might tip over and touch the image. They replayed the video twice more.

Hooley was the first to speak. "That young woman is as tough as they come. You can see what stress she's under — but she's working hard to get that right. Hardly surprising, but victims are usually in tears . . ."

"I agree," said Brooker. "But I'm wondering two things. Why she's trying so hard? Maybe she wants the bad guys to think she is no problem for them. And why is it directed at Jonathan?"

They both looked at him, but he just sat there impassively. If he had an idea, he wasn't sharing.

"That 'running out of time' is a bit of a concern," interjected a worried Hooley.

Roper responded. "I've just been thinking about that. It could be a threat to kill Mary Lou, it could be another attack — or maybe he reckons he is about to escape somewhere we can't find him. I'm going to watch it again to see if there are any clues."

He watched it four more times before sighing with exasperation. "There's nothing there."

At that point, the major walked in, coughing slightly to announce his arrival. He rubbed his hands together and was about to speak when Roper pointed at him. "That's it!" he gasped. "Cough again."

The major knew Roper well enough to carry out the instruction. "Susan, you do it," Roper went on. "And then you, Brian."

After a round of coughs, Roper looked pleased. "Clever woman! She's managed to tell us something!"

All three spoke at the same time. "What?"

He turned the video clip back on. "Watch what happens when she coughs." He played it twice and then waited for someone to spot it.

It was Brooker. "She doesn't cover her mouth properly," she said. "It's like she just rests her index finger over her top lip, then sort of holds her hands out before patting her chest." She paused, seemingly bewildered. "But why is that important?"

Roper smiled. "I didn't spot it straight away, but then I remembered what I'd found in her flat. She must have known we would go there and find something she could tap into to send a message. It was a desperate thing though; there are not many people who could work it out."

The other three were staring at him. It was the major who broke the silence.

"Not sure I quite follow you?"

Hooley shook his head. "Not sure? He might as well be talking in Chinese for all the sense he's making. Come on, Jonathan, this is no time for messing around."

Roper looked offended. "I'm not. I am trying to explain."

"Well, get on with it and do it so that a five-year-old can understand. Try to pretend that we're not all genius-level detectives."

Roper muttered, "I do not need to pretend," under his breath. Hooley let it go and waited for him to tell them what he had spotted.

"Okay," Roper sighed. "As you know, I went to Mary Lou's apartment, and there were a couple of things I saw there that didn't seem that important, but they are now."

He looked at Brooker. "Brian is always telling us to get out and look for ourselves, and I'm glad I did."

"Jonathan . . ." The message from Hooley was almost a growl.

"Yes, yes. I'm getting to it. The first thing you need to know is that I found a Makaton manual there. It's a form of sign language often used with autistic people. When I looked at the video, I immediately felt there was something odd about it, but I couldn't work it out. It was only when I got each of you to cough that I worked it out.

"Each of you used a hand to cover your mouth. It's instinctive, a way of trying not to spread germs. But she quite deliberately leaves her hands open." He paused. "It took me a while, but I suddenly got it. She's making the sign for 'Home'."

He played the tape and held the image. "You can see she's made a shape that could be the roof of a house. Well, we already know that she's not being held at her home so it must be the home of the person who has her.

"The second part of the message is much harder to read. Even though I was looking for something, it was hard to be sure. But then I thought of something else in her apartment. She had a biography about Peter Street in her bedroom, well him and a few other tech people, actually. Let me show you."

He carefully rewound the tape to the point where she coughed.

"Now, watch this. After saying home, she does an odd thing with her hands. I think she's trying to do the sign for 'Street', but to do it properly she would need to push both hands away from her. Obviously, she can't do something so obvious so she gets as close as she can.

"If I hadn't seen those books at her house, I wouldn't have realised what she's doing."

"That's a pretty amazing theory, Jonathan," said Hooley. "But are you sure? What does your Rainbow Spectrum tell you?"

"That's the good news, it totally agrees."

CHAPTER 53

The door to Healy's prison shot open, and she cringed away from the sharp electric light which flooded the room. As her vision cleared, she saw Street standing in the entrance. He looked angry.

Her heart filled with dread. Had he realised that she had sent a message out to the world? Was he now here to punish her? She felt an almost overwhelming urge to confess but managed to get control before she could say anything.

If he had discovered her secret, she would know soon enough. There was nothing she could do about it. Right now, she was going to die whatever happened. Her only other idea was shooting him in the face . . . but she needed a gun for that.

She made herself breathe slowly, concentrating on keeping the fear from creeping up on her. She might be afraid, and she might be helpless — there was nothing she could do about that — but she would hold on to her dignity.

To her surprise, Street held up a bag and shook it at her direction. "I thought you might appreciate a change of clothes and the chance to freshen up a little bit. I'll be back in twenty minutes." He turned away before spinning back to face her, grinning. "Oh and do put on what I've provided."

His voice sounded almost conversational, but she took no comfort from the apparent friendliness. The blankness of his face continued to tell a more chilling story.

He backed out, pulling the door closed but leaving the bright light on so that she was able to see what he had left. At the top of the bag was a packet of wet wipes. After a couple of days without washing, she was pathetically delighted. He had also provided a roll-on deodorant. It was meant for a man, but she wasn't bothered; anything that would help her disguise her own body odour was welcome. There was also a toothbrush and a tube of half-used toothpaste.

At the bottom of the bag was something wrapped in black plastic. She hesitated. This had to be the clothing he had told her she was going to have to wear. Hoping it was nothing weird, she ripped the parcel open.

The first thing she saw was a bright orange. Pulling it out, she revealed a jumpsuit, like the type of thing prisoners wore in her favourite TV show, *Orange is the New Black*. Holding it up, she could see that it was about her size — maybe a bit larger, but close enough.

She shrugged. This was weird, but at least it was bearable. She'd been worried that it might have been some sort of bondage outfit.

Checking the bottom of the bag, were a couple of pairs of plain knickers. As her mother said, you never want to risk being carted off to hospital with grubby underwear. She carefully wiped herself with the baby wipes — her desire to be clean outweighing her fear that one of them could return and find her half-naked. Then, taking a deep breath, she pulled on her new knickers and practically jumped into the boiler suit. Moments later, she sank back onto her cot, her heart pounding but relieved to have escaped any prying eyes.

By the time Street returned, she was back in control. He checked her over and nodded.

"I see the suit fits. I got it a few weeks ago and was pretty confident I'd got the size right. How does it feel? I think it suits you."

She looked at him incredulously. "I'm only wearing this because you told me to." As she spoke, she knew how he was going to react — and there it was, right on cue: the knowing smirk that she really disliked.

"Well, I think you look good. If we need to send your friends another message — actually, hold that; it will be *when* we send another message — this will help focus their minds that you really are a prisoner. I do hope, for your sake, that they're paying attention." The smirk remained in place, but his eyes were glittering. "I thought you might like a change of scenery. Come on, follow me. I think you'll like this."

Street spun around and quickly headed away. Mary Lou hesitated, but finally, she followed him. It felt as if she was stepping into a different world as she left her prison and, after only a few steps, emerged into the main body of the house.

She walked into what was clearly intended as a sitting room, decorated in shades of white and cream, with a pale woollen carpet that felt soft under her bare feet.

Street was waiting for her in the centre of the room and waved his arms around. "Welcome to my little slice of heaven. I'm not here that often so it lacks that lived-in look — but better, I think, than where you've been staying." She shivered. He made it sound like she was a guest, apologetically put up in a shabby spare room.

He pointed out the settee, the large TV placed in front of it and the door in the facing wall.

"Through that door and left is the downstairs toilet, and past that the kitchen, where you can make yourself a hot drink. There are some ready meals if you feel hungry, so do help yourself." He looked at her. "Now, before you go getting any funny ideas, every other room in the house is locked. Including the front door. You can go and have a look if you like — but you won't get out, and this place is so secluded no one will see you." He pointed at the settee. "Make yourself a drink, then get comfortable and watch some TV. I think you might find the news channels quite interesting. Someone, I can't imagine who," he mimed innocence, "has leaked our little video. You're a national hero now."

As he hustled away, she heard the sound of a door slamming shut. She stood uncertainly for a moment, then decided she might as well do as he said. A proper cup of tea would be a comfort.

Soon, she found her way into a light and airy kitchen. Once again, there was no attempt at colour, just neutral tones and clean lines. She had to open all the cupboards before she found what she wanted.

Once the tea had brewed, she cradled the mug in her hands, headed back into the living room and sat down. As she raised the mug, a wave of emotion almost made it slip out of her hands. She was shaking so much she put it down.

Despite herself, she was grateful that he had made her more comfortable. She was under no illusion about her own safety — but at least she was better off than she had been. Picking up the remote, she found Sky news and didn't have long to wait.

The woman presenter started talking.

"The John Ryder story has taken an even more sensational twist with the kidnapping of a key employee. Police are refusing to comment, but Sky sources have obtained the following video which it is believed was sent in the last few hours." She looked especially grave and added, "Viewers of a sensitive nature are advised that the following video may cause distress."

The next second, there she was on the screen — looking terrible. She couldn't stop herself thinking "viewers of a sensitive nature are warned that this woman looks in a shocking state". Then she thought of her parents watching and cried, knowing how frightened for her they would be.

The video ran for its entire length and then ran again, this time with a commentary that it was believed to have come from the Cohort.

The item panned back to the studio, where the presenter still looked grave and solemn. "If this video is true, then it appears a young woman's life is at risk. Norman Smith is our crime reporter at Scotland Yard. Norman, what more do we know?"

The crime reporter flashed into view. He looked tired and was talking slowly to disguise the paucity of hard information that was available.

Looking directly to the camera, he said, "This is a terrible ordeal for this young woman and her family. While the Ryder Corp is saying nothing at the moment, Sky sources have told us their only concern is to get her back safe and well.

"Police are not commenting at this stage and have given no further updates on progress, but I can confirm that the video is being treated as significant evidence."

Mary Lou watched the story unfold with a mounting sense of horror. She couldn't get her head around being on live TV. It was not a comforting place to be, and she sat there fighting back the tears.

"Not now," she told herself. "Don't give in. While you still breathe, you still have a chance."

She leaned back into the settee, and within seconds, she was deeply asleep. She was troubled by strange dreams and kept drifting in and out of wakefulness until Street finally roused her as he called out.

"Don't worry about Marcus and me, we've just got to bring a few sacks through here." As he disappeared, she realised he had given her the name of the large, silent man.

For some reason that didn't make her feel better it seemed as though Street was no longer worried about what she knew and there might well be a simple reason for that; he was going to kill her.

CHAPTER 54

The major ended the phone call and started mock beating himself around the head with his mobile.

"The next time I put out an inquiry about a big bloke with military training, remind me it's a bit like asking does a bear crap in the woods?"

"Having problems?" asked Hooley.

"I was, thanks to Mary Lou, and the ever-amazing mind of Jonathan. You know I haven't seen you guys for a while, but I walk back in and there he is, pulling rabbits out of hats that don't even exist, at least not to most people. I'm just glad he's on our side. If he were a master criminal, like Moriarty, we wouldn't stand a chance."

Hooley could only nod his agreement, and the major waved his phone. "I might be about to have a bit of luck. Someone is going to ring me back shortly. It's a bit complicated, but a friend of a friend overheard someone mentioning a bloke called Street who was looking for a new security chief. He says it stood out because the bloke was offering big money, over a million quid a year, and then my mate says he heard nothing at all, so he reckons the job must have been filled."

Roper and Brooker pounded their keyboards as they looked up details about Peter Street.

"He's the head of Street Industries and Britain's biggest name in mobile phone manufacture and sales. He's in second place to John Ryder. He fits the profile. How long before you hear anything?"

"Soon. But I can't put a time on it. It's a bit of a 'man who knows a man who knows the man' situation."

"What have you got, Susan?" asked the DCI, his urgent tone underlying his desire for action.

Brooker flagged up some more background information on Street: "He's said to be worth more than £500 million — but he's always seen as coming off second to John Ryder. Where Street is a big name in the UK and the market, he doesn't have the same standing in the rest of the world, including North America and Asia. He once sued *Time* magazine for an article that compared the two men. It claimed that Street was 'always the bridesmaid' when it came to producing mobile phones and bringing new products to market. The American courts dismissed the claim out of hand, although not before Street had spent a couple of million on case preparations, hiring teams of lawyers and public relations people. Against advice from his own people, he went on a tour of TV studios. Viewers said he came across as 'weird', 'creepy' and a 'loser', and those are just the descriptions I am happy to read out loud."

The major's mobile phone rang, and everyone fell silent as all eyes swung towards the handset. Major Phillips picked up, identified himself and listened intently. Then he thanked his caller and hit the end call button.

"Looks like confirmation. A year ago, Peter Street let it be known he was looking for improved personal security. He'd hired one of those expensive protection companies to sort the details but wanted his own, self-contained, system. More 'proactive' was how it was just described to me. The name I've got is John Marcus Edwards. He's ex-Foreign Legion and, even though he's a Brit, he's spent most of his time in French territory. That seems to be the reason he's stayed under the radar. In every other way, he's a big player.

He stands six feet six inches, weighs in at over 280 pounds and has a reputation for being utterly ruthless. He's said to have superb contacts and would have had no problem organising the three hits. My contact says that, if the money's right, there's nothing that he won't do."

Hooley was shaking his head. "Do we know anything about his personal background? You can't imagine a man like that being able to stay out of trouble while he was growing up . . ."

The major shook his head. "Nothing. He seems to have appeared out of thin air as a fully fledged giant killing machine."

CHAPTER 55

Healy flicked through the news channels in an attempt to find one that had something new. She'd never really watched rolling news before, and it was clear that, without further developments, the reporters had to keep going over the same old ground. It was also bizarre to be at the heart of a story that was dominating the news.

As she watched, her captors were toiling past with heavy-looking bags. The man she now knew as Marcus was carrying one in each hand, while Street was bringing one at a time, staggering slightly at the weight.

She tried to ignore them, but an unpleasant idea lodged in her brain. Street had never been one to enjoy physical exercise — but here he was, grinning as he toiled backwards and forwards.

"Last bag!" he called out, as he made his way towards her prison cell. A few minutes later, he was back, spooling out a length of wire behind him.

She felt sick as her worst fears were pretty much realised.

"You've gone pale, my dear." If he'd hoped to sound concerned, his flat tone undermined the attempt. "Why don't you come and look at what we've been doing? It's something you really need to see with your own eyes."

Dread settled on her like a heavyweight. It took all her willpower to move as she used her hands to lever herself from the sofa onto her feet. With legs like jelly, she followed him back into the secret rooms.

The space was piled high with bags of fertiliser, but it was the object in the centre of the pile that made her blood run cold. A small block of grey material with two electric cables pushed into it sat in the centre of the room. A solid power board connected to the two cables completed what she could see. She knew what this was — it had to be a bomb.

Street studied her carefully, his eyes narrowed. "Impressive, isn't it?"

She didn't bother to answer. This wasn't impressive; it was plain terrifying. The sight was so chilling she felt frozen to the spot. She had to put her hand against the wall to fight off a wave of light-headedness.

Her discomfort made Street gleeful. "There's getting on for two tonnes of ammonium nitrate fertiliser in there, a little bit of plastic explosive — and Marcus, an expert at this sort of thing, will be adding some sugar. Apparently, that will make sure everything goes boom."

He said the last word quietly, almost reverently.

Suddenly, he straightened up. Healy was looking straight at him and was horrified to see his mouth drop open, his features distorting as though his face had slipped. For the briefest moment, his eyes were blank. It was as though he had briefly lost control, allowing her to see the inner darkness at the core of his being. She recalled newspaper reports about a school shooting where survivors spoke of the shooter seeming to lose control of their expressions as their facial muscles went slack. She wondered if it indicated he was experiencing some sort of psychotic breakdown, brought on by the pressure of what he was doing.

Then he was back and acting as if nothing had happened, the entire performance serving to convince her — as if there could be any doubt — that she was dealing with a man whose mind was on the brink of disintegration.

Street grinned. "Now, I expect you're wondering what happens to you in all this? Well, I'm afraid it's going to be bad news. You see, we're going to make you part of the bomb, as it were." He paused, taking in her reaction. "But you do have a tiny chance of survival. We're going to rig this so that you'll be ultimately responsible for when it explodes. You'll be the one holding the switch — and, once you let go, it will set it off. This house, and you, will be blown to tiny pieces."

He looked sly again and pulled his phone out of his back pocket. "Now, I can see that you have your own ideas. After all, how can I force you to sit around holding a detonator? You could just set it off the moment we hand it to you."

He handed her his phone. The screen showed a couple of video feeds, although she couldn't make out what they were.

"You might want to enlarge those."

She clicked and nearly dropped the phone. The feed — with a timer proving it was live — showed the outside of her parents' home on the outskirts of Bromley.

"The second one, please."

She prepared herself and clicked again. It was her sister's little semi-detached in Milton Keynes, where she lived with her two young daughters, Mary Lou's much-loved nieces, and husband. She sagged. She knew what was coming.

"As I'm sure you've guessed, we have people at both these locations. If I give the order, I can have them killed. If you blow me up, they'll also be killed." He paused and grinned as if something amusing had occurred to him. "Just think you can save innocent lives if you follow my instructions. Mary Lou, I know you fancy yourself as a do-gooder."

When she didn't reply, he patted her shoulder. "Good, good. You're being sensible." He pointed up at the ceiling. "There's a camera in the ceiling light fitting, so we'll be able to see you after we leave. Oh . . . and there's one other thing you should know. There are two ways of setting off the bomb. Either with the switch we give you, or by remote control. So, even if Mr Roper works everything out — and he just might, by all accounts — we can still make sure you go up in smoke. As I said before, I need you to encourage your fellow workers that they would be better off no longer working for the Ryder Corp."

He turned to leave, walking a few steps before coming to a stop. With his back towards her, he said, "Just to give you something to think about. I think I'm a reasonable man. I give people a fair chance." He turned back and poked her sharply in the chest. "Wouldn't you agree?"

"Sure, whatever." She couldn't be bothered to argue.

He carried on. "So, what I've done is to keep the bomb simple. That means someone with the right experience could dismantle it. You might just get away with your life. I didn't have to do that. Marcus wanted to fit a special anti-tamper device, but I overruled him. While you're sitting here with the switch, you can decide how lucky you feel today."

She felt she no longer had anything to lose. "Can I make one request?"

"Try me."

"Will you leave it until the last moment before I have to hold the switch? If I have a long wait, there's a danger I'll get cramp and just let it go."

He sketched a bow. "Of course. Never let it be said that I would leave a damsel in distress."

Mary Lou Healy just stared at him. He was a mad man. There was nothing to be gained in pointing out the obvious flaw in that statement.

CHAPTER 56

Roper announced that he might have cracked the answer to "home".

"That was quick, even by your standards. Tom only came up with confirmation about ten minutes ago."

Roper shrugged. "Actually, Susan and I have had Peter Street's name for a little while."

The DCI looked incredulous. "Don't you think you should have mentioned it?"

Another shrug. "You know Susan and I have been working with algorithms. Well, Street was one of about 500 names we came up with. We didn't have anything to mark him out, so we were still looking when Tom got the name.

"The good news is that we already had quite a bit of information about him — his company HQ, which is quite close to where we are now, his declared home address in Audley Square, Mayfair, and various other properties. But I also remembered reading that he had grown up in his family home in Leatherhead and once gave an interview saying how much he loved the area. Out of interest, I checked if he had any homes in that part of Surrey and something interesting came up. A company linked to him bought up his family home a few years ago after his parents died.

"The old house has been demolished and a huge mansion, practically built out of glass, has gone up in its place. Given that he has never publicly acknowledged owning the house, I think it might be the 'home' Mary Lou alerted us to.

"I don't think he could possibly be holding anyone at the company HQ, so I suggest we leave that to operational command. His address in Audley Square could be the one, although I only rate that a twenty per cent possibility."

Hooley interrupted. "Why so low if it's his actual home address?"

"Simple really. He's having a huge renovation done. A lot of his neighbours are very angry with him for digging a huge basement out. So I think that would be too high profile. He may not even be there, given all the work that's going on."

Major Phillips knew that area of Surrey reasonably well and was already thinking of bringing in a couple of snipers since it was likely trees would surround the house. This meant good cover if they were shooting from a distance — and not so good if it meant charging, unprotected, over a manicured lawn.

"I'm guessing you've narrowed it down to the Surrey place?" he said. "Tell us more."

Roper took a moment to read over some notes. "I don't have loads to go by, but my Rainbow Spectrum says it seems the most likely place he would hold someone. It's isolated, he has a history with it, and he knows the area."

Hooley was briefly awestruck. "I don't know how you do it. Actually, I don't know how either of you does it."

Before he could say any more, Brooker interrupted, "I've found a picture of the security man. He *is* a huge man." She spun her screen so that everybody could see.

The major whistled. "Might need to bring a bazooka with us. Let me get on to operational command and update them. Meanwhile, let's get out to Leatherhead."

CHAPTER 57

Healy had only been on her own for minutes but it felt like a lifetime, which it might prove to be. Her thumb was resting on the detonation switch, and she could feel a low ache developing in her hand. She wondered how long she would last.

She thought again about running and seeing how far she could get — but that was for the desperate moment in the future when she could no longer hold the switch.

Marcus had told her that he and Street were still at the house, working on something outside and he assured her that any attempt to loosen the wires connecting the switch to the bomb would set off the Semtex. Then it would be game over.

Speaking without any apparent emotion, he had added, "If by some miracle you outrun the blast, I will have the pleasure of shooting you myself."

At least she could swap the switch between her hands, so long as the button remained depressed. That would give her a little longer before the pain made it impossible to hang on, allowing her more time for her rescuers to arrive. Even then, they still had to disarm the thing.

Her imagination was running wild. Her thumbs already felt swollen, and the stress was having a strange effect on her, giving her vivid daydreams. At one point, she was sure she'd had a long conversation with her mother. That was especially odd as the woman rarely went in for big chats.

In her more lucid moments, her survival instinct was screaming at her, telling her she had to do something to try and get away.

Suddenly, she could feel a sort of vibration in her chest and a sense of pressure in her ears. She couldn't work it out. Was it something to do with her captors? She didn't know if they were still here.

At that moment, Marcus burst in, ran into the safe rooms and came out with two rifles in his hands. She didn't know that they were Kalashnikovs. Nothing fancy, just efficient, and very lethal.

The vibration was getting stronger and was building to the point where it became obvious that a helicopter was getting very close to the property.

She felt a burst of adrenaline. Could this be a rescue mission? Had someone had worked out her message? It sounded like the helicopter had set down at the front of the house; the rotors were powering down when she heard the sound of gunfire.

* * *

Even before the helicopter had touched down properly the major and two of his men were leaping out and racing towards the house. This saved their lives.

Bullets banged against the fuselage, and some hit one of the pilots, the man shouting out in pain as he fell forward. The SAS team didn't hesitate. They were returning fire with a vengeance.

The major took a nick on his shoulder. It was savagely painful, but he ignored it and kept firing. A brief lull allowed him to charge forward, reaching the relative safety of a sidewall. One of his men tossed a grenade which detonated moments later.

Set on a short fuse, it landed precisely in the middle of Street and Marcus. At such close range, the explosion killed them instantly. The man who had thrown the device checked the bodies and then called the all-clear. Both of their faces had escaped unscathed, so identification was easy.

The firefight was over in less than sixty seconds, but the major wasn't going to abandon protocol. He wasn't going into the house until he had checked it thoroughly.

Hooley, Roper and Brooker climbed out of the helicopter and joined the SAS man at the side of the house. Breathing hard, the major was bleeding but not seriously injured. When a second helicopter touched down seconds later, a medic tried to tend to his wound but he brushed the man off and got his men checking the outside areas and looking through the windows.

It was the team covering the back of the house that called in.

"Hostage in sight! Repeat, hostage in sight!" They were equipped with HD quality cameras and sent a live stream over the command net.

Hooley took a deep breath as the video went live. Mary Lou was sitting on a settee, wearing an orange jumpsuit and looking distraught. As he watched, she transferred something from her right hand to her left hand. She flexed the fingers of the empty hand and grimaced in obvious pain.

She fell back against the cushions and, holding her left hand against her chest, started to weep, her shoulders convulsing. The DCI felt his temper rising and was glad when the major interrupted his train of thought.

"I think she's holding a detonator switch. Well, we already know our man isn't frightened of leaving explosives behind . . ."

Confirmation that it was Mary Lou came quickly. The major decided he'd had enough of waiting. He charged through the front door, followed by his men. They rapidly established Mary Lou was the only one left inside.

Hooley was the next one in and quickly made his way to her. At first, she shrank away from him, looking wild-eyed and shaking her head.

He knew what was going through her mind. "I know you have a detonator there. One of the men who ran in ahead of me is one of the best bomb-disposal people in the world. You're safe now. We need to get you out of here."

Despite her ordeal, Mary Lou put up quite a fight about handing over the detonator. "This is my fault. I need to do it."

It was the major who persuaded her. "In a minute my man and I have to go in there and try to defuse that bomb. You're getting cramp from holding the switch so you might accidentally set the thing off." With a wicked grin and a wink, he added, "We bring the chief inspector along for these things because he's so ugly it makes him bombproof."

His attempt to break the tension worked a little. Reluctantly, she agreed to hand it over to Hooley and was carefully led away from the house.

Major Phillips directed Hooley to hand over the detonator switch. The offer was declined. "I'm the oldest one here. If I go up, it saves me having a heart operation — and, anyway, you're going to make sure that everything is okay, so I'm not at all worried."

The major gave him what might be described as an old-fashioned look. "Don't think this discussion is over. We shall be having words."

Hooley winked at him. "If you're that confident, why are we wasting time? Go and put those bomb-disposal skills to good use. Oh, and could you arrange a cup of tea for me?"

"Don't push your luck," said the major, as he followed the wires back towards the colossal fertiliser bomb. He was followed by one of his troopers, the rest withdrawing from the house, a move that did not fill Hooley with joy.

Despite his determinedly light-hearted tone, Hooley was scared. He'd have to be a fool not to be. But he knew he could never have left the young woman there in his stead.

He had the detonator in a firm grip in his right hand, holding the switch down with his thumb. To his horror, his hands started to sweat, and it felt like the detonator was moving around in his hand. He thought he had a tissue in his jacket pocket and began to search for it with his left hand. Sweat poured off his head, and he felt sick with anxiety. He'd scrunched his toes up, and this triggered cramp in his feet. He nearly wept as he fought against the pain, trying to keep a grip on the switch.

At last, he found the tissue. He was breathing heavily and needed to calm down. Despite his earlier brave words, he very much wanted to live and enjoy more life.

He got his breathing back under control and mopped his brow, just as the major reappeared, looking sombre. "I've had a quick look at the bomb, and it is a bit unusual. I've got one of my best bomb people here, and he's working on it now, but he says the next five minutes are crucial. I won't kid you; this isn't looking good. Are you okay to keep holding that switch?"

Hooley decided he'd had enough of bravado. "The honest answer is no. But I volunteered, and I will see it through."

The major patted him on the shoulder.

"You're a brave man, Brian Hooley. Please don't hold your breath, but we're getting out of here. I can feel it. Try not to look at the clock. I'll be back when we have some information."

Despite the advice, the DCI couldn't keep his eyes off his watch.

With a little over four minutes gone there was a terrible commotion.

Suddenly the major and his man came flying out at a dead run.

"Get out!" he shouted as he ran past. "Save yourself!"

Hooley was stunned. *So*, he thought, *this is how it ends — me looking like an idiot, holding a switch.*

He waited for his life to flash before his eyes — but, finally, the major reappeared, wearing a big grin. "You're a hard man to scare, Brian Hooley. You can let go now; it's all fine."

He didn't know whether to laugh or cry.

"If you've given me a heart attack," he said, "we shall have words."

EPILOGUE

Two days later, a small group were accompanying Hooley to Guy's Hospital. It was the night before his heart operation. Arguing over who was going to carry his bags were Roper, Brooker and the major. He was still apologising for the bomb joke, assuring the DCI he hadn't known about his heart condition. After the fifth apology, Hooley had told him: "No more."

The DCI had tried to talk them out of coming in, but not one of them would be deterred. Arriving at the heart unit, they were met by the administrator, Cheryl McConnaughey.

The other three stood back as she ushered Hooley onto the ward. To his utter astonishment, he was met with warm applause that grew and grew as more people joined in.

The previous day, the story had emerged about how he had insisted on taking the detonator, knowing that it could cost him his life. It seemed that all those at the hospital were waiting to share their approval.

The DCI could not remember being more embarrassed, but he put on a brave face and accepted the praise before finally retreating to his room. As the other three piled in, he darkly muttered, "If I ever find out who spread that story . . ."

But the innocence in the room was palpable.

* * *

Two weeks later, the operation was hailed a success, and Hooley was installed in Roper's flat with a team of medics coming in to monitor his progress. He'd tried to fight off the attention but Roper, backed up by Brooker, had become very angry — so he'd taken the path of least resistance.

The DCI was in the spare room in a new bed that Roper had purchased especially. It had electric switches so he could raise the mattress if he wanted to sit up.

He was pressing the button when there was a knock on the door. The first to appear was Roper, followed quickly by Brooker and the welcome sight of Julie Mayweather, who had been spending her time in round after round of committee hearings. She was holding a bottle of champagne.

"This needs saving for another day, but you earned this. I'm glad the op went well," she said, "but we still need to discuss that foolhardiness back in Leatherhead."

Hooley grinned goofily; he was still on quite strong painkillers. "No alcohol just yet," he said , "it tends not to go with the morphine. Leatherhead is old news . . ."

Julie smiled at that. "We'll see about that, hero." She turned to look at Roper. "How is Mary Lou getting on? She went through quite an ordeal."

"She contacted me," said Roper. "Wanted to thank all of us and to let me know that Miss Kitty was safe. She said that the cat would help her get better." He paused and frowned. "But Susan and I don't understand that." Hooley and Mayweather exchanged a wry look before Roper continued:

"She also let us know that John Ryder has made a slight improvement. Mary Lou says that although he's in a coma, visitors are encouraged to talk to him. She sat at his bedside told him what had happened and thinks it was hearing the news that did him good. There's a long way to go yet, but it's a start."

Brooker had one thing to add. "It was all a bit late in the end, but those financial checks on Ferrari came back totally clear. But we probably guessed that anyway. Jonathan reckons the accountants need to work faster."

Hooley settled back on his pillows. It didn't take much to tire him out.

"Your thing about the cat. Put it down to one of those things, Jonathan. Put it down to one of those things . . ."

THE END

Made in the USA
Monee, IL
17 April 2023

31963893R00163